# Pride and Persistence

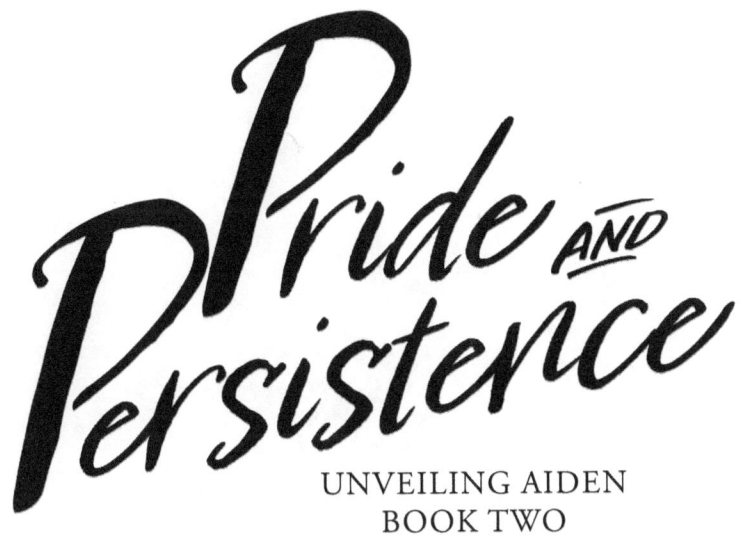

# Pride and Persistence

UNVEILING AIDEN
BOOK TWO

What are We Fighting for
if Not Each Other?

# JOE
# CHIANAKAS

BESTSELLING AUTHOR OF *SINGLETS AND SECRETS*

*an imprint of*
Roan & Weatherford Publishing Associates, LLC
Bentonville, Arkansas
www.roanweatherford.com

**Library of Congress Cataloging-in-Publication Data**
Names: Chianakas, Joe, author.
Title: Pride and Persistence/Joe Chianakas | Unveiling Aiden #2
Description: First Edition. | Bentonville: Mad Cat, 2024.
Identifiers: LCCN: 2024943689 | ISBN: 978-1-63373-981-9 (trade paperback) |
ISBN: 978-1-63373-982-6 (eBook)
Subjects: | BISAC: YOUNG ADULT FICTION/LGBTQ+ |
YOUNG ADULT FICTION/Coming of Age |
YOUNG ADULT FICTION/Loners & Outcasts
LC record available at: https://lccn.loc.gov.2024943689

Mad Cat trade paperback edition August, 2024

Cover & Interior Design by Casey W. Cowan
Editing by George Mitchell, Lindsay Flanagan, & Don Money

*For Tami.*

*Although we were separated by decades and thousands of miles, you amaze me with your constant support and love. To you and to all, especially parents, who fight for and celebrate love and equality like Aiden's mom does in this story—you are all heroes.*

# *Acknowledgements*

PREVIOUSLY ON *Singlets and Secrets*… why don't books have recaps like TV shows? Why don't we change that right here?

In Book One of *The Unveiling Aiden Series,* titled *Singlets and Secrets,* Aiden joins his high school wrestling team to get tough, but he's bullied by a terrible coach and homophobic teammates. Mateo, the JV captain, stands up for Aiden, and Aiden falls madly in love. Aiden's gay, but he's not out yet. He even had a girlfriend, Camila, who got terribly mad when Aiden ignored her and lied to her. When the bullying on the wrestling team becomes too much, Aiden turns to his English teacher, Mr. Samuels, who also knows karate. Mr. Samuels teaches karate to Aiden and Mateo, and eventually opens a martial arts club for anyone who feels like an outsider or never fit in with other sports.

Soon, a big challenge presents itself: The new martial arts club against the state-winning wrestling team. And for the main event? It's Aiden versus Mateo.

Now, spoilers ahead: When Aiden first comes out to Mateo, it backfires. Aiden tries to kiss Mat, and Mat kicks him out of his house. Heartbroken, Aiden turns to his friends—Tisha, DeMarcus, Tony, and Amanda. Mr. Samuels also starts dating Aiden's mom. And when we get to our final chapter in book one—Aiden discovers the secrets of his karate and nearly beats Mateo at the tournament. However, Mateo wins but has a huge confession. He's in love with Aiden. He comes out to Aiden and kisses him in front of everyone at the tournament. Fear held him back, among other things (Mat's parents didn't react the best when his older sister came out as queer). Oh, let's not forget the town's police captain, Claude Decker, is a bully just like Coach Krake. Decker was Mr. Samuels's karate teacher, who opened his own martial arts club. One of the biggest surprises in book one is that Camila turned to Decker for martial arts lessons when her stepmother started abusing her. She kept it a secret, and we've got so many other secrets, surprises, twists, and turns to go.

So, now that you are kinda sorta caught up (I do think you can read *Pride and Persistence* without reading book one first, but you will certainly enjoy it more if know *Singlets and Secrets),* let me share some extra thank yous.

Everyone I thanked in Book One, please know you are included here. You know who you are—my agent, Amy Brewer, my publisher and cover designer, Casey Cowan, my editors George "Clay" Mitchell and Lindsay Flanagan. But I'd like to spend a page or so talking about the amazing local support I had for *Singlets and Secrets.* In no particular order (and my deepest apologies for anyone not included who should be, it is so not intentional, only my poor memory):

To Chad Kautz at Tails of a Bookworm who bought more copies of Singlets than anyone else locally, I think: I love your bookstore, I love your support, and I can't wait to do more! To Zak Kalina of Zeek's Comics and Games—wow, we've had a journey, from *Rabbit in Red* to now, and I so appreciate you! This book should be released around your tenth anniversary and congratulations!

To Cheryl Langley of the Book Nook who even went on TV with me to promote a signing, to Deb Galloway, manager at Peoria's Barnes & Noble—thank you for displaying *Singlets and Secrets* on your Pride table and always supporting me! To Elizabeth Aspbury of Bobzbay Books for relentlessly supporting queer books—you are awesome. To all the wonderful schools I visited and to the brilliant students I was fortunate to share *Singlets and Secrets* with Richwoods High School (thank you, Ms. Maughn!). To Bloomington/Normal schools and the many pride/GSA clubs I visited: you all are some of my favorite people (thank you, Ms. Knowles, Mr. McMorris, Ms. Long, Ms. Hutton, and of course to my wonderful friend Ms. Rachel Heckman!). To Galesburg GSA (thank you Ms. Stegall and Ms. Plemmons), Mortan's Diversity Club (thank you Ms. Kolls), Eureka College (thank you Dr. Jarvis), Bradley University (thank you Ms. Gunn and BU Common Ground!), Illinois Central College (thank you to Dr. Oliver)... and on and on and on.

To Adam Scachette at the Peoria Public Library for hosting book clubs—you are inspiring and amazing in all you do!

To Jennifer Flaig and Jessica Stephenson at Lit on Fire! To Teri and Mark at Wordsmith Bookshoppe! To Danny at Youth Outreach, wow, what amazing things you are doing! To Peoria Proud, thank you for sharing my work, too. To my friends Heather and Nate Monroe at Pour Bros—I hope you know how much you are respected and appreciated.

Ya'll—I hope to see you again to discuss this new book, and again, I know I left out dozens of other visits and events I did last year. Please know I greatly appreciate all of you.

But most of all, most importantly, thank YOU to the person reading this book. If you enjoy it, post a review online and share this story with others. Let's keep changing the world with beautiful, entertaining, meaningful, diverse stories.

# Pride and Persistence

# 1

## *Black Belt Surprise*

TWO MONTHS OF lonely nights without even a text from Mateo made this summer unbearable. I hold the one and only letter he sent me during his absence. *Do not open until I tell you! Seriously, Aiden! Save this, and I'll see you August 20,* he wrote on the outside of the envelope. The day is finally here.

Mat spent the summer in Brazil. Brazil! His father traveled for business, and his family spent no money on international phone charges. At least they used that excuse to keep Mat from talking with me. Before he left, Mateo told me his parents fought nonstop about money. It's why his dad had to take this international job for the season. But I also don't think they like me.

I'm the boy he kissed in front of the entire school, after all.

So, my boyfriend—can you believe I get to use that word?— left the country. I spent the early part of summer training with Mr. Samuels. Tisha, DeMarcus, Tony, Amanda, and I practiced all summer, and we've been brainstorming ways to expand the martial arts club when school resumes. But then Mr. Samuels left for the last half of summer. He spent time in Japan training with genuine martial arts masters.

Japan and Brazil sound like great adventures.

What have I been doing?

Mostly watching social media videos about fashion, dance, music, and even makeup. I never realized how boringly straight-white-boy my wardrobe was until I discovered Beyoncé. But I'm nervous to ask Mom to buy me anything different. Especially at Washington High.

*You know the hip thrust lesson Mr. S taught us? Bet he's shown ur mom that move!* DeMarcus texts me.

*You are nasty,* I text back.

DeMarcus's text reminds me that Mr. Samuels returned a few days ago, but so far, he's spent all his time catching up with Mom. While Mateo has been out of the country, DeMarcus and I have gotten closer. No flirting, no kissing without consent. I'm learning it helps to ask first. Haha. No kissing at all. I'm a proud, loyal boyfriend, but that doesn't mean I haven't thought about it.

Moving from my bed to my mirror, I lift my shirt. I have abs now. Like, totally legit abs! I flex my stomach in the mirror, and it makes me laugh.

So, I'm stronger, I have friends, and I have a boyfriend. I also don't hate my body for once. Looking in the mirror, I wonder how I'd look with a little eye shadow. My sand-colored hair has lengthened to cover my ears, but I style it in different, fun ways. I love my emerald eyes, too, mostly because Mateo told me how much he loved them.

Life should be great, right?

But success and friendship also bring enemies and jealousy. I look over my shoulder constantly. I've lost track of how many times some homophobic jerk has jumped me in this stupid town, but it's been calm and quiet for the summer.

I've been training, thinking about boys, and diving down rabbit holes to learn about gay icons. It's amazing how much you realize you don't know until you start to learn.

I dance across my room, grinning. Mateo will be home today! Why would his family wait until the day before school starts? My fantasies of long summer days and even longer summer nights exist only in my dreams. So much for summer romance.

*Bing.*

It's a notification on my computer, which I ignore. I flipped it open to write a stupid paper that is due tomorrow. Can you believe our teachers assigned summer reading? We're supposed to have a summary of what we read as part of our first day of class tomorrow.

*Bing.*

*Bing bing bing bing bing.*

I grab my computer with a grunt, curiosity capturing me.

Tisha shared an article in a group message, to which DeMarcus, Tony, and Amanda keep replying.

*OMG,* DeMarcus texts. *And we thought last year was intense!*

It's an article titled "Only the Strong," featured in our local newspaper.

> *Last spring, local high school students made history in a mixed martial arts competition that engaged the local wrestling team and a small martial arts club. Washington Police Chief Captain Decker and state championship-winning wrestling Coach Krake proudly announce the 2nd Annual MMA Teen Challenge.*

Sighing, I grab my laptop and sprawl on the floor to read the rest.

> *The 2nd Annual MMA Teen Challenge will be held on the first of March and will feature the talented Tanner McQueen, a Washington High graduate. McQueen continues to train with Captain Decker and will join a traveling UFC circuit in the new year for competitions around the world. At the tournament, he'll be available for pictures and autographs.*
>
> *"I'll never forget my roots," Tanner says. "I always support my hometown."*

Does that mean Tanner won't be fighting? Good.

*And that's not all. The tournament will also feature multiple surprises. "You won't want to miss it," Captain Decker says. "This will be an event people will talk about for the rest of their lives. This is more than just bragging rights and a trophy. We have an anonymous donor who has made it possible to award a cash prize. A huge, life-changing cash prize."*

I shut my laptop and shake my head. I don't want to care about competition or any of those jerks. I don't need a tournament. One was enough.

Tisha's name and photo light up my screen as my phone vibrates in my hand.

"Hey."

*"Did you read it?"* Tisha asks.

"Some."

*"Oh."* She pauses, and my stomach drops. *"Did you get to the end?"*

"No. What is it?" I take a swig of water from what turns out to be an empty bottle and sigh. Nothing to quiet the itch in my throat.

*"Let me read it to you. 'At my school, we celebrate what it means to be a real man and a real woman. We invite only real, strong men and strong women to compete. This isn't a competition for those who need handouts and handicaps.'"*

"So, he's still an asshole." I scratch the top of my head. "You think he's trying to get us to have a reaction and fight? Or is he trying to keep us away?"

*"I dunno,"* she says. *"It's interesting timing. I got a friend request from a new student. Michelle something."*

"Oh, yeah. I saw that, too."

*"Check out her profile,"* Tisha says.

I scroll on my computer. "HOLY. CRAP."

*"Yep,"* Tisha agrees. *"I already sent her a message to sit with us at lunch tomorrow."*

*Michelle Kameade. Tae Kwon Do Black Belt. Martial arts is my life! She/her or they/them.*

"Not only a new black belt. But she also used to go by Michael," Tisha says.

I swallow hard and close my eyes for a moment, remembering all the hate from last year. "We need to be there for her. I don't want anyone ever going through what I went through."

*"That's why I called you,"* Tisha says. *"I'm not letting anyone get bullied again, either. It stops this year."*

Nervous butterflies wage war in my gut. A trans student who is also a black belt would be awesome. We'll accept her. Whether our school will or not is another thing entirely.

## 2

## *So Much Kissing*

MY PHONE VIBRATES, a text from Mateo. When I open it, he's smiling wide, those shiny white teeth contrasting perfectly with his raven-dark hair—a selfie, followed by a voice memo. *"I miss you! Come see me. I'm home!"*

"Tisha, can I call you later? Mat just got home."

*"Yeah, yeah. I'll bring an extra Chapstick for you at school tomorrow."* She giggles as I disconnect.

Quickly, I check myself in the mirror, pulling up my shirt one more time. What kind of shirt would fit my body better? I don't know what to wear.

No. That's a lie. *But what will happen when a wrestler sees you wearing a shirt like the one you're thinking about?*

I sigh. I just want to be me, but just because I finally told people I'm gay doesn't mean I fully feel like myself. I only recently found the confidence to say I'm gay. But that's not all I am.

Ugh. This lazy T-shirt will do for now.

Shaking my thoughts, I focus on what's most pressing. I need a heavy make-out session.

Grabbing my phone, I open my ride-share app and select a driver. Mr. Samuels and Mom bought a nice gift card to use for rides when they aren't available. Guess they don't like me walking the streets alone.

Doesn't it suck that there are towns where queer kids don't feel comfortable walking the streets alone?

Patrick, my driver, approaches in a silver Ford Focus. Once in the back seat, I glance up to see a young man in his twenties wearing a Green Bay Packers hat with messy red hair popping out underneath. He nods at me but doesn't say a word. It takes only a few minutes to get to Mateo's house. I tip Patrick twenty percent—that's what Mom taught me—give him five stars, and race to Mateo's front door.

The front door swings open, and he runs right toward me. His thick, dark hair, perfectly styled, doesn't stir at all. His jawline looks sharper, more defined. Since when did I notice jawlines? I dunno, but it's hot.

But it's that smile. It's the fact that I light up that beautiful smile.

He takes two steps at a time, grabs me tightly with both arms, scoops me right off the ground, and spins me around.

I'd roll my eyes at the sight of us if I wasn't so deeply in love. My stomach leaps to my throat. His strong arms hold me, now stable on the concrete walkway leading up to his door. Then he kisses me.

After a very long minute, he lets go. "I missed you so much!"

"Me, too."

Mat wears tight athletic shorts and a sleeveless shirt. My heart pounds against my chest. I take a long breath and kiss him again.

This time for several minutes. I take in his smell—it's sunshine, sand, and lavender. I could breathe it in all day. Finally, when I need oxygen, I let go.

Mat glances at my T-shirt. It's a plain yellow shirt, and I wear blue shorts.

At this moment, I could simply die. I have a boyfriend who is the hottest and toughest guy in school, and—*shut up, brain.*

Mat kisses me again. Right outside his parents' house. If I could freeze this moment and live in it forever, I just might.

When he needs to breathe, he lets go, reaches for my hand, and leads me inside. *Please don't let his parents be home. Please, please, please!* I could continue kissing Mateo all day.

"Hi, Aiden." Mateo's mother greets me when I step inside. She's got a rag in one hand and some kind of spray cleaner in the other. She opens windows and curtains, bringing fresh life into the room. Sunshine attacks the dark, dusty living room for the first time in months. His father sits on a recliner, eyes glued to the tablet he holds in his hands.

"Hello, Mister and Missus Hernandez. *Como estas?*"

"*Bueno,* Aiden. *Gracias,*" Mrs. Hernandez says. Mr. Hernandez glances at me, grunts, and returns to whatever is so fascinating on his tablet. Mateo's parents previously struggled to accept their queer daughter. It has been a very long journey, according to Mateo, for his father to shift from criticism to grunts, but I can't help but feel nervous every time I'm around him.

Fortunately, Mateo found the right attitude. It doesn't matter what they think. We all deserve to be ourselves and to find happiness. One's parents can accept that or get out of the way. Sometimes I think about what my mom would do in my shoes. Or in Mateo's. She'd never let anyone make her smaller. I think of that when I'm nervous.

"We'll be in my room," Mateo says, leading me upstairs.

"Did you see what Decker just—" I start to ask when we get to his bedroom.

Mateo presses his lips against mine again. "I don't care about him," he says quickly. "I care about you."

My worries and thoughts melt away in the passion of his kisses. And boy, do we kiss. He guides me to his bed. We lay down, and my heart—what's happening? Is this a heart attack or euphoria?

Before I know it, the sun sets, but our lips can't keep off one another. But we need food—more fuel for making out—and Mrs. Hernandez offers us tacos, my absolute favorite.

We eat a record number of tacos in one sitting. My gut produces some odd noises. Mateo laughs at my rumbling, making me laugh.

Which then makes me fart.

My face feels lava hot, and my mouth opens in a silent scream. No, the hot guy I want to make out with cannot hear me fart like this, too!

Mat laughs even harder, leans to one side of the chair, and lets a loud one loose.

Somehow, I love him more.

After a few more minutes of laughing and gas passing, Mat says, "I have a present for you. From my trip! It's in my room. C'mon!" He grabs my hand, and we run back to his room. He opens his top dresser drawer, turns, and hands me a beautifully wrapped gift.

"I love you," I say. I can't help it. It's been bottled up for months, making my brain feel like a cage full of trapped animals. I love Mateo. I don't care what anyone says or thinks about that. I love him. And I've thought about everything, too. Every crappy little thing he did. I'm bruised, but I'm not broken.

"Just open this," he says, with a joyful, coy smile.

"What about the letter you mailed? When do I open that?" I ask.

"Not now," he says seriously. "That's for, well, a much later time, okay? Just save it. I mailed that to you early because… well, a story for another day. Open the present."

Feeling like a kid at Christmas, I tear into the wrapping paper. Inside a box no bigger than my hands is some kind of… tree? It looks like a red bonsai tree. The tree's roots settle in some kind of purple crystal, and a dozen small multi-colored gems act as leaves. It's beautiful.

"It was something homemade from Brazil," Mateo says. "Something about it reminded me of you. The roots in the crystal. The bright colors on the leaves and gems. Like, you know." He pauses, smiling, finding the right words. "You're strong, Aiden. You're strong where it matters most. You're brave. And you're kind. And what happened last year—" He chokes up, and his dark eyes glisten with tears.

I reach for his hand. "Let's not talk about it."

"No, Aiden." Mateo clears his throat. "I have to. Don't you see?

I've thought about this a lot." He wipes his eyes. "I will not bury my mistakes. I owe you more than that. This little gift—it doesn't make up for anything. It's just how I see you." He makes eye contact with me and blushes. "Strong and beautiful. Not like anyone else."

A tear rolls down his cheek, and I kiss it. Then he kisses me.

For the first time in my life—

A tear rolls down my cheek as I return his kiss.

More tears follow.

The gay karate kid who got bullied all year and once upon a time thought life was hopeless is now the luckiest boy alive. The luckiest!

# 3

## *You Won't Believe This*

THE BEST NEWS on the first day of school is that Mateo and I share the same lunch period.

Unfortunately, I do not have Mr. Samuels for English. He teaches freshmen and juniors. I will miss his English classes, but at least we have the martial arts club.

The first morning at school goes by smoothly. Mr. Samuels contacted the principal over the summer to help with class schedules. He did everything he could to separate us from last year's bullies, and we shouldn't see much of them at all except for one class.

There's one thing he couldn't do, though, and it's the worst possible scenario. We have Coach Krake as a teacher. He teaches health classes, and he's the only sophomore health teacher. That class isn't until the afternoon.

So, yeah. Maybe *that* explains why this town is so unhealthy.

At lunch, though, Tisha beams with excitement. Tisha pulls at her long brown hair. Sometimes she braids it, sometimes she wears it long, but she has some of the most beautiful hair I've ever seen. It frames a thin face with gorgeous golden eyes. Tisha. smiling proudly, invited Michelle to join us.

DeMarcus, Tisha, Tony, Amanda, Mateo, and I share a table. And now Michelle. Across the room, I catch a glance of Camila and Logan, sitting together. Mom made me promise to help her get away from bad influences, and I plan to stick to that promise.

"So, you're already a black belt?" Amanda asks Michelle. Michelle's dark hair covers her ears, and she wears a T-shirt that says "Badflower" on it. She has a tough, round face—pretty but hard, and there's something about the deep brown in her eyes. She's been through some stuff. We might have a lot in common.

"I started training the moment I could walk." Michelle laughs, confident and attractive in tight jeans and a touch of makeup. I envy her appearance. She's beautiful in her authenticity. It's not obvious at first that she's trans. Of course, whether or not anyone in the LGBTQ+ community is "obvious" is a problematic thought, I realize.

I hate that people have told Mateo, "He doesn't act gay." No one tells me that. I don't want to feel bad about that, either. Sometimes I think we were brought up to innately hate ourselves, and I'm trying to unlearn that. Michelle's delicate facial features make her look more effeminate, anyway.

"My mom was always into Tae Kwon Do," she says, "and I picked up my joy of it from her."

"What made you move here?" DeMarcus asks, taking a bite of a hot dog. Never expect anything fancy for lunch on day one from the school's cafeteria. Today was hot dogs or cheese pizzas. Exciting. DeMarcus's arm muscles pop out of his T-shirt. He looks almost as strong as Mateo now.

I reach for Mateo's hand and squeeze it. He gives it to me, no questions asked. I had no idea how he'd want to act at school, but I had high hopes. After kissing me in front of everyone at the tournament, I had hoped he could be fully out. It's so hard for us to step out of the closet, and I never want to go back. He squeezes my hand in return. So far, so good.

"My dad got a new job," Michelle tells DeMarcus. "That's why we moved."

"Can I ask about, um, about... um, you know?" Amanda gestures at Michelle, but she can't form the right words.

Michelle smiles, but behind her—a few tables away—Camila glares at us. What's up with her?

"I have no problem talking about myself," Michelle says with an energetic grin. "Tisha told me you all were cool. Yeah, okay, here's the short of it. I knew when I was a little kid that I didn't feel like a boy." She shrugs. "I identified with girls. Boys were always so stupid." We laugh, and Michelle takes a deep breath. "But, of course, it's a lot more than that. It wasn't just that I felt represented by girls. I *feel* different-ly. I *am* a girl on the inside. I hear a girl's voice in my head when I think. That's all there is to it, and making my outside match my inside changed my life."

"Are your parents cool?" Mateo asks.

Michelle nods. "It was hard at first. I was fortunate that they tried hard to listen instead of forcing their perceptions on me. Of course, I didn't know how to articulate half of who I was, either. It's been a long road to get here." I instantly like her—she's confident and self-aware, the opposite of everything I was last year. It's refreshing.

"There are people who go their entire lives without accepting their true selves," Tony says. "You're amazing."

I look at Tony closely and smile. He's a fifteen-year-old straight boy, and he just told a trans girl that she's amazing. It makes me love Tony more.

Michelle blushes at the compliment.

"So, we have a martial arts club," I say. "You have to join! And, well, something else." Nervously, I glance at my friends who nod with encouragement. "There's a history of hate here. Hate, against, um, LGBTQ+ kids. But we're all trying to stop it."

Michelle's lips tighten into a frown, and the rest of the table nods in agreement. Michelle starts to say something when Camila appears behind her.

Camila puts a hand on her shoulder. Wow, Camila came dressed for the first day of school. She wears super-short camo shorts that must violate the dress code, but the smirk on her face tells me she doesn't care. On top, she wears a tight, white sleeveless shirt, totally form-fitting. Damn. Everyone grew up over the summer.

"Oh, hey," Michelle says to Camila and then turns to us. "Camilla filled me in on all that. My parents researched martial arts schools before we moved here. I think we signed up for that school before they closed on the house. My family is intense like that." She laughs.

My jaw hits the floor. Michelle's already enrolled in a school? Um, there aren't exactly a lot of options around here. I gulp, thinking of this beautiful person taking lessons from Captain Decker.

Camila's eyes burn into my skull. She looks at me, then at Tisha, then at Mateo. Her silence scares me.

"Have you heard of Decker's MMA Academy?" Michelle asks. "That's our school. Why don't you all train with us?"

The bell rings, and we have no time but to gasp. How is that possible? How can she be training with Decker? He hates people like me, doesn't he?

I have so many questions, but I can't be late for my next class. It's my first one with Coach Krake, and my goal is to be invisible. I sit in the back row and keep my head down.

Krake introduces himself and passes out the syllabus. He's as gross-looking as ever, a human being shaped like a garbage can. He's awful. "As you will see on my syllabus," Krake says, "athletes on an *official* state sport, as is sponsored by our state's high school sports association, may use notes on the weekly quizzes. That is to encourage you to get involved. I know first-hand that those athletes devote hours each day to training, and that is why they get to use notes. The rest of you can either join an official state-sponsored activity or use that extra time to study harder." He grins, a line of pure red evil from ear to ear that reminds me of the Joker.

*You kidding me, Krake?* This can't be legal. Or at least not ethical or fair.

DeMarcus leans over to me and whispers, "So much for our GPAs. He'll make the tests extra hard for us." He's the only other karate kid who has Krake this period, but at least we have each other.

"DeMarcus," Krake calls out. "No talking during class without permission. You've earned your first detention."

DeMarcus's mouth pops open as wide as his eyes, but he doesn't release a word. Krake makes it very clear what kind of year we can expect.

"Now, our first lesson," Krake says, scratching at the top of his ugly, buzzed head, "is sure to get your attention. State-mandated health lessons. We will separate this class into boys and girls for our first unit." I lock eye contact with him, which I realize is an immediate mistake. "Aiden, which group will you be joining?" Krake cackles. The rest of the students look at me, then at him. They don't laugh, not at first, anyway. Even the bullies understand this is wrong.

"What, you don't find that funny?" Krake asks. "You all can laugh. Go ahead. Laugh! Gayden knows I'm only kidding with her, isn't that right?"

Honestly, I'm not sure if I want to cry, die, or scream. What kind of adult gets kids to laugh at another kid?

*Please don't laugh. Please don't laugh.*

# 4

## *Class with Krake*

THE CLASS DOESN'T laugh.

That's hope.

Krake ignores them, clearly unhappy. "Gayden, I asked you a question. When I ask you a question, you answer."

My knuckles turn pale white as I clench my fists and bite my tongue.

"Still no answer?" Krake shakes his head. "That will be your first detention, too, then."

If I allow myself to speak, I may not be able to control the words that come out of my mouth. Today, I decide to accept the detention and keep my mouth shut and my head down.

"Well, anyway, think about your gender overnight, Gayden. You can choose who you want to be tomorrow. That's when we will split into boys and girls."

If Michelle witnessed this behavior, she'd know to get the hell away from anyone who associates with Krake. But she's not in this class. I'm scared for her, and I'm also annoyed and angry. This is not okay, and I will not tolerate it this year.

When the bell rings, I grab my books and sprint toward the exit.

"Excuse me," Krake calls out. "Aiden. DeMarcus. You both stay here a moment. I want a word."

*Oh, I've got some words for you.*

But I bite my tongue. Again. I already have a detention. I don't need anything else today. I'm not going to run to Mr. Samuels every time Krake picks on me, either. I want to fight for myself.

Once the classroom empties, Krake walks toward us. He stands about four inches taller than us. One more good growth spurt and maybe I'll be able to look down on him the way he looks down on me.

"Yes?" I ask impertinently.

"I wanted to talk to you," Krake says with an ugly smile.

DeMarcus and I remain silent.

"You're an embarrassment to our school." His tone changes. What was once sarcastic and insulting is now purely bitter. "You took the best wrestler we'd have this year and made him into… what? A sissy. Nothing but a sissy and a pussy. You got him kissing boys instead of wrestling boys, and you have destroyed his future. It's a complete waste."

My face burns, and my heart leaps into my throat. I fantasize about punching his ugly, crooked nose.

"He would have had a full ride to any university in the country. He'd be the best wrestler at any school. A full education and a life of championships." Krake shakes his head. "You took that away from him. All for what? Your queer hormones?"

"His *what?*" DeMarcus snaps. "You think it's easy to be who he is with people like you in his life? You don't know what you're talking about. Mateo and Aiden, living their truths, are stronger than you'll ever be."

Krake tilts his head back and laughs. "I so enjoy it when you talk back to me. That's another detention, DeMarky Mark."

DeMarcus looks like he also wants to punch Krake. And kick him, spit on him, toss him in a dumpster, report him to the ACLU, and get him banned from ever entering a public school again.

Krake sighs. "I'm sick of both of you. Get out of my class."

I push DeMarcus out the door and into the hallway. Krake doesn't have to tell me twice to leave.

"What are we gonna do?" DeMarcus asks. He takes several deep breaths, and his eyes look wet. "We can't put up with this all year."

"I don't know."

"He should be fired!"

"He should be. But the fact that he's still here shows how stupid some people in this school and town are."

"We could record him," DeMarcus says. "Record what he says and put it on social media. Get some bigger attention outside of this stupid town."

I put my arm around DeMarcus's shoulders. "That's a good idea."

From down the hall, Mateo runs toward us. I shouldn't feel weird, but I slowly remove my arm from around DeMarcus. Mateo notices, though. His eyes look curiously at us. But something else captures his mind.

"Have you seen this?" he asks, putting a flyer in my hands.

I read it out loud. "Community assembly to discuss teen relationships, PDA, and sexuality. Parents, faculty, and staff are invited. Tonight. Six p.m."

"So, they're gonna try and create some rules for us or something? Like we don't get a say? This is bull," Mateo says.

"Welcome to Washington High." DeMarcus shakes his head. "The high school B.S. capital of the world."

THAT EVENING, MOM walks through the front door, and I can tell by her face that she's pissed. I have the flyer in my hand to show her, but I hesitate.

"Oh, I've seen that crap," she says, rolling her eyes. "Parents received an email today, Aiden. You're on your own for dinner, sorry. I've got plenty I want to say at this assembly."

She sets down her bag, her work-related stuff spilling out on the dining room table. Mom doesn't give it a second glance. She puts her arms around me and hugs me tightly, and the scent of strawberries and coconut wafts over me, probably leftover from the conditioner she uses. Her cherry-brown hair tickles my face.

Mom leaves as quickly as she had arrived, and I send a group message to the karate club.

*I've got a plan. Meet at the school's tennis courts right now.*

I grab my bike and pedal hard. I can't wait to get my driver's license. Soon, but not soon enough. When I arrive at Washington High, I cut through the student parking lot and go around the back of the school to avoid the parents and staff. Tisha arrives first, followed by Amanda, DeMarcus, and Tony. Still no sign of Mateo.

"What are you thinking?" Tisha asks.

"I want to know what they say. Not second-hand." A sly smile forms on my face as I reach into my backpack and take out a few supplies I had packed before leaving the house. "You up for sneaking in?"

# 5

## The Whole Town Talks

"ARE YOU KIDDING?" Tony asks. "You'll get caught."

Shrugging, I put on a gray Washington High baseball cap, followed by an oversized blue hoodie Mr. Samuels left at my house. "If I keep my head down, no one will notice. Once I'm inside, I'm ducking under the bleachers anyway."

"I'm coming with you," Tisha says.

"Where's Mat?" Tony asks.

"Dunno," I say. "Never replied to the group text. Okay, how about me and Tisha go, and the rest of you wait out here?"

"Record it," Amanda says.

"It's about to start. We can duck in with the crowd and then beeline to the back and hide." Tisha nods, and we take off.

"Maybe I'm being impulsive, but I want to hear this for myself. See what's going on," I continue, even though Tisha is already on my side. It's a bit past six, and a final group of parents makes their way inside Washington High's gymnasium. We run to the back of the group, and Tisha takes my hand. We're so close to the people in front of us that we'd tackle them if they stopped walking. Thankfully, they don't. Once inside the school, we slip to the back of the gym, find a gap in the bleachers, and hide underneath.

"My heart is racing," I whisper, adrenaline rushing through my veins.

"Shh, they're starting."

*"Good evening. I'm Mister Evans, your assistant principal. We wanted to have a community forum on these important issues, and we thank you for joining us today."* He pauses, and Tisha and I peer through the bleachers, trying to see. I look beyond the hundreds of pairs of shoes at my eye level and focus on Mr. Samuels and Mom, who sit together. Front row. Closest couple to the microphone.

I love them.

*"Last year, we are aware that we suffered significant interruptions to the learning environment,"* Mr. Evans says. *"After the wrestling and martial arts event, more students became open about their sexuality."*

"You'd think that would be a *good* thing," Tisha mutters, while I dig my fingernails into the palms of my hands.

*"The school board has decided it is important to teach students when it is appropriate to share their sexual orientation and when it is not. Last spring, some students passed out rainbow stickers in class, interrupting important lessons. At our school events, same-sex couples kissed publicly. We want to be inclusive, but not to the point where it disrupts the learning environment."*

"He doesn't even know what inclusive means," Tisha snaps.

*"So, we have a few rules to announce from the B.O.E. Number One— there will be no stickers or flags or signs of any kind allowed on campus this year. This has nothing to do with those items or what they represent, but rather the distractions and disruptions they cause. Number Two—no kissing is allowed between students, regardless of gender or sexual orientation. We will add to these rules as needed. Learning is our top priority, and we cannot have these disruptions."*

The auditorium erupts with noise, and I jump, almost hitting my head. There's a mix of applause and boos.

*"Now, we are going to open the floor for thirty minutes of questions and comments. Coach Krake has volunteered to take a microphone around the gym for you to speak,"* Mr. Evans continues.

"Oh, I bet he has." Tisha sticks a finger in her mouth, gagging.

Peering out through the bleachers again, I audibly gasp, but no one can hear. Mom marches directly to Mr. Evans, ignoring Krake, and grabs the microphone out of his hand.

*"As a parent of a son who is gay, I have a lot I need to say, and I'll take as much time as I need to say it, so you can sit back down,"* she says directly to Krake, who approaches the microphone. *"First, these actions send one message and one message only—that being a member of the LGBTQ+ community is wrong. I will not tolerate that. Second, what we need to be talking about is the safety of our students. My son was bullied right in front of your eyes. These policies are not inclusive. If anything, they will add to the bullying because you are telling our children that being LGBTQ+ is— what did you call it? A distraction? Is skin color a distraction? Religion, too, I suppose? I want to know what you are doing to prevent bullying and to keep our children, especially our LGBTQ+ children, safe. What are you doing about that?"* Mom passes the microphone back to Mr. Evans and gives him a look that brings out his scared, inner child.

*"Ma'am, I assure you we have a zero-tolerance policy on bullying."* His voice shakes.

*"Bullshit!"* Mom snaps.

*"We also have a zero-tolerance policy on that language,"* Mr. Evans says. Mom gives him a sharp look, and Mr. Evans shuts his mouth and swallows hard.

Mom steps right up to his face and snatches the microphone back away from him. She glares at him for what seems like several long seconds. The rest of the audience becomes very quiet. Slowly, Mom turns away from Mr. Evans and faces the crowd.

*"What are you all scared of? Love? Of your children being happy? I'm scared that one day I'll get a call from the hospital and that Aiden will be dead. Think about that for a moment. I'm scared for my child's life. Kids bury their identities because the adults they look up to—"* She pauses and glares again at Mr. Evans. *"Those adults create an environment that*

*leads to bullying and hate. Kids get hurt because of your fear. Kids lie to themselves because of your fear. Some kids—"* Mom touches her throat with her free hand and takes a deep breath. *"Some kids have even killed themselves or have been killed because of this. You think banning kissing and rainbow stickers helps anyone? You should be ashamed of yourselves. I swear.... This year, I have zero tolerance. Zero! If any kid is bullied or hurt.... It must stop, and this is not how to stop it."*

She shakes her head. She wipes her eyes and drops the mic. Mr. Samuels, who has been standing a few feet behind her this entire time, puts his arm around her. He whispers something in her ear, and they leave.

There may be a few hundred people in the gym, but it's impossibly quiet right now.

Tisha holds my hand. "Your mom is my hero."

"Mine, too," I say, wiping my wet eyes. "Mine, too."

# 6

## *Who's the Bully?*

THE GYMNASIUM ERUPTS with chatter. Tisha and I scramble for the exit and run back to the tennis courts. Mateo stands in between DeMarcus and Tony. When he sees me, I flash a smile, but he doesn't return it.

"Where were you?" I ask.

"Parental problems," he mutters. "Tell you later."

"So, what happened?" Amanda asks. She's the shortest of the group, and she nervously bounces a little when asking. She runs her hands down tight blue jeans, crosses them over a tight black T-shirt, and fidgets some more.

"You won't believe—" Tisha starts.

"Hey, losers." The voice comes from behind me, but I'd recognize it anywhere. My heart pounds in my ears. A shot of PTSD finds its way to my nervous system when I hear his terrible voice.

Taking a deep breath, I clench my fists, trying to get my emotions under control. Then I turn and face him.

"What do you want, Logan?" I ask as calmly as possible.

He raises his arms. The sun shines on his pale skin. The school stands behind him, framed by a blue sky, the grass around us freshly mowed. It would be pretty here if not for the ugly in front of me. "I'm not here to fight." He lowers his arms and runs a hand through his red hair. He wears a shirt with the American flag that reads, "If this offends you, you can leave."

"What do you want?" DeMarcus asks.

Logan breathes hard through his nose and forces a crappy grin. "I wanted to share the latest news. You haven't heard? My dad is running for mayor next term. We've got Coach Krake, Captain Decker, and soon...." He laughs so hard he starts to cough. "Oh, I can't wait to see the looks on your faces when my father becomes town mayor. He helped get the init—uh, initial—um, you know the new rules the school board passed."

Bigoted and brainwashed. How surprising. Can we move out of this town yet?

"What initiative?" Mateo asks. The wind picks up, but his perfectly styled hair remains still. Sadness saturates his eyes. What parental problems could make him so sad?

"Who do you think organized this assembly?" Logan chuckles and locks eye contact with me. "You won a battle. You won't win the war."

*"War?"* Amanda asks, rolling her eyes. She approaches Logan, who is easily a foot taller than her, but she looks straight up at him with confidence. "We want you all to leave us alone. There's no war."

"Oh, there is. And you're all gonna regret the day you ever—"

"Shut up!" DeMarcus snaps. "All you are is an asshole who sees anyone different as a threat. That's a stupid way to live."

Logan glares at DeMarcus, takes out his phone, sends a text, and puts it back in his pocket.

"When will you stop treating us as enemies?" Amanda asks. "No one wants to fight you."

Logan's eyes narrow, and the color on his face mirrors his hair.

"When you view people who are different as enemies, then it makes sense that there's nothing left to do but fight. That's what people like Krake do. Why can't you see that? Leave us alone," DeMarcus snaps. "That's all we want."

I step closer to Logan, too. "Yes. Leave. Us. Alone." I clench my fists. Truly, I want to slug him, and it takes all my willpower to remember karate is for self-defense only.

"What the hell are you all doing?" The voice comes from behind Logan, and I recognize it, too. Camila. She comes from around the corner of the school and speaks to someone we can't see yet. "Do you see this? This is what I'm telling you about. This karate club is a bunch of bullies."

Rounding the corner, Michelle joins Camila, and they walk toward us. Michelle's wide eyes and dropped jaw tell me she doesn't understand what's happening here.

"No, Logan came out here and started threatening us again," I say.

"Oh?" Camila asks, shaking her head dramatically for Michelle's sake. "I'm sure."

"I don't know what you've been taught," Michelle starts, "but six on one is not cool." Michelle makes eye contact with me and Tisha, specifically. "I thought you all were better than this."

Something changes in Michelle's eyes, the way a friendly animal can turn fierce when exposed to a threat. Her gaze moves quickly to each of us, sizing us up, and there's a subtle shift in her stance that a trained fighter would notice.

Michelle braces herself for a fight.

## 7

## *The First Fight*

"TOLD YOU," CAMILA says. "They say they're the good guys. But did they tell you that both Aiden and Mateo dated me, lied to me, and cheated on me with each other?"

Camila steps right up in my face.

"You're *not* the good guy, Aiden." She turns to Mateo. "And neither are you."

"What does that make you?" Tisha asks.

"Heartbroken!" Camila snaps. "Especially when it comes to you. You were supposed to be my best friend, and you chose these liars over me!" Spit flies out of Camila's mouth when she talks. My heart races, and my skin warms. Mom made me promise to help Camila. To apologize and to help her get away from bad influences. What would Mom say now?

"Mila, I'm sorry—"

"Oh, no, you don't get to call me 'Mila.' That's for friends. And you know what? I'm sick of sorry. You said that before. Sorry isn't enough."

"Then what is?" Mateo asks. "I apologized, too."

"You're scared and selfish. Not sorry."

"You're full of shit! We tried to help you! And now…." Tisha shakes her head as incredulously as I feel.

"No friend of mine would choose guys who lied over me! I'm nobody's second or third place."

Tisha cries in frustration and charges at Camila. *No! Tisha, stop!* But before I can open my mouth, Tisha shoves Camila, rage overpowering all logic.

Michelle grabs Camila, which steadies Camila's balance. Michelle glares at Tisha. My stomach flips. This can't be happening! A cool black belt who should be our friend defends Camila. Michelle blinks, and before Tisha sees it coming, Michelle drops low, spins like an action star, and sweeps Tisha's legs.

Tisha falls hard to the ground.

Mateo and I glance at each other, and when we look back, Michelle stands right in front of us. Glaring at us.

"You liars. It's my first day here, and you try to talk to me about bullying. Some sick joke. Sick! People have played jokes on me my entire life. But I never thought it would come from... come from...." Michelle covers her face, burying her feelings. When she removes her hands, her expression has shifted to a stoic fierceness.

What do we do? How do I explain?

Logan walks up behind Camila and Michelle, laughing. Mateo and I shift into a defensive stance.

When we move, Michelle yells, a spirited *kiai,* and then, with one leg, she kicks Mateo in the head, pulls her leg back without setting it down, and thrusts her foot right into my chest. *Dammit! No! Don't fight back. She misunderstood! It's just all a big misunderstanding!*

With the wind knocked out of me, the words refuse to come out.

DeMarcus lunges at Michelle, but she easily steps to the side and sweeps him. He falls face-first on the ground, right next to Mat and me.

A throbbing pain in my chest and Logan's laughter in my ears consume me.

Michelle stands tall, and the turquoise shorts she wears reveal strong thighs and lean, powerful muscle. Mateo turns to me, wearing a fierceness on his face I've only seen in his most competitive moments. I shake my head at him, willing him not to fight back.

"I'm not scared of anyone. You hurt my friends, and I'll hurt you," Michelle tells us, keeping her fists in front of her. "That's a promise I made to myself long ago. I don't turn the other cheek to bullies. I face them head-on. Understand?"

"Michelle, you don't understand!" I argue, holding my chest with one hand and taking deep breaths. Mat's not hurt, but his ego may be, and he's ready to retaliate. I've got to cool things down. "Listen, please, you guys!"

"No more lies!" Camila yells. "You want to be left alone? Stay out of our way." Camila puts her arm around Michelle's shoulders. Camila wears a revealing white top, her belly fully exposed. It's not her skin, though, that catches my attention. It's the bruises on her arms and one on her neck. Last year, she hid her bruises. Maybe it's because she can use training as an excuse, but now her bruises are visible for the world to see. Does her stepmother still hurt her?

She's my friend, not my enemy, and I need to convince her of that.

Taking one last glance at us, Logan, Camila, and Michelle leave.

"I just wanna go home," I say. "I don't know what to do."

"Talk to Mister Samuels," Amanda says.

"Yeah," Tony agrees.

Tisha shakes her head. "Mila didn't give us a chance to speak for ourselves. Why would Michelle listen to her and not us?"

No one answers.

"Can I come with you?" Mateo asks.

I smile. "Of course."

He grabs his bike, but we walk to my house. I need to process what happened, but other problems plague Mateo's mind.

"I need to talk to you," he says.

My stomach drops. "That's never good to hear."

When he doesn't smile at me, my stomach sinks even deeper.

**8**

*Don't Say Gay*

"IT'S MY PARENTS."

"Oh." We stop, and I kick at the concrete nervously.

"They don't want me making any more *scenes.*" He uses air quotes. "We've been home like a day, and suddenly everything's changed."

"What do you mean?"

"They were cool in Brazil. At least I thought they were." He scratches the side of his head. I miss his smile. When he fully smiles, nothing else matters. "But come to think of it, they were only cool because we never talked about anything. Day one here at school, and they get this notice that the entire community has something to say about queer kids. They flipped out. I can't even say the word 'gay' around them."

I set my bike down and take Mateo's hand. "I'm so sorry." I love holding his hand. Electricity buzzes through me. Just his touch magnetizes me.

"It's like, I think they can handle me being gay if they don't have to ever hear about it," he says. His dark eyes melt my heart as they turn wet.

"Can you stay over this weekend? It's, well, maybe it's selfish, but you're scaring me. I don't want to go backward, you know?"

He nods. "They'll say no if it's only me and you."

"So would my mom, I think. We'll make it a slumber party. Invite Tony, DeMarcus. Make it a guys' night."

He flinches at the mention of DeMarcus. So, I had my arm around a friend—Mat shouldn't be jealous of that. "Yeah, maybe. That might work."

I let go of his hand and hug him. "I need you. We'll figure everything out. It will be okay. If we've got each other, everything will be fine."

And there it is—that million-dollar smile, the one that erases all my worries, the one that makes me feel alive. He kisses me, right there on a public sidewalk. It's not a long kiss, but it fills me with warmth.

"I hope you're right," he says after pulling back. He swallows hard and wipes his eyes.

"What do we tell Mister Samuels?"

"Everything. No lies. Lying caused all the problems between us last year." He takes both of my hands and faces me. A car drives by quietly, and cute houses sit in the background. It feels picture-perfect. One of these homes could be ours someday. To be a happy gay couple in a community like this, though— it feels like queer people have so many extra steps to climb. "You are my everything, Aiden. My strength. I dreamed about you every night this summer. I don't know what I'd do without you."

"I love you." It's all that matters. We can overcome anything with love. "I love you so much it hurts."

I kiss him again, and then we hop on our bikes for the last part of the journey.

Mom must have been waiting for us because the moment we set our bikes down outside my house, she runs to us. She puts her arms around me and hugs me tightly.

Oh, yeah. She doesn't know I heard what happened at the assembly and the beautiful words she spoke. I hug her back harder than ever.

"I love you, Mom."

Mr. Samuels walks outside. "There's a lot to tell you both."

When Mom lets go, I hurry to Mr. Samuels and hug him, too. I haven't been able to spend any real time with him since he returned from Japan. I'm surrounded by my absolute favorite people, and I just want to feel this joy for a moment.

"Sorry," I mumble. "I missed you." My face feels red hot, but I'm trying to be more expressive, not less. That's something I thought a lot about these last few months.

Mateo smiles. I'm not embarrassed to speak this way in front of him, either. "Mister Hernandez. You gonna get in here, too?" Mr. Samuels asks Mat with a joyful smile.

He walks over, and Mr. Samuels grabs him, hugging us both. "I've missed my boys and our training. Should we start up again at six a.m. tomorrow?"

We all laugh.

"How about after school?" I ask.

"Deal," he says. "First practice is tomorrow, then. Tell the others."

"Sir, we have something we need to tell you," Mateo says.

Mr. Samuels sits on the steps that lead to our front door. His happy expression turns serious. "We have some things to tell you both, too."

I'm sure he's talking about the event at school, so I don't follow up on it. "First, can we tell you something? It's about a new student. A black belt."

"With a heck of a kick," Mateo adds.

"Uh-oh." Mr. Samuels sighs. Mom takes a seat next to him.

"What happened?" they both ask.

We tell them everything.

# 9

## *Training Time*

"WELCOME BACK," MR. Samuels tells the martial arts club at our first after-school practice this year. We're all gathered in the middle of the room, sharing our grins and gripes about the day. "Line up."

I do my best to hold back my smile, but anyone looking surely would see my lips curl into a prideful grin. We line up by rank in karate, and I'm the highest-ranking student—a purple belt. Mr. Samuels promoted Tisha and me to purple belt before he left for Japan. Mateo, Tony, DeMarcus, and Amanda are blue belts but will have the opportunity to advance this semester. Mateo needs to catch up with the lessons he missed last year, but he makes everything look easy with his natural athleticism. We have about twenty other students joining us today, mostly white belts but a few yellow and green belts, too.

And it's the kids people don't usually see on athletic teams. Girls who look like boys, boys who look like girls, people who don't want to look one way or the other—our club attracts a diverse group of students who would never feel comfortable on Krake's wrestling team.

Our numbers grew after the tournament, but so did Decker's. Not that I've ever stepped foot inside Decker's Mixed Martial Arts Academy, but the students share pictures and videos on their socials. He has two to three times the students we have. More jocks and wannabe jocks, which is why I don't understand how Camila and Michelle like them so much.

"Aiden, warm them up," Mr. Samuels tells me. He wears a traditional white gi, and his black belt has seen better days. It's beginning to fade, and some threads have loosened, but *Sensei* says that's a symbol of pride—the worse the black belt looks, the longer that person has been training. I bow, move to the center of the study hall that transforms into our after-school dojo, and lead the group in a series of warm-up exercises. Mr. Samuels uses this time for announcements and stories.

"Today, we practice our falls again. DeMarcus, why do we practice how to fall?"

"Because everyone falls," DeMarcus answers. He wears the red and black uniform Mr. Samuels gifted the tournament competitors last year.

Mr. Samuels smiles. "Correct. Everyone falls. Amanda, what do we do after we fall?"

"We get back up, sir," Amanda says.

"Fall seven times," Mr. Samuels says, "and?"

"Rise eight," we say in unison.

"Yes. Fall seven times. Rise eight. That's a Japanese proverb, a martial arts lesson, and a lesson for life. Mateo, what does it mean?"

"It means we always get back up, *Sensei*."

We practice our falls—and getting back up—for most of the class. In the cluttered study hall room, we still kick random worksheets, paper clips, pens, and pencils out of the way. This room doesn't exactly help morale.

Not every lesson features punches and kicks. We've repeated white belt lessons so many times that I have dreams about them. Mr. Samuels reminds us regularly that advanced techniques mean nothing without a solid foundation.

Before practice concludes, Mr. Samuels asks us to sit in a circle.

"Class, as you know, Decker is promoting another MMA tournament. There's no doubt he wants you to compete. I am going to tell you something you may not want to hear," Mr. Samuels says. "I don't think we should."

A few students erupt into passionate whispers. I glance at Mateo, who raises his hand.

"Sir, why not?"

"Last year, we fought to stand up against hate. You all faced your fears. You all grew from that experience. You have nothing to prove, especially to bullies. We train here for self-defense. To improve our minds and bodies. You get to choose the fights you have, and do you really want to fight them again?"

Tisha raises her hand. "Sir, can we enter the tournament if we want to enter?"

"Why do you want to enter?"

"You know what happened after the assembly with Decker's students, don't you?"

Mr. Samuels nods.

"I don't understand, then," Tisha says. "If we let bullies get away with this, then when will they stop?"

"Maybe we need a different question," Mr. Samuels replies. His hands grip the ends of his black belt, and he stands incredibly tall, looking over us as we sit cross-legged on carpet in desperate need of vacuuming. "What happens if you become the bully? We must be careful not to become the very thing we have tried to stop."

"So, what are we training for?" DeMarcus asks.

I'd be happy to never fight in a tournament ever again. But everyone speaking seems disappointed in Mr. Samuels.

"Many of you have been part of traditional sports that prioritize competition. High school athletes need to know that they won't always have cheerleaders or Friday night lights. If the competition is the only joy, then life will be very depressing after high school." *Sensei* crosses his arms and walks around the room. "I want you to find joy in the journey, in the training itself. That's what creates a lifetime of joy."

I hesitate to speak up. But I do. "*Sensei*, most of us in this room never had anyone cheer for us. We never had a Friday night lights experience, and we never will. All we have is this." I look at my friends, who I want to support. I look at Mr. Samuels, who I never want to disappoint. But I speak my mind. "I think it should be up to us if we want to compete."

"All right. Tell you what," Mr. Samuels responds, an open-mouth grin forming with a dash of mischief sparkling in his eyes. "I'll give you my approval to enter the tournament to anyone who can beat me in a traditional three-point match. Deal?"

It's an awful deal because none of us could beat Mr. Samuels. Still, he knows how to cut the tension. The class breaks into laughter.

"At the end of each practice, I'll ask for any volunteer who would like to face me. Beat me, and not only will you have my support for the tournament, but I'll also train you for it, too."

"Starting now?" Mateo asks, his hand high in the air, an ambitious grin on his face.

"As you wish, Mateo. You versus me." Mr. Samuels matches Mateo's smile, and I sit up straighter. This will be a fun match.

# 10

## *Foursome Sleepover*

MATEO LOST TO Mr. Samuels. Three to nothing in less than thirty seconds. *Sensei* did not take it easy on him. I have a dozen questions, but there's only one that takes priority now that practice is over, and it has nothing to do with karate.

When am I making out with my boyfriend?

We set up a group sleepover so our parents would approve. Even Mateo talked his parents into letting him stay, although I wondered if he had to lie. It's Tony, DeMarcus, Mateo, and me on Friday night. I can't wait!

As the week passes, I keep my nose in my books and my body active with karate. Let the parents fight over the rules on PDA and sexuality. The only tumor we can't destroy comes in the form of a wrestling coach teaching health class, but I keep my mouth shut there all week, too. For now.

"I know the other boys are all sleeping in your room, but I want Mateo on the floor with them, and you alone in your bed," Mom says, after making me vacuum my room. "This may be new territory to me, and you know I support you, but that doesn't mean I want my teenage son to sleep with his boyfriend at this age. Understood?"

"Yes, Mom," I say, blushing while she strives to mess up my hair. "Stop!" I bolt to the bathroom to comb it again, adding a little more gel. There's a spot in the back that always wants to stick up, and I want to look good tonight. More than good. I want to look hot.

Once everyone arrives, Mom orders pizzas. Mr. Samuels comes over, too, with a bottle of wine for Mom. "Excuse me," I say to them. "Is Mister Samuels sleeping on the floor tonight like Mat?"

Mom glares at me, and I turn, giggling and running to my room.

We play racing games, and the loser has to take a big gulp of an energy drink each time. Eight races in, and DeMarcus bounces off the walls. Literally. He does several sprints from one side of my room to the other in between every game. He's lost six out of eight games, and the caffeine pulses through his body. Tony, Mateo, and I can't stop laughing at him.

"You guys!" DeMarcus says. "My toes are vibrating! You ever feel your toes?" He looks extra cute—he wears comfortable running shorts, and his legs look amazing.

A blue tank top frames his body nicely over the gray shorts. *His eyes are up there, Aiden.* I've had to remind myself a few times.

Tony throws a pillow at him, and I'm grateful for the distraction. I must admit I was a little worried that Mateo and DeMarcus would be awkward. Of course, DeMarcus has never officially come out. I don't know what his sexuality is, but I'm learning about something people call *gaydar,* and *my* dar screams rainbows at DeMarcus.

DeMarcus leaps at Tony, and they dive backward on my bed. Tony rolls with DeMarcus, and they fall off the opposite side, making a loud thump and causing Mom to shout, "Boys!" It makes us laugh more.

We watch scary movies next. Tony picked out a few that were streaming, claiming no sleepover is perfect until someone screams in horror. We watch some new slasher, and I sit next to Mateo on the floor by my bed. Each time I jump, he holds me tighter. No wonder people like horror movies.

At midnight, we switch back to video games.

"So, Tony," DeMarcus starts. "We know these two—" he gestures at Mateo and me— "are horning out over each other. What about you? Got anyone you like?"

"Yeah." Tony blushes. His long, dark hair sticks up in all directions, and his smile reveals adorable dimples. He wears a baggy gray sweatshirt over blue jeans, completely different from DeMarcus on so many levels.

Tonight, I took some nail polish from Mom's purse, thinking maybe I'd bring it out and see what kind of reaction the others would have. But so far—not even knowing why—I keep it to myself.

"Who? Who? Who?" DeMarcus asks. Still hyper from all the energy drinks, he jumps on the bed.

"Promise you won't say anything? And promise you won't, um, make fun?" Tony's face turns an impossible red, and I hold back the urge to laugh. We all nod in enthusiastic agreement, though.

"I, um, I… well, I want to ask Amanda out," Tony says.

"Oh, yeah?" Mateo asks, holding my hand. "She's cool. Why don't you?"

Tony shrugs. "I don't want to make karate weird. You know?"

Mateo raises his arm, still holding my hand. "Take it from us. It might seem weird at first, but if she says yes… I mean, it could be awesome?" Mateo smiles at me, and I want to kiss him so hard. But not in front of the other guys. Checking the time, I hope Tony and DeMarcus will crash soon. Not to be rude, but I'd like a little private kissing time with Mat.

"Well, don't wait too long to tell her," DeMarcus says. "A girl as awesome as Amanda won't be single forever. She kicks ass."

Tony smiles. "She could beat my ass any day."

We burst out laughing.

"What about you?" Tony asks DeMarcus.

Suddenly, I sit up much straighter. Mateo adjusts himself, too. It's the million-dollar question, and I panic. If DeMarcus comes out, will Mateo worry? Or be jealous? I might enjoy a little jealousy.

Another thought enters my mind, too. I'll be so disappointed if DeMarcus doesn't like boys. Tony's straight enough for all of us.

"I dunno," he mumbles, much quieter than normal.

"Oh, c'mon!" Tony says. "There's got to be a girl or a guy you like. Who you into?"

I can't help but crush a little on Tony, too. Why can't all straight guys be so cool? People respond better to well-phrased questions that come from open minds.

DeMarcus fidgets, takes a deep breath, and exhales slowly. "All right. Since we're all being honest. I guess I should tell you guys that, um, well." He coughs and scratches his nose. "I'm not… um, I'm not…."

# 11

## *Peacock*

"I'M NOT STRAIGHT," DeMarcus says finally.

Mateo stops breathing. Am I still breathing? I can't even tell right now. The veins in DeMarcus's arms pulse. He's cute, sexy, strong, and so not straight.

What's there not to like?

Oh, no. What if Mateo finds DeMarcus attractive? Or what if De-Marcus finds Mateo hot? Dammit, brain, shut up, shut up, shut up!

DeMarcus looks at Mateo and me. "You two are so awesome. Honest. It's weird not to talk to you about what I'm feeling when you're going through similar things, too. But it's hard to bring up. Sometimes, I guess. You know?"

"I know exactly what you mean," Mateo says. His grip on my hand loosens.

"So, any dude you like?" Tony asks, grinning from ear to ear.

"Well, that's just it. I like girls, too," DeMarcus says. "Wow, this feels so weird and yet so cool to say at the same time."

No one knows how hard this may be for someone. No one knows the anxieties and worries someone has.

"I've never told anyone. But I guess, um. Well, I've always known." He shrugs. "So, yeah. I'm bisexual. There, I said it!"

We laugh with him, certainly not at him.

"That's cool," I say. "Thank you for telling us."

A knock on the door makes us all jump.

"Oh, hey, Mister Samuels," DeMarcus says, as our teacher's face appears slowly through the doorframe.

"Just wanted to say hi. It's good to see you all together. Do you guys need anything before bed?"

"Ooh, teach us something cool!" DeMarcus says. "Something you picked up in Japan, maybe?"

Mr. Samuels steps into my bedroom, nodding enthusiastically. "You know what? I've got just the thing. I was saving this for a special practice, but why not?"

"Tell me it's a secret!" Tony says. "I never understand the karate secrets like Aiden does."

"It is a secret," Tony. *"Kujaku."*

"Ku-*what?*" DeMarcus asks.

"It means peacock," Mr. Samuels says.

Tony and Mateo immediately chuckle.

"Is peacock funny to you guys?"

Tony and Mateo laugh harder, and DeMarcus joins.

"Peacock. Peacock. Peacock," Mr. Samuels says, egging us on. He laughs with us, and then says, "Get it out of your system. Now stand up. It's a cool form."

He demonstrates the technique, and it's unlike anything I've ever seen before. He steps low to the right like a lunge, his left knee bent to the floor, his right leg strong. He places his hands against his hip, both palms still open, one hand a few inches above the other. Then his left leg springs out into a horse stance, and his hands drop low, open palm, one on each side like open-handed low blocks. He brings both arms up wide and slowly. In a quick transition, his arms come together, forming an *X* in front of his face, his forearms facing out toward us. With a wide grin, he pushes forward, striking with two tiger claws and then he tears at the air in front of him. He ends the form with a series of rapid strikes.

"Your turn," he gestures at us, smiling, not even out of breath.

"What are we doing exactly?" Tony asks.

"Peacock is a secret defense against multiple attackers. Picture two people holding your arms and shoulders, one on each side. Picture another in front of you, ready to strike. This move will show you how to defend against them all."

We each attempt *kujaku* several times, but we're somehow all too tired and also too hyper to understand. We keep falling over ourselves, unable even to get the footwork down tonight.

But every fall elicits a laugh, and it's the best night ever.

"All right. We'll practice that again another time. Why don't you all get some sleep soon?" Mr. Samuels shuts the door on the way out but then pops his head back in at the last minute. "Peacock!"

We laugh until Tony and DeMarcus fall asleep. I've still got other things on my mind.

"SHH," MATEO TELLS me when I make too much noise. I can't help it. His body feels amazing against mine—even his most gentle touch awakens every cell in my body. When he gets passionate, it's like my body is a Fourth of July celebration. DeMarcus and Tony are asleep on the floor. Mateo sneaked into my bed after I kicked him a couple of times to get his attention.

So far, we've only kissed. Heavy kissing that is—tongue in mouth, hot breath against my neck, muscles hard as wood pressed against my body. It's the kind of kissing I've only seen in movies.

Hard as wood. I chuckle at my thoughts. Mateo puts his hand over my mouth. "Stop! I feel so weird doing this with them in the room."

"We're never alone," I whisper. "Those hornballs would do the same thing. Don't you think?"

He answers with his lips.

Both of us are shirtless, and that's a first for me. I run my hands over his chest, loving every second of this until—

A memory flashes in my mind.

Confronting Mateo outside of the Chinese restaurant before the tournament. The look in his eyes. The words he said to me.

The words he said about our previous friendship.

About everything.

*"It wasn't real, Aiden. None of it was real."*

I should let myself feel pleasure, but my mind returns to pain. To the pain I felt when my best friend—no, the first boy I ever loved— lied to me, betrayed me. He couldn't have apologized *before* the tournament? No, he waited until he beat me. Then he confessed everything.

"Stop!" I say, louder than I intended.

"Aiden," he whispers, "what's wrong?"

"Just stop," I say again, and Mateo does. He rolls off me. I wanted to make out so badly, and I was enjoying it so much.

Until my brain screwed it up. I wanted to kiss him all night. I wanted this to last so, so much longer. Skin to skin for as long as we could stay up.

But my mind kills my joy, and what should have been a long, awesome night ends abruptly.

Why do I always feel so messed up?

# 12

## *PTSD*

TANNER, LOGAN, JEFF, Coach Krake, Captain Decker, Camila. Their faces race through my mind. The pain they've caused me moves from memory to muscle, and I ache.

Without warning, my face betrays me, and I cry.

Mateo hugs me close and breathes into my ear. "What is it? What's wrong?"

I wipe my eyes.

"What's wrong, babe?" *Babe.* It sounds so sweet. He's apologized like a hundred times, and he's told me he loves me. And I believe him.

So, why do I feel such pain?

*"It wasn't real, Aiden. None of it was real."*

I sit up, softly clearing my throat. Checking to see that Tony and DeMarcus still look asleep, I turn back to Mat and ask, "Is this real?"

"What? What are you talking about?"

"This isn't, you know, a game? This is one hundred percent real?" I wipe my face, trying to hold back tears.

"One-hundred, Aiden. *Mi novio.* I'm so sorry." He kisses my cheek.

I've killed the make-out mood. He lies by my side, and every silent second chills the air until he speaks again.

"What are you thinking?" he asks.

"Sometimes… I wish I had never started wrestling in the first place."

"Then we wouldn't have met," he says, kissing me gently. "I know you went through hell, but I don't know what I'd do without you, Aiden. I promise I will never hurt you again."

My heart quickens, wanting to believe him. All I wanted was to be loved. I never thought someone like me—a queer kid who didn't know how to be honest—would ever find love. Love lies right by my side. My breath quickens, worrying that love turning out to be a lie would be a fatal blow for which there's no recovery.

"I know." We lie in silence again, and a little while later, Mateo's soft snores bring a smile to my face.

Eventually, he wakes and returns to the floor. I watch as he curls into his sleeping bag. DeMarcus stirs, and I panic. Did he or Tony see or hear anything?

DeMarcus wakes up and walks to the bathroom.

I toss and turn. DeMarcus takes too long. Maybe he's doing a number two, but now I need to pee. And I'm nervous, worried he heard my conversation with Mat. Leaving the room quietly, I tip-toe around Tony and Mateo, both sleeping soundly.

I pause at my dresser, thinking of what I have buried in the top drawer. Mateo's letter. The one he mailed to me over the summer but won't let me open until he says so. Many nights have passed when I think about opening it, and tonight is no exception. Still, I choose to wait and instead look for DeMarcus.

The bathroom light guides my way. When I approach, the door pops open a crack. It never latches entirely unless you lock the door. I thought I told the guys that, but it's easy to forget in someone else's house in the middle of the night.

DeMarcus sits on the toilet, tinkering with his phone. "Oh, hey," he says, catching me looking in on him.

"Sorry. You got to lock the door, or it doesn't shut all the way."

"I'm not doing anything," he says. "One sec." The toilet flushes, he washes his hands and opens the door, an awkward smile on his face. "I couldn't sleep and thought I'd play on my phone. Didn't want to wake anyone up with the light or anything."

"Oh."

"You okay?" he asks.

I shrug.

"I, um... heard some of what you said. You guys weren't exactly quiet at first." DeMarcus grins slyly at me, and I'd laugh under other circumstances. "But as for you what you said to Mat... I understand, dude. It's totally normal. You went through hell. Got beat up. Made fun of. Came out. You can't just smile and forget everything, you know? That stuff's gonna take time. Mateo will understand that."

Without warning, I hug him. Exhaustion hangs on every muscle, and I almost cry. DeMarcus understands. And he isn't judging me. Sometimes you need a good friend, even if you have a good boyfriend.

He hugs me back.

When we return to my bedroom, Mateo's eyes pop open. DeMarcus slides back into his sleeping bag, and I go back to my bed.

"Good night, Aiden," he whispers to me. I wish I knew how to forget the weird tone in his voice.

"Night," I say back.

MR. SAMUELS AND Mom prepare a huge Saturday breakfast for us. Chocolate chip pancakes, bacon, scrambled eggs, and English muffins. Tony shoves an entire pancake in his mouth, leans back, and pours syrup until it runs down his face. DeMarcus takes a bite of bacon with his left hand and a forkful of eggs with his right. Mateo and Tony exchange goofy faces with mouths full of food. We're all sleep-deprived and giggly at my dining room table. Mateo rubs his foot against mine a few times, which makes me smile.

How can I not be perfectly happy right now? Sunlight, sleep, and

Mat's smile elevate my mood. I have the boy of my dreams, but something feels off. It's not him, either. Which means something is —My stupid brain loves over-thinking and ruining things.

"My dah is alreffy texxing me," Tony says with a mouthful of pancakes. After he swallows, he continues, "I gotta go. Sorry guys. It was awesome, though."

"It was the best," DeMarcus says. "How about my place next weekend?" Mateo turns his head quickly, his foot finding its way off mine and back on the floor. His face may remain stoic, but his eyes flash with something I can't quite grasp. What's he thinking? "Or, Mat, what about your place? I've always wanted to see your dojo. Aiden says it's awesome."

Mateo nods and swallows down his food with a big gulp of orange juice. Even in the morning, he's super cute. His normally styled hair sticks up on both sides, and his face radiates from the sunlight pouring through the window. "Yeah, man. We can do something at my place whenever. Your place is cool this weekend, though, if it's cool with everyone else."

"Absolutely!" Tony says on his way out, and we all agree.

Relief washes over me. Please let Mat and DeMarcus get along. I don't like any weirdness between them.

After breakfast, the boys go home. Mateo leaves without kissing me goodbye, but I guess that's okay. Maybe he doesn't want to kiss in front of Mom or Mr. Samuels, and I don't blame him.

Once they leave, I shower and return to bed, a nap on my mind. Sleep comes quickly, and I wake up to Mr. Samuels knocking on my bedroom door.

"It's dinner time, kiddo. You hungry?"

I rub my belly. Napping is hard work. "Always." I could get used to only eating and sleeping. Mr. Samuels loves to cook. Tonight, he and Mom made chicken enchiladas, and they're easily the best I've ever had—tender with a spicy aroma.

"I had something I wanted to talk to you about," Mr. Samuels says.

"Oh?" I shove in a mouthful of rice.

"I want to suggest something, but I don't want to force it on you."

"What?"

"Your mom and I have talked. She completely agrees, and I asked if I could suggest this idea to you as your teacher. As your *Sensei.*"

I force a smile. "Which means I don't get to say no, then."

"No, Aiden, nothing like that. It's your choice. But this isn't just a mom wanting this for her son. It's a teacher wanting this for his student."

"Um, okay?" Nervousness makes it hard for me to swallow the rice in my mouth.

"We want you to start seeing a therapist."

"I don't need—" I stand, insulted.

"It's not about need. To be honest, we all should have a therapist. The world is dark, and when that darkness takes up space in our heads, it makes it harder to experience joy. You have the best mom, but you know that don't you?"

I nod.

"Your mom is worried that you aren't as happy as you could be. I'm worried, too. I see it in how you practice. You're good, but you could be better. And you're happy around Mateo, but it's… unstable. Are you two okay?"

How does Mr. Samuels have this sixth sense?

"We're good."

"Nothing's wrong?"

I hesitate.

"We want you to talk to us when you're ready. But in the meantime, we want you to talk to a professional therapist."

Sighing, I search for a distraction. The dishes need washing. Boards need breaking. "Aiden, you should know that I see a therapist, too. I plan on going for the rest of the semester at least."

"Why do you need a therapist?"

"Ask a better question, Aiden." Disappointment lingers on his tone, and my skin heats up.

"Sorry," I mumble.

"It's okay. I have some issues I need to get off my chest, too. Issues with Decker and Krake especially."

"Is something else going on? I mean besides the fact that they are super D-bags?"

Mr. Samuels sighs. "Unfortunately, yes, something else is going on that you don't know about yet. Something about the tournament. I wasn't planning on telling you, but I will. If you agree to see a therapist."

I take a deep breath.

"Okay," I say.

"Okay," Mr. Samuels says. My stomach tightens, and Mr. Samuels continues.

# 13

## *Dream Match*

"I DON'T KNOW what's wrong with Decker," Mr. Samuels tells me. "He wasn't always so toxic. There were a few years that I enjoyed working with him." Mr. Samuels shakes his head and rests his chin on his palm. It's odd to see him discouraged or depressed.

"What's the deal with the tournament?"

"First, do you want to keep competing in tournaments? What do you want to get out of your training with me?" He sits up straighter.

I shrug. "I never thought it would be for me, you know? Facing Logan and Mateo last spring—that was gut-wrenching." I scratch the side of my head. Although I like competing, something has been missing. "But I never felt braver or stronger. And you know what? I think losing to Mateo made me feel even stronger. I didn't need to win. I needed to know that I could fight anyone."

"I'm proud of you for that. I don't want anything to be about revenge if we were to compete."

"Wait, *if*? You changed your mind?"

"Things change quickly when Decker or Krake don't get what they want." He took a deep breath and rubbed his nose. "I'm torn because I don't want to support something that risks your safety." My eyes must be as wide as my mouth, curiosity killing me. "Your mom trusts my judgment, and wants you to make your own choices. But if you get hurt…."

"Can we run *kata*? It will clear my mind."

A spark in his eyes tells me he understands. His smile—this must be what fatherly pride feels like. We head to the basement. I haven't trained here much recently. If the weather is nice, I practice outside. The last time I was down here was before the tournament. It was such hard, exhausting training. If I go through that again, I want a clear purpose.

Once in my little dojo Mr. Samuels motions for me to join him side-by-side. He bows, and we run through *Wansu*. This *kata* has the cool throat-and-groin grab I showed Mateo. Aching memories hurt my muscles like I'm being attacked. Until Mateo's secrets were revealed, those were the hardest days of my life.

We run through *Anaku* next, the form that taught a different hip movement for rapid punching. Sometimes speed wins over power, just like mind over muscle. I know what I want. I need to trust myself.

But before I say so, we run *Nihanchi Sho,* the last *kata* Mr. Samuels taught me before leaving for Japan. This brutal *kata* teaches cornered self-defense, as if one was pinned against the wall by an attacker. As if one is forced to make a choice. Sometimes it's good to be forced to choose.

When we finish, he asks, "What do you think?"

"I know what I want to do."

"And?"

"It's not about a trophy." Putting my hands in karate's formal position for ready, I find the words I always wanted to say. "I want to stand up against hate. I want to fight for equality. I want to be the queer karate kid! And I've got something that most other kids don't have."

"What's that?"

"You." Mr. Samuels smiles but takes a long time to respond. He walks around the dojo he made down here, brushing some dust off an unused punching bag.

"There's something in you, Aiden. You may not see it yet, but you're gonna change the world."

My cheeks burn at his kindness. Mr. Samuels raises his arm, makes a fist, and holds it out for me.

"Do we still have to beat you in sparring to be able to enter?" I ask as I bump his fist.

"Maybe we'll save that for your black belt test."

"So, what's this other new challenge? What's bothering you about Decker and Krake?"

"I wanted to make sure you were committed before I told you."

"Well, now you're scaring me." I laugh nervously.

"Decker is offering scholarship prizes to the winner. It could change your life or Mateo's," Mr. Samuels continues. "Whoever wins will receive a large prize, something unheard of for high school competition. He's committing to twenty-five thousand dollars for the first-place winner."

"Wow!"

"But there's a catch."

"Of course," I mumble, rolling my eyes.

"Decker wants to make sure we have a big crowd for this event. He's pulling no punches. Tanner, as a future UFC competitor, will attract plenty. Michelle, an incredible black belt and a trans student under Decker's wing, may attract attention. But he added one more event, and he's made it clear that no scholarship prizes will be available if this one match doesn't take place." Mr. Samuels scratches the back of his neck. "Small minds have big egos. Decker has a legal contract guaranteeing that any winner of the tournament—his or ours—will receive this money. But he's only signing it if I commit to one thing."

"What is it?"

"A special exhibition match. Coach Krake versus *Sensei* Samuels. Yeah. He wants the wrestling coach and me to go head-to-head in a special karate versus wrestling match. And you know what, Aiden? Don't tell anyone else this, okay?"

I nod.

"But I can't wait to kick that jerk's ass."

Laughter replaces my initial shock. Krake versus Samuels? So, to make sure Decker follows through with the scholarship money, all Mr. Samuels must do is fight Krake? That's an easy answer. *Yes!*

"Oh, my gosh. I can't wait for that either! OH. MY. GOSH. This is going to be the best tournament ever!"

# 14

## *A Big Date*

TODAY, I HAVE a date with my boyfriend. A *real* date! Finally.

Mom drops us off at Mateo's favorite Mexican restaurant.

"Thanks, Miss Rothe. I mean, Miss Gardner. Sorry, I still forget you and Aiden don't go by the same last name."

"Thank you," Mom tells him. "Text me when you need a ride, okay?"

"Yeah," I say, half-listening and exiting the car. Mateo speaks with the host in Spanish. I love that he speaks two languages fluently. I wish I did.

*"Como estas?"* The host greets me when they have finished.

*"Bien!"* I say too enthusiastically. *"Muy bien! Yo quiero mi novio."*

The host laughs, and Mateo blushes. At least my weak Spanish skills are somewhat cute. We slide into a spacious booth, and we dive right into the chips and salsa.

During dinner, his foot rests on mine under the table. His mouth opens wide with laughter at almost everything I say, even my bad jokes. When our bellies fill to capacity, we decide on a romantic walk.

"I, uh, had a special request," Mateo says, with a grin.

"What is it?"

"Just follow me."

He wears these athletic jeans that make his thighs look like they could burst out at any time. Wearing a tight maroon polo, he doesn't even have to flex—the lines and muscles in his arms are enough to drive me crazy with fantasy.

"Around the corner up there," Mateo continues, pointing. "Know where we're going now?"

"The playground. We played on the swings. It was one of the best afternoons of my life. Until—"

"Until Decker showed up and threatened us," he says, finishing my sentence. "I hate him, Aiden. I hate him and Krake and everything they stand for."

"Me, too."

"I don't wanna talk about them, though. What I wanted was… well, I wanna finish that afternoon. I wanna swing with you. I wanna jump off the swings. And I want—"

"To kiss me?" I ask, incredulous at the words flowing out of my mouth without me thinking about them first. I landed on him the last time we were here. I almost kissed him then. Believe me, I wanted to kiss him. Would it have been different if that had been our first kiss instead of me ruining everything that awful night in his bedroom?

"If you had kissed me then, I, um, I dunno," he says, looking down at the sidewalk. "I'm so ashamed of how I used to act. I feel shame every day, Aiden."

Shame. A chill rips through me at the word. My past contains stories I haven't told anyone, not even Mateo. Stories I've buried because they bring me shame, too.

"I had a best friend in seventh grade," I say. "David. I did something, well, shameful, too."

"What did you do?"

My stomach sickens at the memory, and I can't bring myself to talk about it yet. Shrugging, I say, "I'll tell you one day. I promise. But not today. Today is a happy day."

We turn the corner, and the park comes into view. The swing set stands empty. Once we're off the busy street, Mateo puts both arms around me, turning me so we face each other. "I'm here now. I'm ready now."

He kisses me. His tongue warms my mouth, and electricity vibrates through my body. It's like I can feel every synapse, every hair on my skin, each individual cell. Why are we not always kissing?

After a minute that I wish would never end, he pulls away. He takes my hand, and we walk toward the swings. "I don't wanna ruin the vibe," Mateo says. "But can we talk about that sleepover?"

"Sure. What about it?" He's worried about DeMarcus, I bet. Wonders what we were doing outside of my room in the middle of the night, maybe?

"We were making out. And then you, um, kinda freaked out...."

"Oh." I kick at the sand as we approach the swing set. He's worried about me. "I was just nervous Mom or *Sensei* would walk in."

He holds eye contact with me, dark and powerful eyes sizing me up. "Is that all?"

A thought comes to mind. A thought I can't say out loud. The thought I had that night. The one that torments me in my nightmares.

*I don't know if I can trust you.* I won't tell him that, though. I am in love with this beautiful boy, and I'm so scared I'll ruin it.

I've ruined many things before. Things I don't like to remember.

My shoulders feel heavy, and I worry I could cry—should I tell Mateo about my fears?

# 15

## *Kissing Makes Everything Better*

"IS THAT ALL?" he repeats.

I answer with my mouth but not with words. Kissing Mateo passionately, I pull him against me. My body doesn't care if my mind doesn't trust him, at least right now.

When we finally pause, Mateo says, "I'll take that as a yes for now. But I hope you'll talk to me. Be honest with me. Can I, um, can I... I may not ever make up for everything I did to you." Mateo pauses, searching for the right words. "But can I promise you something?"

I nod, but there's a tightening in my chest. Every time he wants to talk to me about something, I can't help but be terrified.

*It was all a lie.*

*I was never your friend.*

*I don't like you like that.*

*I'm not even gay. I was using you.*

My heart pounds so hard I feel dizzy. Was it karma all along? Karma for how I treated my best friend in junior high?

Mateo puts his hands on my shoulders, turns me squarely toward him, and then gently places his palms on my face. He kisses me sweetly and then says, "I promise to never stop trying to make it up to you."

*Don't cry, Aiden. Don't cry!* My eyes feel like dams holding back the pressure of my pain. Why am I always so emotional?

"I love you," I tell him. And I do. Even with all my anxieties and fears, love remains.

"I love you, too," he says.

I hope love is enough.

THE NEXT WEEK, our wonderful Washington High School Board of Education holds its monthly meeting. I sure wish there was more than one high school in this town. The priority on the agenda? "Don't say gay."

*"Have you seen this crap?"* Tisha asks me on the phone. We're on a video call, and she texts me a link to a local news article.

With a heavy sigh, I read it.

> *In response to community concerns, last night the Washington High BOE passed a new set of rules to be effective immediately. Nicknamed by opponents as the "Don't Say Gay" initiative, the Board has informed all faculty and staff of Washington High to enforce the following:*
>
> *Rule number one—no student will talk about sexuality during class time. It is the Board's opinion that such personal matters, especially about sexuality, create a distraction to the learning environment.*
>
> *Rule number two—no Pride flags or LGBTQ+ clothing, symbols, or artifacts are to be worn at Washington High.*
>
> *Rule number three—students who express their sexuality will be removed from the classroom and required to seek counseling.*
>
> *The Board emphasized that, "We are not homophobic or anti-LGBTQ+. We are simply focused on making sure students at Washington High receive the best education possible, which requires the minimization and removal of distractions."*

The article continues on with other specifics, but I'm too sick to read them.

"*I hate this town!*"Tisha yells. She pulls at her long, leaf-brown hair. "What the hell?"

"*I'm not tolerating this,*" Tisha says. "*What do you say we gather the karate club and protest this bull?*"

"What do you have in mind?"

"*For starters, we all get some pride stuff and wear it. They can't kick us all out.*"

"I like the way you think," I tell her, but I bet she's wrong about that.

"*I'm the smart one.*" She laughs. "*Maybe Michelle will wake up and realize we were telling her the truth. She must see this crap, too. What's she even thinking?*"

"I've also wondered that. And what's happening with her and Decker? Do you think he's mean to her?"

"*Oh, I'm sure. With any luck, she'll already have quit his school and will join our team any day. She needs to wake up.*" She groans. "*All right, I'm gonna send a group message. Figure out how we can protest this BS.*"

"Thanks, Tisha."

"*Hey, I always have your back, but this isn't just about you, you know.*" She blows me a kiss and disconnects.

Groaning, I get ready for school. I search through my clothes, trying to find something protest-worthy. Everything I have is so… well, straight. I find an old wrestling T-shirt with pride colors, one Finn Balor used to wear. At the time, I argued that I just liked the colors.

*Are you gay?* My best friend David asked when I wore it. That feels like years ago. Have I not worn this since then?

The school day progresses like normal at first—boring, in other words. No one notices me. No teacher says anything to me.

Until class with Coach Krake.

"Mister Rothe," Krake says to me. "It is still *mister*, isn't it?" He laughs, saliva flying out of his mouth, vomit about to project out of mine. "To no surprise, you are violating school rules with that shirt within hours that they were passed. Off to counseling you go, and how about detention after class?"

Anything to not have to see Krake is perfectly fine with me. I clench my fists and bite my tongue to keep words from coming out of my mouth.

"Off you go."

I glance back at DeMarcus, the only karate club member who shares this class with me. He smiles extra wide. Too wide. I know that grin—it's the same one Tisha flashes me when she's up to something mischievous. He winks at me. Then he pushes out of his desk, standing tall.

"Are you planning on joining him, Marky?" Coach Krake asks.

To my great surprise, DeMarcus takes off his clothes. The students gasp. Some start to laugh. A few even applaud. I remind myself that not everyone here is a jerk, and it doesn't hurt that DeMarcus is hot, too.

"DeMarcus, what in the world are you doing?" Krake asks.

DeMarcus removes his shirt, revealing his toned, strong arms. He looks like a Black Bruce Lee.

Then he removes his pants, taking one leg out at a time, smiling like the crazy fool he must be to piss off Krake like this. What is he doing? And why is my heart racing so fast while he's doing it?

He's not naked.

He's wearing a singlet.

One of Krake's wrestling singlets for his precious team. And damn, does DeMarcus wear it well.

"Out right now!" Krake snaps, pointing at the door. The class erupts in a mix of *oohs* and laughter.

"I just need to clarify something, Mister Krake," DeMarcus says. "Are you saying these singlets that your wrestlers wear are, um, *gay?* That they violate the new dress code? I mean, we all know these singlets are pretty gay. I just didn't think you'd be the one to admit that."

My jaw hits the floor, and my eyes pop out of my head. DeMarcus, the health class hero!

# 16

## *Trouble*

"OUT! OUT NOW, you little—" Krake stops himself from finishing the sentence. What a sad, pathetic man to take out such anger on a kid. DeMarcus picks up his clothes and leaves with a prideful smile on his face. Krake steps up to both of us at the door. "You will face consequences you can't even imagine. And get out of my wrestling singlet. You dishonor it."

DeMarcus takes a giant step back. "I'm sorry, Mister Krake. No, I won't take off this singlet right now. That would be child nudity, and I'm pretty sure there are much stronger laws against that than whatever rules you think you're enforcing right now."

DeMarcus grabs my hand and pulls me down the hall.

As we walk out, the class—all but the wrestlers, of course—applaud for us.

DeMarcus and I run, laughing down the hall to the counselor's office. "I can't believe you did that!"

"Tisha told me what the school board did last night, and this was my first idea."

"I could kiss you!" I say, and we share a hearty laugh.

When we enter the counseling office, we're still holding hands and laughing. Screw this school. If only I could talk all the boys into holding hands—that would send a heck of a message.

Once we're inside, Mateo jumps up to see me. What's he doing here? Did he get into trouble, too? I can't wait to tell him what De-Marcus did!

But Mateo looks down, sees DeMarcus and me holding hands, and my stomach flips. I let go of DeMarcus's hand and reach enthusiastically for Mateo, but he takes a step back from me.

"Mateo Hernandez," a counselor says, stepping out of his office. "You can come inside now."

I don't get a chance to explain, but he'll understand once I tell him. DeMarcus is a hero today.

Still, my gut clenches with tension. Mateo will be disappointed, and I fear the words that may come out of his mouth.

*It's okay, Aiden. It was all a lie, anyway. I never loved you. You and DeMarcus go and enjoy yourselves.*

Why can't my brain stop tormenting me?

Mr. Underkofler, one of the guidance counselors, sees us and says, "DeMarcus and Aiden, you better join us, too." When he shuts the door behind us all, he turns and says, "Look, guys. I don't like these policies any more than you do."

"Then why do we have them?" Mateo asks. Subtle anger vibrates within his voice. Seeing me hold hands with DeMarcus clearly enhanced whatever anger Mateo feels. But why is he here in the first place?

"Well, don't repeat this to anyone else here at this school, but we have a spineless principal who is completely whipped by toxic, homophobic ideas. We have a school board of homophobes elected by homophobes. It sucks." He takes a stack of papers from his desk and puts them in a folder. Then he sits down and motions for us to do the same. Mr. Underkofler looks bi-racial, but I don't know his background. He wears a white dress shirt with a *Star Trek*-themed tie. "They should be the ones sitting here having a talking-to, but they are the ones with power right now. And trust me, kids. The only thing a person in power wants is more power. I don't care if it's the school board president or the principal. Small-minded leaders see progressive movements as threats to their power."

"Why?" I ask.

"*Some* groups will always prioritize self-preservation over helping others. Whether it's logical or not, they see equality as taking a seat away from them at the table." Mr. Underkofler shakes his head. "The reality of equality is that we want everyone to have a seat at the table. No one is losing their seat. But that logic doesn't fly if fear and hate rule one's heart." He clears his throat. "So, tell me what got you all sent here."

DeMarcus and I recap our story, and I study Mateo's eyes. They widen at first—impressed perhaps. But they narrow a bit whenever he looks at DeMarcus, and I can't help but think there's some jealousy there.

"Wow." Mr. Underkofler fails to hide the grin on his face. "And what about you, Mateo?"

"I had, um, a run-in with, um, well, I mean some words were exchanged with—"

"Me," a voice says as Mr. Underkofler's door opens abruptly. "Miss James said to walk on in."

"Yes," Mr. Underkofler says, pointing at the last empty chair. My heart races at the sight of Michelle. Tall, beautiful, and strong—Michelle represents pure athleticism.

But right now, she looks pissed off with a lot to say, and I'm so ready to hear it.

"All right. Mateo, you go first. Then Michelle," Mr. Underkofler says.

"He called me a disgrace," Michelle snaps, ignoring the counselor's instructions. Anger flashes across her face, and Mateo doesn't deny it.

"You *are* a disgrace," Mateo says. "You of all people. How could you be on their side?"

"Decker warned me about your hate," Michelle says. "Look, I

get it." Her voice calms slightly. "I've been where you all have been. Trying to come out. Making peace with myself. Y'all got a lot of misplaced anger."

"Misplaced?" Mateo's cheeks flood with a crimson hue as he tightens his grip on the arms of the chair. "You don't know what we've been through."

"And you don't know what I've been through," Michelle counters. "Let me tell you something." Mr. Underkofler opens his mouth, but Michelle raises her left arm, stopping him. Talk about confidence. "It's important to have empathy for our community. But empathy also creates enemies. It's that simple. To feel for someone who has been wronged, there must be an enemy. I learned that the hard way." She pauses, and I wish I knew her background and her stories. "Someone to blame for that pain. You've made Decker and Krake and even some of your friends the enemy." Michelle shakes her head. "I mean, you both dated and lied to Camila. Isn't that the truth?"

Silence fills the room.

Mr. Underkofler clears his throat. "Why do you say that about empathy? That empathy creates enemies?"

"Because it's true," she says, arrogantly rolling her eyes. "I care about Black Lives Matter. But that movement—*any* movement—creates a bad guy, someone to blame. Same goes for me. Of course, I care about trans rights and equality. But why do I have to label anyone as the enemy? That only leads to more fighting and less understanding."

"Um," I mutter, half-raising my hand and incredulous that I have to say this. "I got beat up. Repeatedly. Would you just have me stand there and take it? Because that's what you're doing now! This school is passing homophobic rules literally right now. The people responsible for that—if they aren't the bad guys, then what are they?"

"It's so much more complicated than that," Michelle says calmly.

"How does Decker treat you?" DeMarcus asks.

"He treats me like an athlete. We don't talk about our sexuality. I know you're pissed at this school right now. But you want a shock? I'd rather not talk about it. I'm not here to be someone's poster child or spokesperson. Sorry, but I just want to live my life. At Decker's, I show up to train. He trains me," she says. "That's what I want and that's all there is to it."

"But don't you care about these homophobic rules?" Mateo asks. "You know your teacher tried to arrest our *sensei* for no reason at all last year. He threatened me and Aiden directly, too. I don't think you know who he really is."

She takes a moment to respond, and I hope she can believe us. "No. *You* don't. You want to change the world? Be who you are without picking fights with everyone around you. Or lying to everyone around you."

"Us, picking fights?" I stand.

"Aiden, sit down," Mr. Underkofler says, the white in his eyes wide and worried.

"No! You need to understand," I argue, looking down at Michelle, who sits peacefully in the office chair. "They're just all... ugh! They're stupid! Evil, even! Why can't you *see* that?"

Michelle stands, and I gulp. She's taller than me, and every part of her physique reminds me that she's way out of my league athletically.

"Not everything is good or bad or right or wrong. Some things are more complicated than that. Look," she sighs, "you think it was hard for you to come out? It was hard for me, too. I'm lucky that I had good parents, and they taught me one thing about the world that's helped me avoid the conflicts you have. Choose curiosity over clash." She takes a breath and crosses her arms. "Understand how and why they think. Why don't you show some empathy for that? Show them you're still willing to listen. You want to change minds?" Michelle laughs. I don't find any of this funny, and I can't believe she's laughing. "You do it from within. But none of you would know that, would you?" She shakes her head, chuckling again. "You're all quitters. You gave up on people a long time ago and decided to fight them instead. Don't tell me you're the good guys. 'Cause from where I'm standing, you're the problem. And I choose not to be a part of that problem."

Michelle doesn't ask for permission. She turns around, exits the office, and slams the door shut.

All of us, even Mr. Underkofler, are left speechless.

# 17

## *Aiden and Mateo's Fears*

DURING A BREAK in one of our practices later that week, Tisha asks, "Mister Samuels? We had an idea we wanted to run by you. What if we do a demo for the school? Like at a halftime show? The club needs a boost in morale."

We had new students join after the tournament last spring, and our numbers were pretty good when this school year began. But Decker continues to offer incredible deals and gets students to sign exclusive contracts. Michelle signed a contract for three years, which I can't believe. Decker's a master manipulator.

"That's a great idea," Mr. Samuels says. "We can run some *kata*, break some boards, and…." His eyes twinkle, and I know that look. "Yes, I've been working on a little surprise for you that is absolutely perfect for a public demonstration."

"What is it?" Tony asks.

"It might get me in trouble." Mr. Samuels rolls his eyes. "I can handle some good trouble, though. One of my heroes, John Lewis, used to say, 'Get in good trouble. Necessary trouble.' That's what we will do."

"What kind of trouble?" Amanda asks.

"Don't you all love surprises? Let me arrange the demo first with the school, and then I'll tell you." Mr. Samuels laughs. "Okay, back to training. Everyone line up."

I sigh, wanting to know the secret. We get in our warm-up positions in the study hall dojo.

"Today, I want to talk to you about empathy," Mr. Samuels says, walking the room.

We have eight students at practice today, more of a group than a team. Hate and rules put people back in the closet, and we lost the very crowd we had hoped to attract. We stand in our white gis. Mateo, Amanda, Tony, DeMarcus, Tisha, and I stand in the front row, proudly wearing our purple belts. Mateo has caught up quickly, and Mr. Samuels has been teaching us a new *kata*. I wish we would practice that more—it's by far my favorite form so far. It's called *Empi Sho*, and it features all sorts of new moves, including leaps and jumps. The rest of the students—all three of them—are white belts. Are they LGBTQ+ or other outsiders? I don't know.

It doesn't surprise me that Mr. Samuels wants to discuss empathy. We told him everything Michelle said at the counselor's office, which still confuses me.

"Empathy is feeling what another person experiences, and it's important because we will never truly know how each of us sees the world. For example, some of you won't know the fear that pulses through me when I'm pulled over by a police officer. The color of my skin changes things. That doesn't mean, though, that I view police as bad guys." He clears his throat. "In this town, I haven't had the best of experiences. But it's not always like that. Some of you will never know what it's like to torture yourself about your sexuality. We can imagine and assume, but we never fully know. Now, if empathy points out a problem—systemic racism with some law enforcement, for example—then it's worth addressing the problem. But it's not about painting people as solely good or evil. It's often about the systems and structures in which those people live and work." He takes a deep breath. I'm trying to follow, but I have no idea what he even means by systemic problems. "I know this is a lot to understand. Partner up. I've got an exercise for you."

Mateo smiles at me, and we face each other.

"Everyone, close your eyes. Tell your partner about something that hurt you recently, a physical or emotional pain," Mr. Samuels instructs.

Which one do I choose?

Silence fills the room, and then a few whispers emerge. Talk of break-ups. An argument with a parent or friend.

Courage rumbles through me. I feel the words coming, but I pause for a moment. Letting them stew for a few extra seconds in my brain, I search for courage.

"Be true to your inner selves," Mr. Samuels says. "If you can't be honest with yourself, then how can you ever be honest with others? Honesty, integrity, character—you develop these by first being honest with yourself."

I speak my truth.

"I'm scared that any minute you'll tell me this is all a lie," I tell Mateo. "That *we* are a lie. That you're *still* lying."

My face burns with red-hot fear.

"Now, take it in. No response. Just take it in. Picture how they feel," Mr. Samuels says.

Mateo sighs heavily.

A long minute passes, and then Mr. Samuels continues. "Now, I want the other person to speak. Tell them what worries you now. Tell them your pain, your fears, too."

I gulp, bracing myself for what Mateo could tell me.

He doesn't hesitate. "I'm worried I'm not strong enough to be honest. I'm worried I'm weak. Remember when I told you how strong you were? I wasn't lying. You're so strong on the inside. That's where I'm weak. I'm worried that someone like Krake or Decker could manipulate me again. I hate that you worry about things like that, too, because you have every right and reason to be worried. I'm not as strong as you, but I'm trying, Aiden." He clears his throat. My eyes remain closed, but for a moment I wonder if he's choking up, holding something back.

How can I ever fully trust someone who was manipulated before and could be manipulated again?

My heart sinks.

"Highest rank, open your eyes," Mr. Samuels says. "Lowest rank, take a ready position, keeping your eyes shut. Now, high ranks, you will practice your techniques with control. I want you to strike near the head so that your partner's hair moves. But you aren't to make contact. Build trust. Build control. It's fifty push-ups for every time you hit skin. Ready? Corkscrew punches first."

Mr. Samuels counts, and I throw punches at Mateo's head. His eyes stay closed, but a tear runs from his left eye down his cheek. Mr. Samuels has us switch to round-house kicks. We keep practicing with control. The wind from my kick wipes Mateo's tear away.

When the exercise concludes, I'm drenched in sweat. I've thrown a hundred moves at Mateo, never hitting him once. It feels good to release the frustration.

Mr. Samuels has partners switch, but Mateo raises his hand.

"Sir, can I be excused for a moment?" He opens his wet eyes.

Mr. Samuels nods, and Mateo exits the study hall dojo.

I watch him leave.

He doesn't return.

Practice ends, and he's nowhere to be found on campus. No messages sent to my phone.

He doesn't text me that night, either, and I can't find the courage to be the first one to text him. Why does he get to be upset? I'm the one worried he's gonna break *my* heart!

I love Mateo so much that my chest could explode. I think about him virtually every waking second. Why does love hurt so much? If I'm not lonely, I'm sad. If I'm not sad, I'm scared. And at all times, I feel exhausted. Before bed that night, I take his letter out of my dresser, the one he says I must wait to open. Why should I wait any longer?

What are we fighting for if not each other?

# 18

## *Gutter Balls*

A TEXT MESSAGE wakes me the next morning.

*I love you.*

That's all Mateo says. That's all he needs to say. With Mat's letter unopened in my hands, I text him back.

*I love you, too.*

Sure, I'm curious what Mateo wrote me, but I don't want to be the guy he can't trust. I'll wait to open it until he tells me to.

In our group chat, Tisha suggests dinner and bowling for some Friday night fun. I enthusiastically say yes, hoping Mateo will join, when my phone rings.

"Hey," I greet Mateo.

*"Hola,"* he says. *"Lo siento. I can't go."*

"Why not?"

*"Mi padre. Ugh! I got detention, you know, for getting sent to the counselor's office, and he grounded me. It sucks."*

"Yeah, it does."

*"I gotta go. He's coming."* Mateo disconnects, and I stare at my phone. My brain urges me to ask why he left practice and why he didn't message last night, but I barely had time to say hello. At least he's still allowed to text me. I keep waiting for the day he asks to message using a different app, in case his parents check his messages.

I read through the group messages, and everyone's cool with dinner and bowling. Everyone but my boyfriend.

When the evening comes, we meet at the bowling alley and eat there. The pizza isn't half-bad, and we get mozzarella sticks and deep-fried mushrooms to share. You can't go wrong with fried food, especially on a teenage budget.

In the eighth frame of game one, my score reaches forty. I try not to intimidate anyone with my natural athleticism, you know. No one cares about winning, and we high-five each other every time we throw a gutter ball.

"If we waited for someone to get a strike," Tony says, "we'd be waiting forever."

"Should we do bumper bowling for the next game?" Amanda asks.

"Nah, it's more fun this way!" DeMarcus says.

"Of course, you'd say that," I tell him, punching him gently on his bicep. "You're winning. The only one to score over one hundred."

We play a second game, and right when we begin, from the corners of my eyes, I see—of course!—a group that fills me with dread. Is there nothing else to do in this town?

The first people I see are Logan and Camila.

Oh, please. They can *not* be friends!

"Are you *kidding* me right now?" Tisha asks. "Why is she hanging out with him?"

Michelle and Jeff saunter in behind Camila and Logan. Jeff attacked me in the bathroom last year, but I surprised him. Michelle looks beautiful—her hair has grown out more. Everything about her looks more—I question my thoughts, trying not to think the wrong thing—well, female.

It's just the four of them, I think, as I hold my breath. Four of them and five of us. That's good. We can handle that if it becomes a problem, which I hope it won't.

No more fighting.

We watch them check in, put on their rental shoes, and walk this way. *Please let them go to the opposite end.*

As if the universe wants to screw with us, the four of them get assigned the empty lane right next to us.

"You gotta be joking," Camila says when she finally realizes what's happening.

"Ignore them," Michelle says. "They're not worth it."

Logan and Jeff remain suspiciously quiet. My heart races. Every time Logan or Jeff takes out a phone, I worry they're texting the rest of the team. I shoot a quick text to Mateo.

*Wish you were here. Jeff and Logan just arrived with Mila and Michelle.*

Mila. She was such a good person, and I treated her terribly, something I want to remedy, if only I knew how. Jeff gets a strike on his first throw. Logan gets a spare. Puke.

"Nice score, Aids," Logan says to me, looking up at our scoreboard.

I roll my eyes. "Your homophobic insults are as out of fashion as that camo shirt you're wearing. You going to war here in the bowling alley?"

"Whatever, Aids," Jeff says.

"Do you not hear that, Michelle? Camila? Are you okay with them calling Aiden *Aids?*" Tisha snaps.

Michelle ignores us, but Camila has no problem saying something. "Stay in your lane." I stare at the girl I used to know—the girl with the cutest freckles, whose smile I envied and wanted for myself, whose dark hair over her brown skin used to be magical to me. Not in a romantic way, but in a platonic way. And now? Now, the smile tuns malicious, and bruises and makeup cover the cute freckles.

Tisha slams her fists on the desk near the scoring computer. "What is wrong with you people? I'm so tired of this!"

"I'm tired of liars and people betraying me. But you have never tried to understand," Camila snaps. "You are all a bunch of pathetic liars."

Tony and Amanda stand and gather around Tisha. "Stop," I say, putting my arm out and holding them back. "Please." I don't know what to say or do, but we cannot be involved in any more fights, especially with people I wish were our friends.

Jeff slams a bowling ball down and stares right at DeMarcus and me. "Where's your boyfriend, loser? Or are you two dating now?"

"Wouldn't you like to know," DeMarcus answers. He reaches for my hand and holds it. "Why, you like to picture us making out? Something for your spank bank?"

DeMarcus surprises me. He's totally hot when he talks tough like this, and I can't help but admire it.

"You mother—" Jeff starts.

"No," Michelle says firmly. She grabs him. She whispers something in his ear. How can she be friends with these two homophobes?

Jeff smiles, and I wish I knew what Michelle said.

But there's no time to ask more questions.

The doors to the bowling alley open. It's another group of wrestlers. And another.

And another.

Some wear Decker's MMA shirts.

Camila approaches our lane with a sinister smile. "I hope your new daddy is coming to pick you up soon, Aiden. Because you *all* are going to get what you deserve tonight. And trust me, it's not going to be enough."

I gulp. So much for four against five. As I do quick math, it looks more like twenty against five.

I'm so tired of fighting like this. We can't live this way. Something has to change.

Before I can figure it out, one of the stupid wrestlers pulls the fire alarm, forcing everyone to take it outside.

# 19

*A Twisted Trio*

"DO WE FIGHT? Or do we run?" Tony asks as we walk outside.

"I don't wanna run," Tisha says.

"We're so outnumbered, though," Amanda whispers.

We need a miracle.

"We can try to run," Tony suggests. "We'd be stupid to fight this many people." The moment we step outside, we sprint toward the high school. It's only a few blocks away, and there's always some kind of event going on. If we can get inside, we can get help. I hope.

I know running away is the wiser option and that it is the right thing to do, better than fighting. But dammit if I'm not mad about it, too. Jeff and Logan deserve a fist in the face, and running away makes us look weak in their eyes.

Risking a glance over my shoulder, I don't see anyone following us. My pace slows, and I find a steady rhythm in my breathing. Maybe I'm overreacting. But when people have jumped out of a vehicle on a public street to beat you up, well, you might develop some paranoia and trust issues, too. The high school's around the corner, so we stop for a breather.

"Was Camila just screwing with us?" Tisha asks, breathing hard. She puts her hands on her hips and bends backward, stretching.

"Makes. Sense." Tony has a harder time catching his breath. "To mess. With us."

DeMarcus spins around, not breathing nearly as hard as the rest of us. Next to Mateo, he's clearly in the best shape. "I don't trust them. They get their kicks on crap like this."

We walk down the street, the high school on the right. When we turn, we stop dead in the road.

There's a small parking lot by the entrance nearest the wrestling room, and police vehicles fill the lot. My stomach drops. It's a fall Friday night, but there's no home football game tonight. Why such a police presence here tonight?

"Something's not right about any of this," Amanda says. "We should go."

Tony nods, but Tisha holds up her hand. "Don't you wanna see what it is?"

"What if it's a setup?" DeMarcus asks.

"Wait a second!" I point with my right hand. "That car—the one on the far left."

"What about it?" Amanda asks.

"That's Mateo's dad's car," I whisper, chills racing down my spine.

"Now we have to see what's going on," Tisha says. "C'mon!" She takes off before anyone can argue, and we follow reluctantly.

Quickly, I call Mateo, but it goes right to voice mail.

We approach the parking lot just as a door to the school pops open. Three men walk out. We duck behind a cop car.

"Is there anything else we can do to help you, Mister Hernandez?" That's Mateo's father, and I'd recognize the awful voice anywhere—Coach Krake.

"No. Mister Krake, thank you," Mr. Hernandez says. I strain my neck, trying to peer around the vehicle. The two men shake hands. "And thank you, Captain," he continues. "I want my son safe. I'm glad you understand that."

"We most certainly do," Decker says.

"It's a shame he gave up his future for that boy," Krake says.

Nausea rises in my throat. "He would have had a free ride to any university in the country. That's why I can't stand that kid. He ruined your son's life."

Mr. Hernandez sighs. "Well, thank you for all the information you've given me. You know you can't trust what a teenager says."

"Especially sexually misguided teenagers," Decker adds. "But don't you worry. We'll straighten him out."

Wait. *What?* What's happening? My heart beats so fast I think it's going to burst out of my chest. I start to move, but DeMarcus grabs me. His powerful grip surprises me, and I stay still.

Mr. Hernandez starts his vehicle and drives away. Decker and Krake return inside the building.

"I wanna know what's going on inside," Tisha says. "Why are there multiple cop cars here?"

"Did you all hear what I just heard?" I ask, my entire body shaking. "What's going on?"

No one answers. Tisha's already half-way to the door, desperate for more information.

"They're training," she says, after a few moments. "The cops. They're training with Krake in the wrestling room."

"Why here?" Amanda asks. "What for?"

We shrug.

"What are you doing, Aiden?" Tony asks when I pull out my phone and start dialing.

"Trying to call Mat. None of my texts are being read. He's not answering. I need to talk to him," I say. I kick at one of the police cars, which triggers an alarm.

"Crap! Run!" Tony says, and we spin around in the parking lot.

But we're not alone.

"Ugh. Something stupid this way comes," Tisha mutters, clenching her fists.

It's the bowling alley crew—Camila, Logan, Jeff, and Michelle.

They're walking right toward us. And they're not alone. Other wrestlers walk behind them. Suddenly, the door opens behind us, and Krake and Decker step out.

The presence of adults should alleviate my fears, especially the presence of a cop. But not in this town.

I've seen this play out before, and it's never been good.

# 20

## *It's Brutal Out Here*

"WHAT'S THIS, GAYDEN?" Krake asks me directly. "Vandalizing police vehicles, now? What's the punishment for that, Captain?"

"We'll start with a nasty fine. Send something home to stress out your mommy." Decker laughs. "What's your mom have in her savings? A few hundred? A few thousand, maybe? It must be rough for a single mom."

"Haven't you heard? His mother sleeps with your former student." Krake chuckles. "How does that make you feel? Maybe your teacher that you admire so much just wanted to get close to you to get in your mother's pants."

What the hell is wrong with these two so-called adults?

"See that anger on his face?" Decker says. "That's the sign of a poor teacher. One must keep emotions calm to win fights."

Krake laughs. "Let them hang out with their friends. All your friends." He gestures behind me. When I look over my shoulder, I see at least a dozen others—Krake's wrestlers and some of Decker's MMA students. Decker snickers and enters the high school, Krake holding the door open for him. Krake winks at me as he walks inside and shuts the door. A few moments later, the lights turn off and the school darkens.

DeMarcus faces his former teammates. "Why can't you all leave us alone? Can't you see that it's that asshole coach and cop making us fight?"

Tisha glares at Camila and turns to Michelle. "Do you hear this? Why are you with them?"

Michelle steps up in front of Camila and faces Tisha. "What I care about is being the best fighter I can be. While you hang out in a study hall room and pick up litter, I'm training for a life you can't imagine."

Tisha snaps. She lunges at Michelle, but Michelle calmly steps to the side, extends her leg, and trips Tisha, who falls hard on the concrete.

DeMarcus runs at Michelle, and Jeff and Logan jump up, physically putting themselves in between Michelle and Camila and us.

"No," Michelle says. "They started this. Everyone saw that, right? We used words, and Tisha attacked me. Tisha—the person who sent me a message inviting me to sit with her on the first day of school. Guess you got a habit of trying to screw with people like me and Camila, huh?"

Logan and Jeff back off, each wearing a sinister smile on their faces.

"I'm tired of this!" DeMarcus shouts. "You don't understand. We're not the bad guys here."

"Sure looks like it from where I'm standing."

Something snaps in me. The false accusations, the misunderstanding, the intentional manipulation from the adults, the fact that Michelle and Camila see us as the bad guys....

Say something enough, and perhaps it will come true.

Anger washes away all logic. She wants a fight. They want to see us as the bad guys. Fine. They win, and I'm tired of it. I push DeMarcus to the side and then execute a side kick right at Michelle's stomach.

She grabs my leg before I make contact. She kicks me in the groin and sweeps my standing leg. My back hits concrete and the wind gushes out of me.

I watch as DeMarcus, Tony, and Amanda rush at Michelle.

DeMarcus grabs her, relying on his wrestling to take her down. She drops into a low stance, elbows him hard in the chest and stomach, and flips him over her shoulder. Tony and Amanda grab Michelle's arms, trying to stop her. Michelle uses their momentum against them. They pull in one direction, and I watch carefully—this isn't a novice fighter. This isn't luck. This is more talent than I've ever seen.

It's as scary as it is incredible.

Instead of resisting Amanda and Tony's pull, she moves with them, executing multiple kicks to both.

Wait a damn minute—is that....

*Kujaku.* Peacock. It was a blur, but I swear Michelle used some of the techniques Mr. Samuels taught us at my sleepover.

The entire thing takes seconds. Michelle takes us all down, and the rest of her teammates stand cockily by her side, laughing. Logan blows on his nails, mocking us in multiple ways.

"Karma," Camila says. "This is what you get for lying. And remember—we just came to talk. You all started this fight."

They turn and walk away, finally leaving us alone. The five of us get up slowly, each hurting in different areas, physically and emotionally. It was five against one, and the one won.

We have no words to say and no energy to speak. Tisha and Amanda check on each other and then on us. We're okay. Hurt but okay.

A flurry of thoughts storms my mind. What was Mr. Hernandez doing with Decker and Krake? How does someone like Decker embrace a trans student and yet hate us so much? And how would anyone—even Mateo—ever beat an athlete as talented as Michelle?

We're losing every fight, and now they're calling us the bad guys. Logan or Jeff, to my surprise, did absolutely nothing. Tisha and I threw the first attacks.

What's happening to us?

# 21

## *Teenage Love*

"MOM, WHAT DO I do?" I ask after I told her about everything.

"Oh, honey," she says, rubbing my back. When I'm upset, she rubs my upper back to relax me. My memories of being ill consist of my whines with Mom right by my side, always trying to comfort me. "Where do you wanna start?"

"With Mateo," I tell her.

"Want me to invite his parents over for dinner?"

"No!" I say too quickly. Mom frowns. "I mean, that's a good idea. I dunno. I'm sorry."

"I was a teenager once, too," she says with a half-smile. "Hanging out with parents is the worst, especially the parents of your partner."

"What were my father's parents like?" My mom lost her parents when she was young. Her mother died of cancer, and her father passed away due to a sudden heart attack. I was a little kid when it happened, and I don't remember them well. Those were my first funeral experiences, and I've never met my father's parents.

"They hated me," she says.

"How could anyone hate you?"

She blushes, looks like she's about to hug me, then just laughs. "Thank you, kiddo. I needed that."

"What's wrong?"

"Oh. Um, work stress. One thing after another. Never mind that." She studies me closely. "Your father was a drunk because his parents were drunks. I don't even know if they're still alive."

"They never asked about me?"

Mom can't hide the disappointment on her face. "Aiden, I want you to remember something. Never let absent people determine your value. They're absent from our lives because of their issues. Not ours."

I fidget uncomfortably on the sofa.

"We may not be able to control the cards we're dealt, but we can control what we do with what we have. You've been hurt enough. You deserve joy, and I want you to fight for that."

"I'm scared Mateo's gonna hurt me." Mom's eyes sharpen. "Not physically. You know, here." I tap the left side of my chest.

Mom nods. "Relationships are difficult, and you have to realize that you and Mateo may not last forever. You may have lots of boy-friends." Mom takes a deep breath. "Or he may be your one true love for life."

It's my turn to sigh, and I look away.

"The best thing you can do is to live in the present, Aiden. Enjoy your time right now. One day at a time, okay?"

"Yeah."

"All right, kiddo," Mom continues. "I've got a plan for you. Lloyd isn't the only one with some tricks up his sleeve."

"Mom, do you love Mister Samuels?"

She blushes. I haven't seen Mom blush like this in, well, maybe ever.

"I do. Is that strange for you?"

I shake my head. "I like that you're happy. He's a good guy."

"He is." Mom wipes the corner of her eyes. "I'm glad we both found him."

"Me, too."

"Okay, so here's what we're gonna do today," Mom says, launching into a plan.

WITH SO MANY problems—Decker, Krake, Michelle, Camila, the upcoming tournament, stupid school rules—I'm grateful to focus on the one that matters the most to me right now.

Mateo and me.

Mom asked, "What makes him happy? Think about what he wants, too. The best romance comes when we can detach ourselves from our worries and wants. Then, ask what would make the other person happy."

So, I text Mateo and tell him I'm coming over. It's a Sunday afternoon. I don't knock on the door. I text Mateo to meet me outside, so I can avoid his parents. I'm still confused about Mat's dad at the high school, but one thing at a time right now.

"Hey," Mateo greets me.

I've got my hands behind my back.

"Are you hiding something?" he asks, a silly grin on his face.

"Maybe," I tease.

"What is it?"

"A gift."

"For me?"

"Yes, but you'll have to earn it first."

His silly grin turns into a sweet smile. He steps closer to me. He beams, revealing those beautiful white teeth. He kisses me. His lips press gently against mine at first, then harder, then he hugs me and pulls me close against him. It takes a lot of willpower to step away.

I show him the gift. It's a picture I drew of Mateo and me from last year's tournament, a drawing of our first kiss with people cheering in the background. I even put it in a small frame.

"Oh, Aiden. Wow. You made this?"

"I'm not very good at art, but I wanted to try... I just thought...."

Suddenly, my face burns. "I thought, um, you'd look at it and think of me. And that you'd remember there are still people who cheer for us even when it doesn't seem like it. Something to think about when you get down."

"You are the sweetest person I know. I love you, Aiden."

He kisses me again, and it takes my breath away.

"Do you wanna go somewhere, um, private?" he asks.

"Yes."

One hundred percent yes.

# 22

## *Girls on Girls, Guys on Guys*

"SO, UM, I guess you wanna know about my dad, yeah?" Mat asks. "I heard you all saw him at the high school."

Mat's parents were home, so we went to our favorite spot—the park with the swings. Unfortunately, it isn't private, so my hopes of a mega make-out session die, at least temporarily. We swing and talk, while a couple of families hang out around us. A dad plays catch with his son. I see father-son bonding moments all the time, and while I try not to think about it, it bothers me. I never got that experience. Sounds like Mat has a cruel father, too, in different ways.

"Way to go, bro," the father says to his little boy when he catches the ball, and I try not to gag. Never mind. There's nothing about "bro" talk that I miss.

Shaking my thoughts, I focus on Mateo. "Yeah, what's up?"

"So, he wants to—"

"Well, hello, losers," a voice calls from behind.

Can we not go *anywhere* in this stupid town without being bothered?

"Screw off, Jeff," Mateo says, recognizing the voice instantly like I do. If it's not Tanner, it's Logan. If it's not Logan, it's Jeff. If it's not a kid, it's Krake or Decker. Maybe I need to convince Mom and Mr. Samuels to move.

Jeff isn't alone. He's with one other person.

Michelle.

Were they—no, impossible, right? For a second, I thought Jeff and Michelle were holding hands. Each put their hands in their pockets the moment we saw them. That's a little sus. Jeff wears black tights. I know they are athletic leggings, but they look like tights. He looks so gay for a straight man, and yes, I hate so many things about having that thought, but I do have it.

Michelle looks gorgeous as always, tight-fitting jeans over her long legs, and a colorful blue and white top.

Could a homophobe like Jeff date a trans student like Michelle? And of course, how is Michelle friends with such d-bags?

"Let's not call them names," Michelle says loudly.

"I'm not," Jeff defends. "Just stating the truth."

Mateo looks at me, but I can't read his face.

"Last year, Mateo won the tournament. You know that?" I ask Michelle. "It came down to Mateo representing wrestling and me representing karate. Now we're both on the same team because of all the crap they put him through. Why don't you ask your team about that?"

"Clearly, the *months* of martial arts experience you all have will pay off," Michelle says sarcastically. "I've been training for years. I'm winning this. You all should know that—"

She stops suddenly. Know *what*?

Mateo's face turns darker. "You think someone like Decker will let you face me? We've always fought by gender."

For once, Michelle looks displeased. "I'm in the girls' division, so you can relax, I guess."

"Is Decker gonna keep you in the girls'—"

"Shut up, already," Jeff interrupts me. "Captain Decker has specific rules. Boys fight boys. Girls fight girls." My head hurts. It's almost a progressive, positive thought, buried by the hate they all have for us, I guess. A terrible smile grows on his face. "So, Aids, which gender will you be fighting?"

He sounds so much like Coach Krake I could puke.

Michelle flashes him a dirty look. Good! These people aren't hiding who they are, and I don't understand how she doesn't see that.

I take a step forward. Jeff doesn't scare me. I've faced him before, and he met my arm bar in the boys' restroom. I'm ten times better than I was then. Mateo holds me back, which is certainly for the best. Maybe I'm better than Jeff, but Michelle is one-thousand times better than me.

Jeff laughs, and Michelle gives him another concerned look.

"Did you know, Michelle," I start, "that your boyfriend here repeatedly insulted my sexuality last year? Is that who you like to date?"

"She is *not* my girlfriend," Jeff says this through gritted teeth, and I'm clearly getting under his skin. Michelle looks hard at Jeff again. I've touched some kind of nerve.

Not backing down, I continue, "Why not? Are you saying you wouldn't date Michelle?"

"Shut up already." Jeff pushes away from Michelle and gets right in my face. The swing set sits behind us, and we stand face-to-face in a sandpit.

"It looks like you would rather kiss me?" My heart feels like it moved to my throat. Something pulses wildly inside me. Mateo looks at me like he doesn't know who I am. I get it. Last year, I'd be running or hiding. This year, I'm standing up for myself, even if I take a beating.

Anger pulses through me. I clench my fists. My arms shake, and all I can think about is taking my fist and slamming it against Jeff's stupid face.

Mateo pulls me back more and steps in front of me. Michelle tries to do the same with Jeff. Now Mateo and Michelle face each other.

I've never seen them side-by-side. Mateo has the muscle. He looks like a wrestler—athletic, strong, and powerful. Michelle is taller and leaner. She looks like she's faster than Mateo, but not as strong.

Chills run through me. Who would win this fight?

"I'd love to face the best wrestler in the school," Michelle says.

"So, do it!" I say. "Not here. At the tournament. Tell Decker you insist. Tell him you insist on fighting the best. Or are you too scared to face Mateo?"

"I'm not scared," she says calmly, not taking her eyes off Mateo.

I force a laugh. "Ha. Maybe Decker's the one scared. Maybe that's why he'd keep you and Mateo in separate divisions."

"Fine," Michelle snaps through nearly clenched teeth. "I'll tell him. But you'll regret it. You will lose."

"I'm not scared of you," Mateo says. I reach for his hand, and it's shaking, though. Michelle and Mat stay like this, eyes locked and unflinching, face to face, for what seems like the longest minute of my life.

Then Michelle smiles. She turns to Jeff. She doesn't say a single word, and neither does he. I'm both disappointed and relieved.

When they leave, Mat releases my hand and crosses his arms.

"I wanna go home, Aiden."

"Mat, why?"

He looks at me with disappointment in his eyes. He's looked at me like that before, and I hate the reminders of it. "Let me choose my battles."

He turns and walks away, but I call out for him. "Oh, Mat! No, I'm sorry. I, uh, I dunno what I was thinking. *Lo siento!* I figured there's no way Decker will let Michelle face you, not with all his gender BS. I just thought it was a way of getting under their skin."

He stops for a moment and turns around. "And what if Decker agrees, Aiden? I mean, you really don't think that homophobe is gonna let someone born a male fight our girls, do you? Think, man! What if this is what Decker's been wanting all along? You might have to face Michelle in the ring, too, you know." He shakes his head and walks away from me.

Why can't I do anything right?

# 23

*Why Protest?*

AT LUNCH, I sit with Tisha, Mateo, DeMarcus, Tony, and Amanda. DeMarcus and Mateo sit at opposite ends of the table. Mateo sits across from me, with Tisha on my left.

"I'm so sick of this school!" Amanda shouts, loud enough to cause a moment of silence among the cacophony of chatter. "I've been researching, and did you know there are even states that have what they call 'don't say gay' laws? Like for the entire state!"

"You sound like my grandmother," DeMarcus says, trying to lighten the mood. "She's already telling me who to vote for and not vote for, and I'm not even eighteen."

"Sounds like you have a kick-ass grandmother," Tisha says. "I'm with Amanda. My parents showed me some of the communication the school has emailed them. I don't understand how any modern school can get away with this crap."

"My grandmother said they tried to ban Holocaust books a couple of years ago," DeMarcus adds. "Seriously, just some graphic novels that show what happened. Why would anyone do that?"

I shake my head. Why *would* anyone bury history? Then a terrible thought comes to mind. *Unless they kinda-sorta-maybe agree with the oppressors.* Sadly, I can see this school siding with the privileged instead of the oppressed.

"What do you think Mister Samuels has planned for the demo tonight?" Tony asks.

"He's been happy about whatever it is." I shrug. "He said I'll find out with everyone else at the demo."

"He's cool like that," DeMarcus says. "No advantages for you just because he's doing your mom."

"Hey!" I say, but I can't be too mad. DeMarcus bursts into laughter when he says it. If there's one thing I've learned, jokes about who is doing your mom never get old, and it doesn't matter if you're gay or straight.

Mateo remains suspiciously quiet the entire time. I still don't know what his father was doing with Krake or Decker. We haven't talked about it. We haven't talked much at all since last weekend at the park. Even our text conversations feel brief and meaningless this week.

"I can't wait for the board breaking," I say. Mateo doesn't look up.

"And Mister S is going to do an awesome break, too. A couple of them," Tisha says. "That should wow the stupid football crowd."

Mateo still doesn't look up.

"Mat, what's eating you?" Amanda gently elbows him in the side. She sits next to him, across from me and Tisha.

Mateo mumbles something, but we don't hear. The cafeteria gets louder for a second, and Mateo repeats his words.

"I said I don't know if *mi padre* is gonna let me go." He still doesn't make eye contact with us. Crap. Am I a bad boyfriend for not asking him more about his parents all week? Sometimes, as much as I love Mateo, he makes me feel even worse about myself.

The bell rings, signifying the end of what little freedom high school gives us, and we move on to our afternoon classes. The rest of the school day passes quickly, mainly because instead of taking notes in class, I use the time to choreograph fight scenes. Little *X*s and *O*s line my notes, with arrows and footnotes of attacks and defenses. I don't know what, if anything, I'll do with these fight scenes, but it's a cool way to pass the time.

Can you blame me for not wanting to learn history from a school like mine? It's the kind of town where white people have a meltdown if you want to change the name of a school from an old white dude to any modern person of color. Mom told me once that someone proposed changing our school's name from Washington High to Obama High, and a school board member suffered an actual stroke.

I'm so tired of people who want to live in the past. The past was only good for very specific people, and it sure tells you a lot about someone when that's what they want.

Later that night, I share my concerns with Mr. Samuels, who drives me to the demonstration at the football game.

He starts laughing and doesn't stop for a full minute.

I blush, worried I expressed something completely stupid.

"Oh, Aiden. I don't mean to laugh." He chuckles in between words. "It's just that I've known what this school is like. I chose to be here because I thought I could make a difference. When I was hired, I was the only Black teacher. I chose to stay here, though, because I knew there would be Black students in my classroom who never in their life even had a Black teacher. Representation matters. Education should be about recognizing problems and inequalities instead of burying them. That's why I love ya, kid. I laugh because you are smarter than the people running this town. You've got a great mind and an even greater heart."

I blush again, for multiple reasons. "Why was it so funny?"

"Lots of reasons," he says, with a huge smile on his face. "Some reasons are depressing, so I don't want to share those now. But other reasons are uplifting. It gives me hope that what we're doing at this demonstration tonight is the right thing. You, kid, just boosted *my* confidence."

"Oh. Well, you're welcome," I say with a laugh.

*"Arigato!"* He chuckles again.

"So, what's the secret? What are we doing tonight?"

"I know you love a good secret. You thought *Wansu* had secrets?

*Empi Sho* has even more. I can't wait for you to discover them. Have you figured out the peacock's secrets yet?"

"You're dodging the question," I reply. So am I because no, I have not figured out the hidden meanings of the peacock.

"You do know, Aiden, that the best defense is simply to avoid the attack altogether."

"Okay. But tonight is not about self-defense. You've got an attack planned. Why is that okay?"

"Great question." He pats me on the knee with his right hand while his left turns the steering wheel. We're seconds away from the high school and our first-ever demonstration—a half-time show at a home football game to a packed crowd.

"So?"

"There's an order to things, wouldn't you agree? Like if you disagree with me, you'd come to me first? But if it doesn't get resolved, you'd go to my supervisor. Then to his or hers. And so on, right?"

"I guess?"

"I haven't told you this, but I am done having conversations with those above me. I've talked and talked and written and written, one concern after another. So has your mom. Oh, is she a firecracker, and I love her for it. Sometimes—only sometimes—you must go on the attack. We're going to make people see us and listen to us."

"But what are we gonna do exactly?"

"You're about to find out," he says, winking at me and pulling into Washington High's faculty parking lot.

# 24

## *Rainbow Protest*

THE SCHOOL ALLOWS us five whole minutes. Football consumes hours and months, but, to be honest, it's a miracle that Mr. Samuels even made that limited amount of time happen.

"Okay," Mr. Samuels says in the high school commons after the football game starts, "here's the plan."

We rehearse the demonstration one more time, with an added surprise. There's just one huge disappointment—no Mateo.

Still, I can't wait to do this. And I guess with all the crap Mateo's going through with his parents, he should be careful about causing a scene. Because we're going to cause one heck of a scene. Finally, halftime comes, and it's our turn.

The crowd claps as we take the field, perhaps out of habit for supporting the dance team or the marching band. We're going first, and then those teams will put on their shows. We wear our white traditional gis with a belt on the outside. It's extra hot, and suddenly, nervousness hits me harder than ever. Perhaps it's the crowd—way bigger than last year's tournament. Where the heck is Mateo? Surely, he at least came to watch and support? Scanning the enormous crowd, I can't find him.

We take our place in the middle of the football field. Mr. Samuels signals to the MC high up in the stadium, and music plays.

We start with forms synced to music—our traditional katas of

*Wansu, Anaku,* and *Nihanchi Sho.* Most faces in the crowd yawn. Others check their phone. My stomach sinks. It's hard to create change when people won't even give you a second of their time.

They won't be bored for long. We've got to give this our all.

We move to the track on the home-team side. Time for board breaking. We've practiced this, too. Each of us has a partner. Since Mateo isn't here, DeMarcus and I team up. He holds a board for me. On Mr. Samuels's cue, I break it with a step-behind-sidekick. We make a domino effect of one board break after another. Then my side holds boards for our partners, reversing rolls, and they break their boards with a palm strike.

Finally, some cheers come from the audience, and more people look at us than at their phones.

DeMarcus, Amanda, Tony, Tisha, and I lie down on the track. Three other students hold boards on one side of us. Mr. Samuels walks to the opposite side. We've practiced this, but I can't help but be extra nervous in front of the crowd. *Sensei's* a big guy, and if he lands on any of us—well, to the hospital we'd go, if not the morgue.

The music changes, which is our cue that Mr. Samuels prepares to fly. He runs toward us, leaps over all five of us who are laying on the track, finds perfect, beautiful form, extends one leg into flawless technique, and breaks the boards with a flying sidekick.

The crowd gasps.

But he's not done yet. And neither are we.

We line up behind Mr. Samuels, who now faces several concrete bricks all set up on the track. He bends down, ignites a lighter, and the bricks catch fire. It's all part of the demo—a little lighter fluid on the bricks to make it extra entertaining for the crowd. Mr. Samuels shouts a powerful *kiai* and slams a clenched fist through multiple bricks.

The crowd erupts in cheers.

"I hope Krake and Decker are watching!" I tell Tisha. "That could be Krake's face!"

Still, it's not our finale. With less than a minute left, we remove our white uniforms. Mr. Samuels decided it's time for a change of appearance for public events.

Underneath, we wear sleeveless black T-shirts and black pants. But the kicker is our new belt.

Mr. Samuels gave us all the same belt. It's what he found on the computer the evening I walked in and found him laughing hysterically at his master plan.

"This is to support our LGBTQ+ friends," he had said in the high school as he told us about the plan. "Evil wins when good people stay silent. You don't have to wear these, but I hope you will."

Every single student of our karate club agreed enthusiastically, although given we have very small numbers. Still, I almost broke down in tears. Yeah, we have a few out LGBTQ+ kids on the team, but the rest of the team, the majority, identifies as straight. For them to stand with us, in front of peers and parents and facing possible punishment—what a joy.

What hope.

Mr. Samuels found pride-colored martial arts belts. Rainbow belts. We each wear one, *Sensei* included.

We pick up a poster board and share a message with our Washington High School community. Once put together, the words are as follows:

*Be yourself to free yourself.*

The crowd doesn't clap. Silence runs through the stadium like someone died. Eventually, a few small groups cheer, whistle, and clap.

The music changes. A new song plays—and it's not one of ours.

*"Ladies and gentlemen, out of fairness, we have another surprise for you. My mixed martial arts school will also do a demonstration for you. Let's get excited for a new martial arts challenge!"* Captain Decker speaks loudly on the mic, making my stomach instantly turn ill.

Michelle runs out to the center of the football field, leading her team. Behind her, Camila, Logan, Jeff, and a dozen others follow. The last one out makes the crowd gasp. They welcome Tanner, who wears a UFC jacket, with a crazy number of cheers.

Nothing is ever fair at good old Washington High.

It's their turn to perform, and I can't help but be scared as to what message they'll send.

# 25

*Counterattack*

FOR A MOMENT, pride pulsed through my veins. Pride in being true to ourselves, true to our karate, and true to our message.

That pride vanishes quickly. People yell at us to sit down so they can get a better view of Decker's MMA team. Money must be falling out of Decker's pockets, and he loves showing off. Multiple MMA students wheel out a stage. They place it in the center of the football field. Fireworks—I shake my head—explode from the rear, once it's set up. Red, white, and blue sparks fill the sky above. This has to be illegal, right?

Decker's students don't show forms like us. Only fighting. One pair at a time jumps on stage, and they swing at each other—not a real fight. It's choreographed, but that doesn't make it any less effective. Their group looks like the military.

They roll, spin, flip, and dodge. One pair after another jumps on stage, fights for a few seconds, and then rolls off. Spin kicks, aerial moves, even some gymnastics—holy crap, how are they so much better than us? As much as I want to hate it all, my jaw remains on the ground during the entire performance.

At the end, Camila faces Michelle. Michelle's impeccable form nearly matches that of Mr. Samuels. Camila surprises me, too. She performs a dive roll when Michelle sweeps at her. Michelle grabs Camila and executes a perfect one-arm throw. With her back on the stage, Camila kips-up, flying just like a stunt actor in a fight scene.

How did she become so incredible? Michelle and Camila may be better than all of us combined.

Explosions in the sky produce magnificent red, white, and blue colors, and the crowd bursts with energy they never had for us.

"Is it over yet?" DeMarcus shields his eyes with his right hand. "I can't watch."

"No," I mumble. "And I think you'll want to see this."

Slowly, confidently, and expertly, two men take center stage, apparently for the finale—one dressed in all black, the other dressed in all red. It's Krake versus Decker.

The two coaches stand face-to-face. Decker throws a punch, and the audience gasps. Krake ducks and dives into Decker's gut, taking him down on the stage. The two wrestle briefly, but then Decker puts his foot in the center of Krake's chest and flips him upside down.

I would cheer for the pain I hope Krake feels, but it's such a perfectly and beautifully crafted throw and fall, I can't help but admire it.

Yes, I dislike these two adults more than I've ever disliked anyone in my entire life. Yet, their form is perfect. I hate how perfect it is. It's stunning. I realize I've never seen either in action, not like this.

It's just as good as Mr. Samuels's form, and honestly—ugh, I hate this—Decker's even better, and Krake's pretty damn good, too. Maybe I'm blinded by my loyalty in thinking *Sensei* is the best and can completely handle himself. That may be true against teenagers, but I've never seen him face an adult of similar or greater experience.

After their excellently choreographed fight, Decker raises Krake's hand. He points to the sky, and more fireworks explode. Then, a banner falls across the stage.

It shares the date of the tournament—December 19. But that's not all. The banner features multiple images, the first a picture of Michelle and Camila facing each other

Underneath their photos, the text reads, *"Introducing the two toughest girls in MMA history!"*

So, Decker plans to keep Michelle in the girls' division, then? Mateo should be relieved. Quickly, I glance at Tisha and Amanda. Color drains from their faces. I know those fears. They can give Camila a run for her money in a fight, but how in the world would they stand a chance against Michelle?

We're going to lose this tournament. It's as clear as day. We should back out now. Do something else. I'm worried our girls will lose to Michelle. And what about *Sensei*? Can he beat Krake? Yes, but it's going to be a thousand times harder than I had imagined. And if today is any indication of future events, Decker and Krake have plenty of surprises up their sleeves.

The crowd applauds more for them, and my stomach turns. I'm glad they are cheering for women—and a trans student at that! Yes, I need to focus on that. Does the crowd know? They must know, right? In a town like this, everyone knows everything. What is it, then, about us? Why do people hate us so much?

Or, at least, why do they hate me?

A second picture on the banner features a scary, larger-than-life Krake and a tiny, frightened-looking picture of Mr. Samuels. Nausea rises in my throat as I read the text under their images. *"For the first time, teacher versus teacher!"*

My eyes settle on the final image on the banner.

Text surrounds a blue-lives matter flag that reads, *"Decker's MMA invites you to join our mission! First month free."*

Mr. Samuels starts to speak to us, but the stadium again erupts in applause as Decker and Krake take a bow. Then both of their teams—the wrestlers and the martial artists—take the stage. The wrestlers sport that stupid singlet that started all my troubles last year. The martial artists wear red and black sleeveless gis. They look badass. I can give them that. And the meaning isn't lost on me. It's a merging of Krake and

Decker. Their styles of fighting and teaching coalesce into one mixed martial arts fighter.

They all bow, and Tanner comes out, sporting his UFC jacket, and waves at the crowd. This stupid audience gives them a standing ovation.

We stand on the track, our pride belts still tight around our waists, but I certainly do not feel prideful right now.

"What were you going to say just then, sir?" DeMarcus asks when the cheers settle.

A vein pulses in Mr. Samuels's neck. "The show is over. Now we train. Harder than ever. All of us." He looks at me first when he turns from the stage, as the wrestlers and MMA teens push it off the field. "It's time we won. A clear victory is what we need, and that's exactly what we're going to get. We must win. We will win."

I appreciate his anger. It's not something I see often.

And I'm one-hundred percent on board. I'm tired of it all. "I'm ready to train," Tisha says. "They're not the only team with girls who can kick ass." Amanda high-fives Tisha. They both look determined as we walk off the field. Whatever we had hoped to accomplish with our pride belts and our message is lost and forgotten. We're not even relevant enough to get in trouble for it.

As we leave, I search the stadium for the one face I miss the most. I scan the wrestlers and the MMA kids again, holding my breath while I do so. I can't help but be nervous. I've been tricked before.

But I don't find who I'm looking for, and I'm left with one big question. Where the heck is Mateo?

# 26

*Shirtless Selfies*

I CALL MATEO. No answer, so I text him. *Where are you?*

He reads the text immediately, and my heart leaps at the formation of text bubbles. But then nothing. He doesn't finish the text, or something happens. I don't receive anything.

Fine. Let Mateo sit at home. I'm going out with my friends.

"Chinese buffet?" DeMarcus asks.

Tisha and I shoot it down. The last time we all had Chinese, it led to a brawl in the parking lot. Those memories sit heavy, especially with me.

I hate that Mateo isn't here. He and I should be going out, holding hands, making out every second we can, making each other laugh so hard that we snort… that's the relationship I want and miss.

Heck, Mateo lost his college scholarships because of me. Sure, he was only a freshman, but everyone said—and it was clear as day if you'd had seen him wrestle—that he would be able to get a free ride at any university in the country simply based on his talent.

He threw all that down the drain. For me. To be with me.

So, why can't I stop staring at DeMarcus right now? DeMarcus with the cute dimples, that bright smile, the adorable way his hair curls, his beautiful Black skin.

Shut up, brain! Checking my phone again, I tell myself to be patient. Still, there's no reply. C'mon, Mat. What's going on?

"How about that grilled cheese place?" I suggest.

"Oh, yeah. That new one with like a hundred grilled cheese variations?" Tony asks. "I've been wanting to try it."

"Let's do it," Amanda says.

Our plan now confirmed, the other boys and I head to Mr. Samuels's classroom to change clothes, and the girls use a faculty restroom nearby. We use Mr. Samuels's classroom to avoid the locker rooms. That pisses me off, too. We must avoid the locker rooms because any wrestler might walk in and assault us.

I put the pride belt in my bag. Because of Decker and Krake's demo, the pride belts may not have had the impact Mr. Samuels had wanted. However, I couldn't have more pride in my teacher. Holding the rainbow belt, I can't help but smile. Mr. Samuels is a straight, masculine man. Yet he puts his reputation and even his career on the line for us.

Or, more specifically, for *me*.

*I'm* the queer kid. I'm the kid who caused these problems in the first place, I guess. No, it's not all my fault. I know that. But I have to remind myself of that every day. I bet just about every LGBTQ+ kid out there has to remind themselves of the same damn thing all the time. It's not our fault that stupid, narrow-minded adults don't understand. It's not our fault that some straight people are so fragile that they don't even want to acknowledge we exist.

I put on clean jeans and hold a fresh gray T-shirt. Even with a school board that doesn't want us to use the word "gay," I've got a straight male teacher who would do anything to make me feel included and supported.

Out of nowhere, a tear emerges in the corner of my left eye. I wipe it away. Tony and DeMarcus get dressed behind me.

I tell myself I'm going to do something extra nice for Mr. Samuels. Something to show how much I appreciate him.

"I want that mega bacon melt they've been advertising," Tony says. "It has like six pieces of bacon in one sandwich. Give me all the bacon!"

"You know Amanda is a vegan, right?" DeMarcus asks.

"So?"

"So, don't you like her?" DeMarcus asks with a cheesy smile.

"Shut up!" Tony says, immediately blushing.

"Be yourself—but maybe not the version that eats an entire pound of bacon in front of the vegan girl you're trying to impress," DeMarcus says.

Tony zips up his duffel bag and sits on one of the desks in Mr. Samuels's classroom. "So, um. What would you do to impress her?"

DeMarcus smiles sincerely, and it's a grin that could brighten anyone's mood. I check my phone again. Still no reply from Mateo.

Shrugging, DeMarcus sits down. "Well, I dunno. Maybe try one of the vegan specials there."

"Vegans don't eat cheese, though, right?" Tony asks. "What will Amanda even get?"

"No worries. They have a whole vegan menu. Fake cheese," DeMarcus adds when Tony flashes a confused look. "So, order something off that, maybe. That might get her attention."

"Okay. Cool. Thanks, man," Tony says, blushing as he walks out of the classroom. I like Tony, too. On the surface, sure, he's another straight dude. But below the surface, mixed in with all those teenage hormones, is a nice guy who has no problem being friends with and standing up for his LGBTQ+ friends.

So, what happened to the likes of Logan, Tanner, Jeff, Decker, and Krake? I've got questions for Camila and Michelle, too. At least with Camila, I kinda get it. She had two gay boyfriends, and both lied to her. But can't she understand how hard it is to come out?

I wish I could articulate these thoughts to her. Memories of Mom's wish to help Camila nag at me. But how do I help someone who doesn't want anything to do with me?

"Where's your boy?" DeMarcus asks, taking me away from my thoughts. He's fully dressed now, which of course is the first thing my hormonal brain notices.

"Dunno. Hasn't replied to me. Never told me what was going on in the first place." Tension laces my words, and I feel bad for speaking so honestly behind Mat's back.

DeMarcus looks at my chest and arms. Have I spent all this time so lost in thought that I forgot to put my shirt on? I've been holding it and spacing out this entire time.

"You're, like, getting really ripped."

I gulp and my arms shake.

"Selfie?" DeMarcus suggests. "Show those MMA idiots that we aren't scared. Show them we're not the same kids as last year, either."

I nod, unable to get words out of my mouth. Am I honestly getting ripped? I can't help but admit that I rather enjoy the compliment.

DeMarcus removes his shirt. He's ripped, too. To be fair, I don't think I'm ripped. I'm much more defined than last year, true. But ripped—that's DeMarcus. Bulging biceps, beautifully defined tris, a chest that you want to snuggle… I try to shake the thoughts from my head.

I love Mateo. He just frustrates me sometimes. And I can't help but be attracted to nice, hot guys. DeMarcus is both.

He holds his phone with his left hand, puts his right arm around my shoulders, and we take a shirtless selfie together.

"Hot," DeMarcus says, looking at it afterward.

I can't help but agree.

And thank goodness I'm not wearing a singlet, or I might have a repeat of one of my most embarrassing moments.

With or without Mateo, it's going to be a very interesting night out.

# 27

## A Secret Kiss

WE ORDER SO many varieties of grilled cheese that I think I've been making them wrong my entire life. I'm a two-cheese-slices minimum guy, butter spread to the edges of the bread. Here—well, if you can think of it, they have a name for it.

Tisha eats the Cheesy Geeky sandwich, which has avocado and tomato on it. It looks gross to me.

"Wanna bite?" Tisha asks as I stare at her sandwich. Amanda takes a picture of her vegan sandwich followed by a selfie. Tony puts his arm around her shoulder, and they take a picture together.

"I'll try anything with cheese on it," I say.

"I'm pretty sure I can think of one thing you wouldn't try even with cheese," Tony says, looking from me to Amanda to see if she likes his sense of humor. Tony turns to me, raises his hand, forms a V with his index and middle finger, and tongue-bangs the heck out of his gesture.

"Ew, Tony! Gross!" I can't help but laugh. "You're right about that."

"You ever been with a girl?" Tony asks, his cheesy grin as wild as his long hair.

I shake my head.

"What about you?" Tony asks DeMarcus. My attention dramatically increases.

"Only playas tell stories," DeMarcus says. He's looking at me, though, and I can't stop staring at his smile. Is DeMarcus flirting with me? And do I like it?

Checking my phone for the hundredth time, I roll my eyes. Still no text from Mateo. I've followed up a few times.

*Hey, we're getting food, wanna come?*

*U okay?*

*Are u mad at me or something?*

All texts have been read. Not a single reply. It's making me crazy. Crazy enough to do something stupid, I think, as I glance up at De-Marcus again.

Tisha leans in my ear and whispers to me. At first, my heart jumps into my throat. Does she know what I'm thinking?

"Look at those two," she says to me, and I realize she's talking about Amanda and Tony. They're holding hands.

"Aww."

"I'm gonna be the only single person in our group," she says a bit louder, following it up with a laugh.

DeMarcus, who sits on the other side of Tisha, elbows her gently in the side. "You and me both."

"I'd ask you out in a second, DeMarcus, if I thought you were interested," Tisha says playfully.

"What makes you think I'm not?" he says back.

What? Um, *what?* My stomach drops, and not even the crinkle fries on my plate look appetizing anymore.

DeMarcus just laughs. Amanda and Tony, previously lost in some privately whispered conversation of their own, sit up straighter and look at him, too.

"I guess if you have to put a label on it, then I'm bisexual," he says. "And honestly, it's nice to be able to tell some friends. I've known who I am for a long time, but it's hard to say the words. You know?"

"I know," I mumble, probably not even loud enough for anyone to hear. My stomach feels sick. Although I know it shouldn't affect me, I can't stand the thought of seeing DeMarcus date anyone, especially a girl.

*Hi, Aiden, you have a boyfriend. A wonderful, hot, sexy boy who lost college scholarship opportunities because he chose to be honest.*

I don't want to talk about sex or who likes who, and my inner voice of reason exhausts me. I open my mouth to change the subject but change my mind instead. This moment is important to DeMarcus. It shouldn't be about me. When someone opens up, shut up and listen, no matter how uncomfortable it might make you.

"So, have you dated both girls and guys?" Tony asks.

"I've never had a boyfriend," he says. "I've had a couple girlfriends, though, yeah."

"Ohh, details!" Amanda grins and snuggles even closer to Tony. They sit so close together now that it looks like their shoulders have merged, and they've become one person. I take a couple big gulps of water, hoping it will settle my stomach. I want that feeling right now more than anything, but my person won't even text me back.

"Well, it was last year, before I hung out with you guys. I went to homecoming with Sherita Jackson. You know her? She's cool."

I know her only by name, but the rest of the group nods. DeMarcus's mouth keeps moving, and he tells some story about Sherita, and maybe even the other girl he went out with. My mind, though, floats away.

What am I doing?

I'm sitting here daydreaming, and something must be wrong with Mateo. I should know better at this point in our relationship.

"Be right back," I tell the group, and I dash to the restroom. Thankfully, no one else is here. I sit in a stall, shut and lock the door, and call Mateo.

The phone rings and rings. He doesn't answer.

I sit here longer anyway, trying to compose myself before I rejoin the group. I can't help that maybe I have a little crush on DeMarcus.

Right? I'm in high school, so isn't it all right to have a few crushes even if you're going out with someone else? I don't know how this life stuff works, but I can't help how I feel.

I wait a moment longer. Just as I have my thoughts under control, my bladder feels like it's about to lose it. I do my business and wash my hands. Right when I'm drying off, the bathroom door opens.

DeMarcus enters.

"You okay?" he asks. He looks cuter than ever, the concern and care on his face enhancing what I already like about him. He looks like he needs a new shirt—not that it's old, but it's tight on him, his strong chest about to burst right through a cute purple T-shirt.

I nod.

"You don't look okay."

I shrug.

He steps closer to me. "What are you thinking about?"

*That you're cute but I don't think I should tell you that. No, I know I shouldn't.* "Nothing."

"For what it's worth, I think Tisha is awesome. Incredibly awesome. But I don't think I want to date her or any other girl right now."

"Why is that?" I ask. "Why tell me this?"

He swallows hard and takes a deep breath, like he's trying to muster some courage. He shrugs a little, smiles wide at me, and then says, "Cuz there's this dude I'm kinda crushin' on. I kinda want him to know I'm crushin' on him. The problem is that he's taken. But, um, his boyfriend never seems to be around. I am, though. I'm here."

"Oh?" I ask, my legs taking the smallest step closer to him.

"But I can't do anything about it," he says. "Can I? If the boy I like is already taken?" His mouth opens, and he quickly, subtly licks his lips. My eyes can't help but focus on the tongue, and my heart pounds like the drums in a rock song.

"You can't?"

A coy smile forms on his face. It's a terrible sight. He could conquer the world with his puppy eyes and smile. "I mean, we're all friends, and it just seems wrong, right? But I want my crush to at least know how I feel. I hope that's okay."

My arms shake. I don't know what to do. He must be talking about me, right? *Of course he is, Aiden. What do you want to do about it?*

*Nothing! Walk away!*

*Kiss him now. Kiss this hot boy right now.*

A debate rages war in my brain, and I'm a bystander to my own thoughts. I'm torn in so many directions.

"Yeah, it's okay. I'm sorry, um, that this boy is taken."

"It's life," he says. "But we're also very young, yeah? Who knows what may happen like next month. Or next week. Or, you know, right now?"

My stomach does some kind of dive-roll, and I step as close as I possibly can to DeMarcus. Our faces, inches away from each other, move impossibly closer. My heart pumps blood to all parts of my body—my face flushes, my arms and legs shake. My mouth opens slightly. I lick my lips.

I want this. I want DeMarcus. I know I shouldn't. It could ruin so many things. But right now, I don't care about anything. Emotions and hormones bury logic.

He puts his hand against my chest, ever so gently holding me back. He whispers in my ear. "I never want to be this guy, Aiden. No lies. No cheating. Definitely don't wanna hurt our friends." He kisses me sweetly on the cheek. He smiles softly at me. Then he turns around. "I just needed to tell you how I feel."

He smiles and holds the bathroom door open for me.

"After you," he says.

When we walk out, my thoughts jump around my brain like raindrops hitting concrete. I can't focus on anything, but I put one foot in front of another.

DeMarcus puts his arm around my shoulders.

He smiles again, and I can't get enough of that beautiful, soft expression. Wouldn't it be nice to be with a guy who shows up, who doesn't fill me with anxiety and worries all the time?

Just then, from the corners of our eyes, Mateo comes into view. He walks into the restaurant. He sees DeMarcus and me by the bathroom. DeMarcus quickly removes his arm from my shoulder, but Mateo sees it.

Of course he does.

But there's something else, too. Something that becomes much clearer as Mateo gets closer.

He's got a black eye and a bruised nose.

# 28

## *An Unexpected Punch*

"MATEO, WHAT HAPPENED?" I ask, running to him, hormones and thoughts about DeMarcus fading as quickly as they came.

"Can we get out of here?" Mat asks, looking around the restaurant. He scans every face, looking for someone. We stand next to the table where Tisha, Amanda, and Tony finish their meals.

"Yeah, of course," Tisha says, tossing her napkin on the plate in front of her.

Perhaps Mat only wanted me to come, but he doesn't say anything. He doesn't even look at Tisha. Mateo does, however, lock eyes with DeMarcus when he approaches the table.

"What's going on?" DeMarcus asks.

"What happened to you?" I ask Mateo again. He grabs my hand, pulls me, and heads outside. I toss Tisha some cash to cover my bill and follow Mateo. "Who did this to you?"

He sighs deeply. Purple bruising radiates around his left eye. Red and brown scratches encircle his neck.

"My father...."

He trails off as the rest of our group comes outside. I wish we were alone. Mateo may not want to be this vulnerable around everyone. Did his dad hurt him? Is that what he was going to say? My palms suddenly hurt, as I realize I'm clenching my fists and digging nails into my skin.

Tony and Amanda walk out hand-in-hand, but the flirty, friendly smiles from earlier have vanished.

"Dude, what happened to you?" Tisha asks.

"Let's go somewhere quieter," Mateo says. We follow him down the street and into an empty storefront parking lot.

"So?" Tony asks, curious, too.

Mateo faces me. The others take a seat on the edge of the sidewalk. "I'm so sorry," Mat says. "I'm sorry I couldn't reply to any of your messages. I don't even have my phone on me, but I took a chance that you guys would still be here."

"Where's your phone?" Amanda asks.

"My parents took it." Mateo frowns. "As punishment. I have to find another way to talk with you all."

"Punishment for what?" I ask.

Laughter bounces around the empty parking lot, but it's not from any of us. "Dammit," I say loudly, not caring. "What the hell?"

Logan, Jeff, Camila, and Michelle walk directly toward us.

"No, I'm sorry," DeMarcus says, holding up his hands. "We need a minute. You aren't invited over here."

"Do you think we want an invitation from you?" Logan asks. He licks his lips animalistically, his hair spikier than normal.

"Go away," DeMarcus says again. "Wait. How did you even know we were here?" I wonder the same thing—this town is small but not that small.

Logan and Jeff laugh.

Camila and Michelle remain stoic.

Then something completely unexpected happens, and a gut-wrenching pain rushes through me. All my anxieties and fears rush back, wondering what's going on here.

"Wait, wait, wait," DeMarcus says, turning and facing Mateo. "Why is it they show up right after you? What's going on?"

Mat's face twists from surprise to anger. I haven't seen that face since… since I first kissed him in his bedroom the night he kicked me out of his house.

"What are you trying to say?" Mateo asks through tight lips.

My mind races, but my mouth freezes. I want more than anything to tell DeMarcus to shut up. Mateo didn't bring them here. They probably stalked one of us on our socials. Wasn't Amanda taking pictures at the restaurant? If she shared the pics, anyone could easily find us.

DeMarcus steps closer. "I'm saying—you weren't here. You're never here. Missing practices. Missing our demo. Then you show up and these jerks are right behind you." He swallows hard, his eyes twitching and glancing over at me, gauging my reaction.

"You have no idea what you're talking about," Mateo says, stepping closer to DeMarcus. "So, I advise you to shut the hell up."

"Or what?" DeMarcus sneers. "You'll start yet another fight? How original."

Something snaps in Mateo. He lunges for DeMarcus and grabs his shirt. "I know what you're doing. You like Aiden. Don't think for one second I haven't seen how you're always all over him."

DeMarcus laughs. "You're always gone, so how would you even know? What kind of friend—no, excuse me—*boyfriend* is that?"

Mateo shakes his head, and I'm cursing on the inside. DeMarcus knows how to press his buttons. Mateo shoves him hard, and DeMarcus takes several steps back. Then he marches right back up to Mateo, face-to-face.

"Is that all you got?" DeMarcus asks.

"Be careful what you wish for," Mateo snaps.

"You're not as tough as you think," DeMarcus says. "And you're not a good boyfriend, that's for—"

Mateo's right shoulder moves back, something a trained fighter notices. It's a threat to punch DeMarcus.

My mouth may not know how to work when I'm in this much shock, but my body does. I jump between them, arms out.

But I'm about a second off.

Mateo swings, his temper getting the best of him, his right fist flying directly at DeMarcus. Instead of connecting with his face, though, Mat hits me instead. I land in between the two in time to save DeMarcus but not in time for Mat to pull back.

"Gah!" Mat's fist against my head makes me dizzy, and Mateo and DeMarcus catch me before I fall.

Laughter fills my ears. Logan and Jeff grab each other and laugh so hard they nearly choke. Camila kicks at them, telling them to shut up. Michelle watches us intently, never taking her eyes off Mateo.

Something about her stare scares me. The focus, the intensity—but I don't have time to consider it long.

Because Mateo isn't the only one snapping aggressively today. Tisha's fed up with Jeff and Logan's laughter, and she has no impulse control. She runs to them and kicks Logan literally and directly on the butt while he and Jeff laugh ridiculously.

Camila steps up and addresses Tisha. "You all really are the bullies, and you can't even see it. You keep blaming us, but haven't you thrown the first strike in every one of these situations?"

Tisha and Camila glare at one another, and I gulp, dreading yet another fight between people who should be friends.

Tisha lunges at her former best friend.

# 29

*Everyone Fights*

MY JAW HITS the floor at the incredible display of talent I witness.

Tisha, her temper as lost as Krake's morals, swings her right fist at Camila. Camila steps outside of the punch and strikes Tisha's arm right below the elbow. Camila steps close with one leg and with the other throws a sidekick at the back of Tisha's knee. With Camila on the outside, Tisha's closed-off, her arms tangled up, unable to defend. On one hand, it's an inspiring display of karate from Camila. On the other, it's terrifying.

Getting right back up, Tisha adjusts her fighting stance, but Camila and Michelle approach her quickly. With her back against the wall, I think about *Nihanchi Sho*. It was designed to teach us how to defend if we're cornered and stuck.

Michelle wears a fierce expression. She comes at Tisha from the left, while Camila approaches from the right. They both step up to her almost at the same time. Amanda races toward them to help Tisha. The boys glance at each other, not wanting to fight any of the girls.

Camila attacks, but Tisha's timing is impeccable. She sweeps Camila's leg. Camila tries to throw a punch, but Tisha blocks it at the same time. The combination of block and sweep knocks Camila right on the ground.

Michelle lunges next, and Tisha times the sweep perfectly again.

But Michelle's experience comes into play. She steps in quickly, then removes her foot. It's a trick. She knew exactly what Tisha was doing with the sweeps. Tisha's momentum is too much, and she can't stop the sweep. She misses, and Michelle pulls some kind of reversal— sweeping her sweep. Tisha falls hard and fast.

Amanda grabs Michelle from behind. She shoves her into the wall where Tisha is trapped. Amanda throws a round house at the back of Michelle's thigh, and Michelle stumbles to one knee.

"Go, Amanda!" I can't help but cheer. Given—it was an attack to Michelle's back, but she attacked Tisha two on one.

"Should we be cheering or helping?" Tony asks.

Or stopping this? Mom's voice speaks in my mind, and this is not what she had in mind when she made me promise to help Camila.

With Michelle's head now at waist level, Amanda reaches and puts her in a chokehold. She finds a good grip, and Michelle's eyes bulge and her face reddens. Great talent and experience do not matter when it comes to sneak attacks. Not at all. Michelle deserves this. She deserves whatever she gets for betraying her people, for hanging out with these homophobic liars!

I blink, and the tables turn.

Michelle elbows Amanda, loosening her grip. She steps backward and performs a perfect judo throw. Amanda flips upside down and smacks against the wall. Tony cries out and runs toward her, but I see something else. Maybe the adrenaline hyper-focuses my brain, but as Amanda hits the wall, Michelle adjusts her position and holds onto the back of Amanda's head. Michelle protects her. Or Amanda's head, at least.

"Tony, stop!" I want to tell him what I just saw. Michelle was defending herself, and she chose to protect Amanda. I don't know who is right or wrong.

But Tony doesn't stop. He flies at Michelle, who steps to the side and trips Tony. Tony smacks into the building's wall head-first.

There's no time to protect his face.

Blood flies out of his mouth, as well as something shiny—possibly a tooth. Tony turns and faces us. He puts a hand over his mouth, yet blood continues to stream out, in between his fingers, below his palm, down his neck, staining his T-shirt. I reach a breaking point and charge at Michelle, but I don't get far. Logan and Jeff grab me from behind.

Instantly, Mateo and DeMarcus toss them off. Logan puts his hands in a defensive position. When Mateo does the same, Logan snaps his head toward Michelle, as if begging for help. Jeff and De-Marcus grab at each other, wrestle, and roll on the concrete parking lot. My body hurts thinking about the rocks and concrete digging into DeMarcus's skin.

"Tony, are you okay?" I ask.

Michelle stares at Mateo and me. Tony shakes his head, makes some feral noise, and pushes Michelle from behind.

Michelle runs right into Mat and me.

"Enough," Mat says. "Someone's hurt. When will you all stop being so stupid?"

"Excuse me?" Michelle snaps back. "We didn't start this one. In fact, it looked like you all were fighting each other. Can't blame us for enjoying the show, until *you*—" Michelle glares at Tisha— "came after us."

Jeff and DeMarcus stop fighting and listen to Michelle.

She gets in Mat's face. "Why don't you all apologize and leave?"

"Us? You want an apology from us?" Mateo asks.

"Yes," Michelle says so confidently. *"You're* the bully. With your privilege and your know-it-all attitude. So, bully, if you want this to stop, then apologize."

I step up this time. "I'm not scared of you."

"That's because you have your B.F. here," Michelle quips. "But I got news for you. He's not as tough as you think." She smiles at Mateo, egging him on.

I hold my breath. I don't know what I want. To go home in one piece, yes. But I also would absolutely love to see Michelle get a taste of her own medicine.

Mat's already on edge, and it doesn't take much. He swings at Michelle. Michelle dodges, spins, and throws a sidekick at Mateo's ribs. He blocks, grabs her leg and sweeps her. He falls on top and raises his hand like he's about to slug her in the face.

She flips Mat over before he can hit her, then she slugs him twice in the gut and puts him in a chokehold. His face turns purple.

Mateo breaks the choke and reverses it. He kicks at her, freeing his legs, which allows him to lock his thick, strong legs around her neck. The color on Michelle's face deepens, and she panics. Mateo's winning.

Until Michelle escapes. They both roll to their feet, running right at each other, two alpha champions refusing to back down.

Then we hear sirens behind us.

"Oh, no," I mumble. I know who that will be.

And it's never good for us.

# 30

*Secrets and*
*Surprises*

CAPTAIN DECKER STEPS out of his vehicle. "You know," he starts, pausing to spit out chewing tobacco, making my stomach curl, "we've had such a peaceful community in Washington since I've been in charge." Decker glares at me, his eyes washed in hate. It disturbs me on a physiological level. My stomach turns. My body shakes. How someone can have so much hate is beyond my understanding. Michelle and Camila must see this.

Decker spits again. That nasty habit alone would be enough for me to never want to train with him. "Not once did we have fights in the street. How many fights have you started now, Aiden? Six, seven?" He approaches with a disgusting yellow smile and crosses his arms. His biceps bulge, and in this moment, he resembles Coach Krake. Both have such big, muscular arms and the same truck-like, boxy physique. They could be related, I think, but then remember they are brothers-in-law. There were women out there who saw these men and wanted more? Gross.

"Sir, Aiden didn't—" DeMarcus speaks up, but Decker shuts him up with one cock of the head and glare from the eyes.

"As I was saying, I was trying to figure out how and when this all started," Decker continues. *Um, it started with homophobic wrestlers who wouldn't leave me alone!* "Then it dawned on me. My former student, Lloyd, started this mess. There wasn't fighting in the streets until Mister Samuels started teaching you all karate."

"Bullsh—" I slap a hand over my mouth. I can't believe my audacity, but maybe it needs to be said.

"And look at the language and character of his students. As the old saying goes, there's no such thing as a bad student. Only a bad teacher," Decker says. "Let me take some responsibility for it. You see, Lloyd was a wonderful martial artist, but he never overcame his weaknesses."

"What weaknesses?" Tisha mumbles. The crimson in her cheeks shows that she surprised herself.

*Don't let Decker get in your head, Tisha!*

Decker spits again. "For starters, we disagree about strength. Equality isn't strength. Equality is weakness."

Anger rises in me like stomach acid. How dare he! I look around, willing someone else to speak. Mateo stares at the ground, avoiding Decker and me. Tony and Amanda look pale as ghosts. DeMarcus wears a "screw you" facial expression, and I want to hug him for it, but he's keeping his mouth shut now, too.

"I can see not all of you agree with me," Decker says. "It's simple, though. The best gifts in life aren't ones given to you by ignorant protestors. You earn respect. You earn a seat at the table. No one should just be given one, especially based on something so ridiculous as who they like to sleep with."

Michelle and Camila nod.

They *freaking* nod, a sign of agreement. What the hell?

*Déjà vu.* Didn't Michelle talk like this, too?

"At my school," Decker says, "there *is* no equality. You want to be the champ? You win. Period. You want to win in life? You put in the work instead of taking the handouts and the scholarships and the unearned seats at the table. You want a real shocker, kid?" He gets right in my face. "I don't care that you like dick. I care that you get special treatment because of it."

My legs turn to Jell-O. I'm staring at an adult, a grown man, a police officer who made it through the ranks to become captain somehow. I can't believe he would talk to teens like that.

Someone needs to punch him in the face, and I wish I was the one who had the strength and confidence to do so.

Tisha speaks up, and my entire body shakes, nervous for her and everything else. "Special treatment? You do realize that the only special treatment Aiden's ever gotten is a fist in the face because people like you keep perpetuating gross narratives? You're the weak one, or equality wouldn't scare you. And you think you've earned everything you've gotten?"

*Jesus, Tisha, thank you but shut up! He's going to kill us!*

"Please! You already had the advantage. White, straight, and male. Wow, please tell us all about all the hard obstacles you've overcome in life." Tisha rolls her eyes, while mine are about to fall out of my head.

Decker shifts his focus to Tisha, and something else catches my attention. Michelle smiled. She smiled at Tisha's comment! I don't understand Michelle at all. She should be standing with us.

"You sound like your teacher." Decker laughs. "He used to come to me for advice when he was your age. He had these fears about police. Thought his Blackness made people like me instantly judge him." Decker shakes his head. "I could arrest any of you, you all know that, yes? So, you're going to sit down and listen to a story I want to tell you." He pauses and motions for us to sit. "I loved Lloyd Samuels. He was my best student. Perhaps my best ever. I loved him like he was a son."

He clears his throat and claps his hands, clearly making sure we hear the next part.

"But your teacher betrayed me."

We all sit, and Captain Decker reaches into his pocket for more chew. He's so gross.

"What did he do?" Tony asks.

*No, Tony. Shut up! We shouldn't be listening to this.* I trust Captain

Decker as far as I can throw him, and despite my desire to throw him into an ocean across the country, I doubt I'd even be able to pick him up.

"You know what?" Decker asks, marching around us, his students on one half of the sidewalk, us on the opposite. "I'm not sure you deserve to know. Starting fights with my students?"

"When we got here, *Sensei* Decker, DeMarcus and Mateo were about to fight each other," Jeff says.

"Oh?" Decker smiles. "Is that so?"

Mateo and DeMarcus look away, putting their heads down.

"It is," Camila answers. "We all saw it. Then they attacked us."

"I suppose the right thing to do here is to notify everyone's parents and let them see if they want to press charges. It's time we get this fighting under control," Decker says. "I won't have it in my community."

Tisha snorts.

"Miss?" Decker says, irritated. "Did I say something funny?"

"No, just ironic and hypocritical, which might be hilarious if it weren't all so depressing."

*Geez, Tisha, are you trying to get us arrested?*

"Mister Hernandez," Decker says, stepping in front of Mateo. "Care to explain yourself?"

"We weren't fighting," he mumbles, his head still down.

"And you," Decker says to DeMarcus. "What's your last name?"

"Freeman," he says. "DeMarcus Freeman."

"Mister Freeman," Decker says with another ridiculous grin. "What happened here?"

"Nothing, sir. We were talking, that's all. Then your students came and started harassing us."

"Is that so?" Decker addresses Michelle this time.

"No, *Sensei*. They attacked us, and we defended ourselves."

Decker walks around, looking carefully at everyone. He pauses by Mateo, examines Mat's black eye, and even rubs his thumb on Mat's bruises. Mateo flinches and pulls back, which just makes Decker chuckle.

"Mister Samuels's students bully each other. Looks like I'll need to have a big conversation with your teacher," Decker says. "After I talk to each of your parents, that is."

Tony and Amanda's faces turn pale. Certainly, this kind of trouble would be a first for them, and I'm sure a run-in with the law, no matter how corrupt or wrong that law is, could have drastic consequences for them at home. But I smile. Mom can and will kick Decker's ass. I'd love to see him try to intimidate her.

"I suggest you all put your excessive energy and tempers into your training," Decker tells us. "This year's tournament is going to be spectacular. I can't wait to see Mister Samuels and Coach Krake fight." Decker leans down close so only we hear the next part. "And trust me when I tell you, I'm making sure Krake knows every trick your teacher ever learned and then some." He stands up straighter, laughs, and walks over to his students. "Meanwhile, we're offering you young adults a scholarship prize to help pay for college. You see, we do these things for all of you and yet look at the terrible disrespect. One of you will win. Some of you desperately need the money." Decker snickers while making direct eye contact with Mateo. "But only one of you will win. Who will it be?"

"Only one?" Michelle asks, a confused expression on her face.

"Only one," Decker answers. "Yes, Coach Krake and I discussed it. Originally, we were going to have one scholarship for the winner of the girls' division and one for the boys' division. But guess what?" He looks right at me when he asks the question. "You all have taught me something about equality. You want equal rights? You got 'em. Let me announce a big change. Our MMA tournament this year will be mixed gender." He walks away from his students, back to us, so that he can whisper the next part. "I wasn't sure which gender some of you would be by then, anyway."

Camila's open mouth reveals this news is a surprise to her, too. That means Camila and I might have to fight. Or Camila and Mateo.

Their teacher blindsided them with this announcement, right in front of all of us. And attacks gender identity right in front of Michelle! Surely, they see what a jerk he is.

"I don't care what your pronouns are or who you dream about," Decker says. "There is no equality in real life. There is no equality in a fight. Period."

Tisha looks at me then glances at Logan. She glares at him, and the glare morphs into a grin. Okay, Tisha likes the idea because she could fight Logan, but could I ever face Camila? She's my friend.

Hesitantly, I raise my hand. "How could I fight Camila? How could Mateo fight Camila? That's not fair."

"Why the concern, Aiden? Are you saying the genders aren't equal? Are you saying you only believe in equality when it benefits you?"

Chills run through me. Decker can't be right, but I don't have the words to argue.

"I suggest you put your energy into training. That is, if your parents let you continue to train. I'm afraid I have a long round of house calls to make tonight." Decker laughs. "Before I go, there are a couple final things I should say. In terms of your teacher's betrayal of me, I encourage you to talk to him. You may not believe me anyway. So, ask Mister Samuels this—what happened between him and *Sempai* Denise?"

"Who?" I ask.

"What's a *sempai?*" Amanda asks.

Decker just laughs again. "I can see you have so much more to learn. Sempai is a term for the top student under black belt, the next in line to test for black belt. Ask your teacher what happened between him and *Sempai* Denise." Decker opens the driver's side door of his squad car. "Oh, one more thing. Mateo—have you told your boyfriend and your friends where you got that black eye yet? I really have been meaning to apologize. When you train with me, I don't hold back."

# 31

## *Mateo's Secret*

"I KNEW IT!" DeMarcus snaps. "You're training with them again!"

Decker pulls away slowly. Michelle, Camila, Logan, and Jeff linger in the background, taking their time.

"Stop!" I shout. "Can't you see through this? This is what they want. For us to fight ourselves."

"I'm not on their side," DeMarcus says to me. "I'm on our side. Mat—whose side are you on? That's all we want to know."

"We?" Mateo asks.

DeMarcus sighs, shakes his head, and looks around at each of us in frustration. "What? Am I the only one who wants to know what's really going on?"

Tisha walks over to me and puts a gentle hand on my left shoulder. Then she faces Mateo. "Mat, I think it's okay for us to want to know if you've been training with them again." She looks more at me than Mateo, trying to read my emotions. Well, I won't hold them back. Not tonight.

"I trust Mateo," I say.

He sends me a kind, warm smile. He wouldn't betray us. He wouldn't hurt me like he did last year.

Oh, please don't let me be a fool.

*"Gracias,"* Mateo says.

"You guys," DeMarcus continues. "You can trust someone and still want to know what's going on. The two aren't mutually exclusive."

Mat holds up his hands. "Fine. Fine! That's what I came here to talk to you all about, anyway. It's why I missed the demo and why I haven't been available. I wanted to tell you about it, but not like this. Not when I'm being accused of doing something wrong. I'm *not* the bad guy here!"

"Who is, then?" DeMarcus challenges.

"Decker," Amanda and Tony say in unison.

"And Krake," Tisha adds.

"Exactly," DeMarcus says. He turns to Mateo. "Are you working with them? Training with Decker or Krake?"

Mateo doesn't answer.

"Don't you see?" DeMarcus asks, his eyes focused on me. He opens his mouth to say more, catches the fear and worry in my eyes, and closes his mouth.

"Mat," I say as gently as I can. "What were you gonna tell us?"

He kicks at a curb in the parking lot, while we stand and watch. Sitting down, he puts his face in his hands. For a second, it looks like he's crying. But then he stands, his face calmer, his voice unwavering when he finally starts to speak.

"*Lo siento,*" he starts. "My parents. *Mierda!* You won't understand."

"Mateo, I…. Give me a chance to understand. What's going on?"

Mat shrugs and scratches the side of his head. "You know my parents expected me to earn a college scholarship, right?" I nod, approach Mateo, and reach for his hand. "We've been fighting non-stop since I quit the wrestling team. It's not even about me being gay. It's that they have no money saved for me to go to college, and somehow that's all my fault."

"But there's community college. Student loans," Amanda says. "Lots of options."

Mateo nods. "I argued all of that. But it's even worse—my father lost his job. Well, laid off, anyway. They make us spend our summer abroad and then slash his job. It's so wrong." He rubs his forehead and looks down, trying to hold back tears. "They think I threw a big chance away. They're so pissed at me."

"I'm sorry, Mat. So, what's this have to do with Decker and Krake?" I ask gently, thinking back to when we saw Mateo's father at the high school.

"My father said—" He chokes on the words, and his eyes fill with tears. "He says we have to move. We move to a new school in a new place where I start over. He needs a new job, and I have a chance at scholarships again. That's what they want."

"No," I say, a headache instantly forming at my temples. Mat can't leave me. Not after all of this—how could I lose him like that?

"He's given me one option to stay here. Only under one condition will he even consider staying. Ugh." He rubs his temples. "They were ready to put our house up for sale this week, too. It's no joke."

My heart sinks. "What's the condition?"

"That I win Decker's tournament. If I win the college scholarship money, we won't move."

"But you *will* win," I say. "You're the best of us."

DeMarcus frowns at my comment but says nothing.

"That's not all. A chance of winning is not enough for my father," Mateo says. "He came up with a plan."

"What's that?"

"At first, he wanted me to quit the karate club and train only at Decker's school," Mat says. DeMarcus huffs in the background, but I ignore it.

"You can't do that. You can't betray Mister Samuels like that," I say. You can't betray me like that. After everything they've done to me, to us, how could Mateo even consider it?

"Dad said I could keep training with you and Mister Samuels," Mat says. "But only under one condition."

"Another condition?" I groan, seeing exactly where this is going.

"Yeah. I can train with all of you if and only if I also train with Decker and prioritize Decker's lessons first. Dad wants me to get every lesson and every opportunity possible." Mat clenches his fists and slams them against his thighs. "You guys, it's either I do that, or we move now. Like this week. They are so not joking." He takes several deep breaths and holds my hand. "Do you want me to move?"

"Of course not," I say.

"Then I have to train with Decker," Mateo says. "And I have to win. Somehow."

Michelle scares him, though. She intimidates him—I can see it in Mat's eyes. He might end up underestimating any of us, like DeMarcus, but it feels like a given that Michelle will be in the final match for the top prize.

"And your black eye?" I ask. "Decker did that?"

Mat's body shakes. He wipes his eyes again. "Dad told him to not hold back. *Mi padre* watched practice as Decker used me as his guinea pig. I was Decker's sparring partner. He beat the crap out of me right in front of my father, and my father cheered it on."

He hugs me and rests his head against my chest, sniffing, trying hard to hold back tears. I look up briefly at DeMarcus, who looks away from me.

"We'll figure something out," I say. "It's gonna be okay."

But nausea rises in my throat. We should call the police. That's my first thought, and then I realize how terrible this town is.

Then my tears come out for Mateo, as I think about his father watching Decker hurt him. How could parents let their kids take a beating from an adult? I don't get it. Not at all.

I just hope that the two adults I love and trust the most in this world will know what to do. It's time to tell Mom and Mr. Samuels everything.

# 32

## A Private Night

"CAN I COME over?" Mateo asks.

"Yes."

The group says awkward goodbyes, and Mateo holds my hand while we walk home. I love his confidence and his strength. A year ago, he couldn't be honest with himself. Today, he holds my hand in public.

I text Mom that we're coming over. She's currently out to dinner with Mr. Samuels, so Mat and I will have privacy for a few minutes.

"*Lo siento,* Aiden."

It's the Spanish phrase he says the most. "What for?"

"Everything." He squeezes my hand, and we turn the corner, my house in front of us.

"Do you wanna talk about it?" I ask.

"No."

"Are you okay?"

"No." He squeezes my hand again.

"I'm sorry, Mat." I open the door. We kick off our shoes and head up to my bedroom, leaving the door cracked open.

He hugs me. I want to kiss him. To tell him it's okay. That I love him. That I trust him.

But do I fully trust him? Is that my inner critic or DeMarcus talking?

A tear rolls down his cheek.

"What's wrong?"

"I think I should just move."

"What?" My heart leaps into my throat.

"Wouldn't it be easier? Start over somewhere new." We sit on my bed. I hop in the middle, cross my legs, and pull him toward me.

"You can't do that."

"I feel like everything I do hurts you. And even if it doesn't, it's like I just have one crappy choice after another, no good options, you know? I can't train with Decker. He *disgusts* me."

"So don't."

"Then my father won't let me train with you and Mister Samuels."

I take a deep breath. "There must be another way."

"There is. I tell my family I want to move. They'd do it in a heart-beat, especially since *mi papa* can't find a job here. Start over in a com-munity that doesn't know they have two queer kids."

"Why does that even matter?"

Mateo jumps at the volume of my words. "It doesn't to me. How do I convince them? It's impossible." He lowers his head, and I pull him toward me. We lay down on my bed, Mateo curls into me, his head now on my chest. I rub the back of his neck, thinking I could stay like this for the rest of my life.

"We'll talk to Mister Samuels. He'll know what to do," I say, hop-ing that I'm right.

*"Bueno. Gracias."*

We cuddle. Just cuddle, I tell my hormone monsters. Several min-utes pass in silence. Mom hasn't returned, as far as I can tell.

After a while, I take a risk. I kiss him on top of his head, then whis-per into his ear. "I know what might cheer you up."

He looks up at me, his lips curling into a beautiful smile. *"Mi gringo cachondo."*

"What's that mean?"

*"Nada."* He laughs, and I kiss him.

When his tongue touches mine, he rolls completely on top of me. My body melts and ignites on fire at the same time. I want more. So much more.

Breaking away to inhale much-needed oxygen, I gulp in air and kiss his neck. Mateo moans in my ear, filling me with dizzying desire. My insides float, the pressure of gravity changing in the room. I kiss harder, even biting his skin a little.

He moans louder, and it's the most beautiful sound. He pulls back a little, smiling at me. A patch of brown skin on his neck turns purple, and I gasp. Oops. "You might have to tell your parents you were working extra hard on choke holds."

Thankfully, he laughs. "When will your mom be home?"

"Any minute now."

"I better work fast."

He goes for my neck, and the blood in my legs turns to oil. Every inch feels alive, the cells in my skin, the smallest details, every sensation fresh and new. On a mission to return the "favor," Mateo bites gently on my neck. His hand runs up my shirt while he kisses me.

Everything feels so....

Hot. And scary. Scary that I want more. Scarier that I'm not sure what step next to take or how.

I pull back, jokingly and gently saying, "You just wanna get me in trouble, too."

"Wouldn't want you to feel left out." He kisses my cheek and rolls next to me. "Just hold me," he whispers, and I do. We embrace, arms around wrapped around each other. If this was my last moment on Earth, I'd be okay with that.

"I love you," he says.

"I love you, too." I don't want the moment to end.

But eventually, the front door opens, and Mom calls. "Aiden, I'm home. Mister Samuels and I brought leftovers for you."

Mateo kisses me on the cheek again and rolls off. This moment was the best part of the day. Reality returns. We need to have a serious talk with Mr. Samuels and Mom. Because I want my life—and Mateo's—to be happy.

And I'll do whatever it takes to make it so.

# 33

## *A Plan is Hatched*

STRANGE PAINS STING my heart. Although I'm happy to have Mom and Mr. Samuels in my life, I wish I didn't need to go to them for every problem. I wish I didn't have so many problems, and I hate more than anything that Decker has planted a seed of mystery about *Sensei*'s past behavior.

"Who is *Sempai* Niecy?" I ask after we tell them everything. "What happened there?"

"A tale for another time," Mr. Samuels states. "Look, none of this news surprises me about Decker. He's highly manipulative. He'll do anything to get what he wants. Krake and Decker may have technically won the MMA tournament last spring, but you both instantly deflated any gloating." Mr. Samuels forces a smile. "To which, I might add, I rather enjoyed."

"Can't we get a lawyer?" Mom asks. "We need someone to put Captain Dick in check."

Mateo's eyes bulge at my mom's wonderful choice of words.

"So, it's another MMA tournament, but no separation for gender. Is that right?" Mom asks. "And what about age? Size? No *equality* in a fight." She shakes her head. "What does he want next, ten-year-olds fighting professional athletes? He's a moron. Worse, he's a *dangerous* moron."

Mr. Samuels sighs. "Yeah, this is Decker and Krake's terribly misguided attempt to make a statement."

"It's a stupid, stupid statement," Mom says. "Maybe they'll let me enter. That's equality, right? I'll knock them all out."

Mr. Samuels releases a small chuckle, but part of me worries Mom is serious.

"Let me ask you guys something," Mr. Samuels says to Mat and me. "Do you want to do this? There is no reason we have to fight. I know what I said before, but this—this feels wrong."

"There's a reason for me to fight," Mateo says. "Not just a reason to fight. I need to win. Or I'll have to move."

"But what if you don't win?" Mom asks.

"I can't think about that." Mateo reaches for my hand. "The stakes are about more than just money. It's my life. If my parents choose to move, what happens to us?" He looks at me with such sadness.

No, no, no. I'm not even thinking about that. I'm not putting that thought into my consciousness or the universe.

"I'm sorry to say this, Mateo, but what if your parents move anyway? They may not have a choice if your dad doesn't find work. And then all of this…." She gestures, turning and looking out the window of our home. "Then all this stress and hard work, even if you win…."

Mateo exhales sharply. His face turns pale, and silence fills the room. After a long minute of fidgeting, he says, "If I have a chance to win, a chance to stay…." He swallows hard. "If I have a chance to be with Aiden, then I want to do whatever I can to make that happen."

My chest bursts with warmth. Suddenly, I'm guilty about DeMarcus—what he said to me, how I let myself crush on him. I'm letting myself get distracted when there's a beautiful boy who loves me sitting right here.

"What about you, Aiden?" Mr. Samuels asks. It takes me a second to realize they are asking about the tournament and not my relationship.

I shake away my distractions. "I want to fight. It's no longer just about me or about me standing up to my bullies. I'm standing up for others like me."

"Just because you can fight doesn't mean you need to fight for everyone," Mom says. "That's not your responsibility."

"I know, Mom. I really do." I try to gather my thoughts. Last year, I wanted my bullies to stop seeing me as weak. I wanted to face my fears, win or lose. This year's different. Before I continue, I reach for Mateo's hand. "Look at what Mateo and I have. We didn't have that last year. I'm not just fighting for me. I'm fighting for us. And for everyone like us, who is exhausted by all the ignorant jerks in the world."

Silence fills the room, while Mom, Mr. Samuels, and Mateo make me feel awkward because they stare at me without responding. But I think they get it. They let the words sit with us for a moment.

"Lloyd, are you still going to fight Coach Cuckoo?" Mom asks, breaking the silence. "Look, I know you're good, but you have to think about this logically. They know you're good. They wouldn't offer this challenge lightly. They've got something planned. I'd bet on that. Something to hurt you. Or embarrass you. Have you thought hard about all that?"

Mr. Samuels holds Mom's hand. It makes me happy to see them together. All this drama aside, I've never seen them so joyful.

"I have," he says. "I've made a simple decision, and I am thinking carefully about the risks. I will not be a teacher who sits on the sidelines. If my students fight, then I will fight, too. We live in a world with so many problems, and our default setting cannot be to let someone else deal with it. That's false hope. I like my hope to come with a healthy side of action. So, we fight."

My heart bursts with pride.

"Okay, let's make a plan," Mom says. "And I'm helping because we've got to get this right. I never want another tournament in my life. If we do this, it's the last one. But how about pancakes first? I think better over food." We move to the kitchen. Mom slaps pancakes on our plates, and we brainstorm ideas. After I've eaten not three but four huge pancakes—I may have worked up an appetite before they came home—we come to some conclusions.

"We flip the script," Mr. Samuels says. "Last year, Krake and Decker used you. They wanted to get under our skin, torment Aiden, even spy on us so they knew what I was teaching you. This year, we can do the same to them. Mateo can tell us everything they're doing. You go from their practice to ours, showing us everything."

"But that risks Mateo's safety," Mom says. "That much training? And with adults who give kids a black eye?"

*"Gracias, Senorita Gardner,"* Mateo says. "I wish my parents thought the same way."

"I don't like the mixed genders, either," Mom says. "It doesn't make sense. They can't go through with it, right? Maybe that's their strategy? You'll prepare and they'll change the rules the day of the event."

"It's a good theory, Susan," Mr. Samuels says. "I wouldn't put it past them. But I also don't put it past Decker to follow through with this."

"So, what do we do?" Mateo asks.

"I have an idea," Mr. Samuels says. "I don't like it very much, but I think it's *exactly* what we need to do."

# 34

## *New Competition*

THE NEXT DAY, we meet up at Tisha's to strategize, but she's way ahead of us.

"Has anyone been paying attention to the new wrestlers on Krake's team?" she asks.

We reply with grunts and shrugs. DeMarcus plops himself on the floor of her bedroom by her desk, where Tisha sits, our high school's webpage displayed on her laptop's screen. Mateo sits on her bed. DeMarcus and Mateo mumbled something inaudible to each other when we first entered the room, but they haven't spoken since.

I've been beating myself up, too. DeMarcus has distracted me, and my thoughts about Mateo have been a mixed bag of sweet and sour. Everything Mat has done recently to me or with me has been so kind. I hate that he must train with the enemy, but at least he's transparent about it. No more lies. That's all I want.

*Are you lying to yourself, though?* DeMarcus looks extra cute in his red, sleeveless shirt.

Shut up, brain! It's only attraction. I'm in love with Mateo.

*Do you even know what love is?*

Shut up!

"I don't know how we missed that!" Tony says, sitting on the bottom edge of Tisha's bed, holding Amanda's hand.

Realizing I had spaced out for a minute, I mumble, "Wait, what?"

"Aiden, anyone home?" Amanda turns around and knocks on my head gently with a closed fist. "Where are you?"

"Here, sorry. What is it?"

Tisha swivels in her desk chair, turning to face us, looking like a badass spy. "Coach Krake has a son, Wyatt, a freshman on the team. How did we miss that?" She looks at Mateo and DeMarcus more than the rest of us.

"It's been months since I've kept up with any wrestling news," Mateo says. "Krake never talked about his family." Mat glances lightly over at DeMarcus, who shrugs.

"Yeah, I don't remember anything about him having a kid," DeMarcus says. "You never saw his son at any of the summer training camps?"

Mateo shakes his head. "If he was there, Krake never said anything about him."

"And he's dating Alyssa!" Tisha says.

"Oh, her," Amanda says. "She's the one you knocked out in one punch at the tournament last year."

"That's the one," Tisha says. "Look at her socials. Lots of pics of Wyatt and her together. And that's not all. She looks like she's been training her ass off. In the last martial art pic she shared, she's wearing a blue belt."

"If she gets the chance, I'm sure she'll be out for revenge," Amanda says. "Maybe she's trying to come up with her own one-punch knockout move."

"I beat her once. I can beat her again," Tisha says. "How good do you think Wyatt is? Oh, wait, let's watch this." As if answering her own question, Tisha finds a video on Wyatt's socials of a wrestling match from junior high.

The video isn't long. It's less than thirty seconds, and it ends in a quick pin and victory for Wyatt.

"Damn," Tony mutters. "That's how Mat wrestled last year."

"He's good," Tisha says. "And Krake has kept quiet about it. A secret weapon, maybe? This is what we need to be doing, you guys. We need to learn about the people we'll be facing. Study up."

"I want to be a thousand times more prepared this year," Amanda says. Poor Amanda and Tony lost so quickly last time. I don't blame them for wanting to make a bigger impact.

"Okay, real talk," Tisha says. "What if it ends up being two of us against each other? How would that work?"

"I don't wanna fight any of you," I say. "I dunno. I think one person should forfeit. Save the other's energy that way, don't you think?"

"But how do we make that decision?" Tony asks.

"I don't like any of this," Mateo says. "You guys know my family needs the money. But worse than that, if I don't win, I move. It's not fair for you to have to back down just because of my stuff. Any one of you deserves to win, and any one of you is good enough to win."

I laugh, and I realize I'm the only one.

"I mean it, Aiden. Look how close you came to beating me last year! That's Mister Samuels's teaching. Anyone can win, and you'd be stupid to give up a chance at the money."

DeMarcus flashes Mateo a fierce look. He's not taking Mat's words as a compliment or any kind of politeness. That's the look of someone who *does* have a chance to win. Yes, all things considered, Mateo is the strongest—the *best*—of us. But competition does have other factors—multiple skillsets, speed, overall knowledge, and, of course, luck.

"I don't want anyone backing down from a fight with me," Mateo says. "We owe it to ourselves to give our best, no matter who we face."

"I agree," DeMarcus says confidently, still staring at Mateo.

I hope I don't have to watch that fight.

*Think about how close you came to winning last year, especially once you learned the secrets in your* kata. And if someone like me can get that close to beating Mateo, then anyone in this room could do the same, including DeMarcus.

Including Tisha or Amanda or Tony.

What about the other team? With competitors like Jeff, Logan, Camila, Alyssa, Coach Krake's kid, and let's not forget the Olympian-like Michelle, one thought is clear as day. Truly, anyone can win this tournament.

Anyone.

That includes me.

But would I do that to my boyfriend? Would I fight my true love again, knowing everything that is on the line? That money would change my life, too. But then I'd lose my boyfriend, not just in a break-up, but in a move where I may never see him again.

The endless possibilities hurt my head as much as the hate hurts my heart.

# 35

## *Falling Down and Getting Up*

FOR THE MOST part, our practices have been fun. I enjoy the workouts, I like the people, and there's something about martial arts that just feels... well, magical. It's like taking science classes for the first time—when you learn how some of the magic works, it's powerfully captivating.

But now, with the tournament approaching, *Sensei* Samuels gets more serious, too.

"Today, we *master* how to fall," Mr. Samuels says. We're lined up in our dojo, aka the study hall room. Our hopes of picking up new members after the demonstration fell flat. Mr. Samuels teaches two karate classes—a general class designed for beginners and a tournament training class, an extra hour, for those entering the MMA tourney.

It's just the core six of us for the second hour—DeMarcus, Tisha, Amanda, Tony, Mateo, and me. Mateo only makes it once or twice a week, depending on his other practices. He looks more and more exhausted every day.

Mr. Samuels demonstrates multiple falls—backward, front, side, and even diving and rolling techniques. It's cool, and we've done some of this before. But those were fun lessons. Now, seriousness spreads across Mr. Samuels's face, as well as ours, although it's buried under a river of sweat.

We spend the hour falling, a full hour devoted to basics that could have been our first class. This part of training is not much fun, but *Sensei* emphasizes fundamentals in every practice.

"Line up," he says, finally. That's the phrase that indicates the end of class, and I couldn't be more grateful. "Listen to me carefully, kids. Falling is an essential skill. Many fights end the second someone falls. They can hit their head, which can result from anything from a concussion to death." He takes a deep breath. "My job is to keep you all safe. But this lesson is more than that. I want you to repeat this next sentence back to me, all right?" He clears his throat. "When you learn how to fall, you learn how to rise."

"When you learn how to fall, you learn how to rise," we repeat through tired breaths.

"Very good. Karate isn't just self-defense. I fell in love with karate more so because of the life lessons it teaches. When you learn how to fall, you learn how to rise. So, how do we rise?"

"With our hands up?" I offer.

"Quickly," Tisha says.

"Safely," Tony adds when Mr. Samuels looks at him.

*Fall seven times, rise eight.* We've practiced falls so much that I could give Mr. Samuels's lecture. Does Decker teach life lessons like this? I doubt it, but then how did Mr. Samuels learn all this?

"Amanda, do you remember what else we did last year when someone fell?" *Sensei* asks.

"We helped them back up," she says.

Mr. Samuels smiles. "You're my best students. Not only do you all have good memories, but you also have good hearts. Well done." He folds his arms and looks deep in thought. "Yes, when we learn how to fall, we learn how to rise. Everyone falls. Every person you know will make mistakes. The smartest, kindest people in the world will make mistakes. When they fall, help them up. When you fall, rise with grace and humility. But rise. Get up and learn from your mistakes. Always try to improve, but never focus on perfection. There is no perfection. There is only progress. Do you understand?"

We nod. Perhaps more out of fatigue than true comprehension.

"Very well," Mr. Samuels says. "Let me conclude with this. Your biggest test isn't about victory or success. Your true strength is revealed only when you fall." He pauses again and scratches his nose. This time, he looks right at me when he speaks. "Do you know how to fall?"

*Um, we just spent the last hour practicing this for the hundredth time.* But that's not what he wants to hear. "Yes, sir."

"How, then? How do you fall?"

"Do you want me to show you?" I ask, his gaze still on me.

"How do you fall, Aiden?" His voice remains patient. I'm at the point where I just want a nap.

Scratching the side of my neck, I try not to show my fatigue and impatience. "We fall the way we want to rise." I cough a little, and Mr. Samuels nods, encouraging me to continue. "We fall with grace and humility, which means—I think—that if we don't fall with grace and humility that we can't rise with grace and humility, either?"

Mr. Samuels nods approvingly. "Think about people who can't admit when they lost. Or made a mistake. Never look up to those people. That's weakness. Strength is revealed when we fall." He pauses for a moment, and I wish I could sit down or something. I'm so tired. "If you fall with arrogance—like you can't make a mistake, like you're surprised you'd even stumble—then how does that person rise? That person rises arrogantly without learning a thing. They will fall even harder next time." He lowers his voice, saying this next part carefully. "Think about it because some people, I guarantee you, are not learning how to fall or how to recover. They don't think they will fall, so why practice it? That's where we will surprise them, class." Mr. Samuels smiles. "We will surprise them with the very lessons karate is meant to teach —grace and humility."

Mr. Samuels bows, and we return the gesture, signifying the end of class. I like his ideas, but how will grace or humility beat someone talented like Michelle? Or stop the hatred of someone like Coach Krake?

AFTER PRACTICE, TISHA and I hang with Mateo to see what's been happening with his training and plan to visit Camila, too. Tisha's determined to make things right with her. "So, do you get to spar with Michelle?" Tisha asks Mat. I'm super curious about Decker's teaching style.

"Yeah."

"And Camila?"

"No."

"Why not?" Tisha asks.

Mateo rolls his eyes. "Why do you think? I mean, Decker hasn't said it directly, but I'm sure it's because Camila's a girl."

"Um, so is Michelle," Tisha adds.

"I know, I know," Mateo says, shaking his head. "It's just. Well, you know. Decker doesn't see her exactly like that, I guess."

"How does Decker see Michelle?" I ask, genuinely curious.

He shrugs. "He doesn't tell us what he's thinking, not about that. As much of a jerk as Decker is, I don't think he cares about her identity, not when she's a badass fighter."

"Can you beat her?" I ask.

"It will be a heck of a fight. She's better than Tanner," he says. "So much better than Tanner, and I lost to him last year."

"Speaking of the devil, do you ever see Tanner?" Tisha asks.

"No," Mateo says. "He's training with certified UFC coaches now and is on an adult training circuit. Decker thinks he'll be on all the premium live events any weekend."

"Gross," Tisha says. "Why do the worst people get the best attention?"

We're walking toward Camila's house, and memories of last year's walk to Camila's come to mind. Tisha and I tried to make up with her then. She had bruises on her body and wore a Decker's MMA T-shirt only sort of hidden under hooded sweatshirts. How do I make things right with someone who sees me as the enemy?

"You know, Camila was my best friend," Tisha says almost like she is reading mind. "She dated both of you. I get why she's pissed, but Camila was, no, is a good person. I forgot that. I let my anger get the best of me. I'm not saying she's innocent, not at all. I'm just saying I understand why she did the things she did. If we can't understand a person's behavior, then how would we move forward? I'm just trying to understand, you know?"

We both nod.

"That's why I want to talk with her," she says. "It's time to put our egos to the side. Just be sorry. What's wrong with just being sorry?"

Are these ideas from Mr. Samuels's lessons? With her impulsive nature, I wonder what kind of student Tisha would be if she trained with Decker.

Our previous experiences with Camila could be described as failures. Or falls. But we didn't fall with grace or humility. When we fell, when she shocked us by training with Decker and fighting against us, we fell with anger.

"And then we rose with anger," I mumble.

"What's that?" Tisha asks.

*"Nada."* I keep thinking about Mr. Samuels's lesson on falling.

"I want to make things right with her," Tisha says. "I want to do whatever it takes to make things right."

"So, what happens if you make up but have to fight her in the tournament?" Mateo asks.

"I'd rather face a friend than an enemy," Tisha says. "Wouldn't you?"

Mateo looks at me, a warm smile lighting up his face. "What if you have to face your boyfriend?"

Returning his soft smile, I say, "Don't you think that's what they want? Decker and Krake and the jerks that look up to them. They win if we fight. We should have learned that last year, but…."

"But you kissed me, and I was too scared to tell you how much I actually really really liked it," Mateo says. "I liked it so much it made me crazy. Made me say and do terrible things. I'm so sorry, Aiden."

I reach for his hand. "I love you, Mat."

"I love you, too." He stops and kisses me, right in broad daylight, right on a sidewalk outside of a row of houses.

"Enough, you two. I'd say get a room, but I know you'd take me up on the offer and leave me," Tisha says, laughing.

When I pull away from Mat, I turn to her. "Maybe there's hope for us and Camila after all," I say, thinking of how much Mat and I have gone through together.

"There is," Tisha says. "There has to be, or… or…."

"Or what?" I ask, curious and surprised that Tisha can't find the right words.

"Or why are we fighting?"

"This 'don't-say-gay' crap. This community. This school. I want to show up, be one hundred percent me, and kick ass. I don't want to be seen as weak or unequal." I take a giant breath. "I want to show them I'm stronger than their hate."

"Yeah, exactly!" Tisha holds out her fist, and when I go to bump it, she pulls it back, laughs, and hugs me instead. "I'm tired of the hate, too. I keep thinking of Camila and Michelle. And even Logan." She pauses for a second, and I wonder if she is thinking about how she dated Logan once upon a time. She probably knows things about him she's never shared with us. "And the real truth—I don't know how we can get a school and community to be better when our own best friends, or former best friends, hate us. That's why I want to talk to Camila. So, let's win this battle today, right now. You both with me?"

"Yes," Mateo and I say right as we turn and face Camila's house.

Then we hear screaming.

# 36

## *The Fight We Should Have Seen Coming*

WHEN WE APPROACH, shouts transcend the walls of Camila's little house. A few remaining fall flowers hold on to the sunshine out front as long as they can. The house looks freshly painted—a blue coat that would suggest friendliness, but that right now seems like anything but.

"Why are you such a terrible brat? I can't stand you!" The volume of the words shakes the glass window on the front door.

"Was that Camila's mom?" Mateo asks.

"Not her mom. Her stepmom," Tisha whispers.

Glass shatters on the inside, and Tisha knocks loudly and immediately. The voices instantly silent. Good. Scare her stepmother. Make her think it's the cops.

My arms and legs shake, nerves flaring up like they have many times before a fight begins.

"Who is it?" Camila's stepmother asks, her voice raspy and horse like she's a heavy smoker.

"What do I say?" Tisha asks.

Mateo and I shrug, so Tisha simply knocks again.

"Jesus, one minute, for Christ's sake." Loud footsteps approach, weighed down by anger and annoyance. What is Tisha getting us into today? The door swings open, and we're greeted by a middle-aged woman with messy hair and dark, tired eyes. "What the hell do you want?"

"Um, we want to see Camila," Tisha says quietly. The woman turns halfway around, and we see a series of objects and trash on the floor—broken glass, magazines, boxes of food.

"She's grounded. For life." She starts to shut the door when Camila kicks it back open with her right foot. "Listen, you little bastard! I told you no karate. You are *done*. No more lessons. No more anything. It's turned you into a super brat!"

"Then what's your excuse?" Camila snaps. She glances at us, and for a moment, I catch a WTF reaction to us showing up at her house, but her attention returns to her stepmother.

Just in time, too. Her stepmother raises her right arm and swings an open palm right at Camila's face. She blocks, and I can tell Camila is fighting every urge not to hit back.

The stepmother screams. Her left arm shoots straight at Camila's throat. She's choking her. Mateo and I exchange nervous glances, not knowing what to do. Tisha, however, doesn't hesitate.

"Leave her alone!" Tisha shouts, forcing her way through the door. The stepmother releases Camila, spinning like a rabid beast, and faces Tisha.

"You will leave my property this instant, or I'm calling the police. You're trespassing!"

"Go ahead," Tisha shouts back just as loudly. "I can't wait to tell them we have three witnesses to child abuse. What is *wrong* with you?"

Camila squeezes past her mother and gently pushes Tisha outside.

"Get back in here, you ungrateful whore's daughter!"

Mateo and I stare at her in total shock. His face turns pale, and I wonder if he's had moments like this with his family. Maybe not the language and the abuse, but the intensity—there's something in his eyes I can't interpret. A quiet sadness.

"I will not!" Camila shouts back. "I'm never coming back!"

"I will report you as a runaway, you stupid little—"

"No, you won't!" Camila shouts back. "*Sensei* Decker said I can stay with him and his wife. What do you think about that? Call the cops and see what good it does when he answers the phone!"

As I stare at Camila's stepmother, something twists and snaps inside her. A monster lives inside her, and it's terrifying. My eyes dart to her hand, as her fingers curl into a solid fist. Camila looks at Mateo and me, and that's when the step-monster attacks.

Her right fist wizzes right toward the back of Camila's head. I open my mouth to warn her, but before any words can come out, Tisha leaps in front of Camila.

*Smack!* Camila's step-monster slugs Tisha right on the jaw.

The step-monster finally has an appropriate reaction. She gasps. Her arms shake. Tears roll down her cheeks. Her screams morph into sobs.

Camila gasps. "Look at what you've done! You've lost it! I am never coming back to this house. N*ever!*"

With each word, the step-monster retreats, one small footstep at a time. The front door closes. No apologies. No more words of any kind.

Tisha holds a hand up to her now red, bruised jaw.

Camila sniffs, wipes at her eyes, and shakes her head. I've never seen her this defeated. The anger she held before deflates like a flat tire. Tisha reaches for her, hugging her and pulling her close.

"Are you okay?" Tisha asks.

Camila cries, and Tisha holds her. We stand out front for what feels like several long, never-ending minutes. The house quiets, and even the flowers look wilted like the shouting poisoned them.

"Thank you," Camila says.

"For what?"

"For being here." She pulls away and looks over at Mat and me. "Let's go to your place," she tells Tisha. "Anywhere but here."

"Okay."

"If you hadn't been here…." Camila's voice fades away, and she sighs. "We haven't had a physical fight in some time. But today, she blew up. I don't know what would have happened if you hadn't been here. I think I would have… let's just say that it was gonna be her or me, but one of us was gonna get seriously hurt today."

"What happened?" I ask softly.

Camila glances at me but doesn't immediately reply. None of us push her to do so. She'll talk when she's ready.

We walk in silence for a long time, and then Camila bursts into laughter. It's the hysterics from someone who just experienced trauma, but Tisha asks, "What's so funny?"

Camila wipes her eyes again. "I just thought, you know, that you could have at least blocked that punch. I thought you were better than that." Camila flashes a smile to let Tisha know she's kidding. Tisha puts her arm around Camila's shoulders.

It's a terrible thing we witnessed, but this moment right here—I can't help but smile. There's a new emotion I'm feeling that I haven't experienced much, and I like this feeling.

It's more than hope. It's a rich optimism, a feeling that friends who turned enemies can still become friends again. Nothing is impossible unless we make it so.

WE HANG OUT in Tisha's bedroom. She grabbed a bunch of drinks and snacks for us. The girls sprawl out on her bed. Mateo and I sit on the floor, looking up. Camila keeps looking at her phone and texting.

"The practices are so hard. But so worth it, wouldn't you say, Mat?" she says, when we ask Mat and her about training with Decker.

Mateo looks defeated. I haven't ever seen him like this, and I feel like I've seen almost every emotion he has. "I'm just a damn puppet."

"Huh?" I take his hand and hold it.

"Decker tells me to do something, and I do it. My dad tells me to do something, and I do it. Mister Samuels tells me to do something, and I—"

"Ignore it," Tisha says. "He's got the least amount of influence on you. Don't blame him or us for the crap you're going through."

Blood rushes from Mateo's face. Squeezing his hand, I glare at Tisha. "Be nice."

Tisha huffs and turns back to Camila. "Who are you texting? You've been on your phone since we got here."

Probably telling Michelle or Logan where we are so they come and—I stop myself from finishing the thought, and I certainly don't say it. What happened to the optimism from a moment ago?

"What makes Decker's practices so hard?" I ask, trying to change the subject.

Camila looks at Mateo, who shakes his head like he's annoyed and doesn't want to be here, but he takes a deep breath and finally talks. "Mister Samuels and even Coach Krake, to some extent, try to keep everyone safe, you know?"

My turn to huff. *Safe* isn't exactly what comes to mind when I think of Krake.

Mateo picks up on my attitude. "I mean, like, most practices you didn't have to keep an ambulance on call. He does still have a school board to report to," he says when I roll my eyes. "And even if that board is a bunch of homophobic jerks, they can't have kids going to the hospital after practice every day." *Um, did you forget about my trip to the hospital last year?* "Decker, on the other hand, acts like we're in a war." Mateo, sitting cross-legged on the floor, buries his face into his hands. I scoot closer to him. The girls look down on us from Tisha's bed.

"What does that mean?" Tisha asks.

"I don't have anything to compare it to," Camila says. "Every day is hard. Every day we fight. We fight until someone quits. It's about toughening us up, emotionally and physically."

"This, um, *war?*" I ask hesitantly. "It's all about us, though, yeah? He just wants to see us lose?"

"Yes," Camila says. "But not just lose. He wants you all to lose so badly that you'll never want to try again."

"Because we're gay?" I ask.

"No," Camila says. "It's nothing to do with sexuality."

"Bull," Tisha says.

Camila gets down from the bed and walks over toward Tisha's desk. For a second, I think she's going to get on her laptop, but she just leans against the desk chair, stretching out her back. "It's not bull. Decker has a gay daughter. Her name is Caitlin."

"What?"

"Yes," Camila says. "Not only that. She's also a black belt."

Mateo looks up at this, and his face says this is news to him, too.

"Um, does Caitlin train with you?" Tisha asks.

Camila shakes her head. "No. *Sensei* told me about her privately."

"What did he say? And why privately?" Mateo asks.

"Look, you guys, I'll tell you, but I want to come to an understanding first," Camila says. "We're not friends. You all lied to me, repeatedly, and I am choosing not to be friends with liars."

Tisha looks at me, her eyes begging me to say something. Mom's words and my promises to help Camila echo in my mind. "Mila, I'm so sorry," I start. "I understand if you never want to be friends. But please give me a real chance to not only explain but to make it up to you. You are one hundred percent right." I pause for a moment, trying to get the words right. "I did hurt you, but that was not my intention. My only intention was to figure out who I was. That's not an excuse, though. It's just a reason, and I need to make it up to you. I want to make it up to you. I'm sorry."

Camila looks at me like she's seeing me for the first time.

"Can you ever forgive me?" I ask.

She shrugs. "I was really hurt, you know. I really liked you. We were going out at the same time my stepmother started, um, well. It was the same time she decided words weren't enough, and she started hitting me." Camila walks over to a bedroom window and looks out onto the street. "I needed someone to be close to me. I thought it was going to be you. Then I felt so betrayed when you came out." She pauses and looks at Tisha. "So, I thought I'd at least have my best friend to help, but you paid more attention to Aiden instead of me. And then there was Mateo."

Mateo and I share uncomfortable glances.

"I should have known it was all a lie," Camila mutters. "Decker will do anything to win." She makes eye contact with me and pauses. "Before you fought with Mateo, Aiden, all he did was ask about you. Once you two got in that fight or whatever, suddenly he seemed interested in me. But that was all a lie, too."

"*Lo siento,*" Mateo says. "You know how persuasive Decker can be, and he told me to date you to get under Aiden's skin."

"How can you train with a man like that?" Tisha asks both Mateo and Camila.

"That's when Decker opened up to me. Told me all about Caitlin. And that's when I told him about my stepmother. Everything changed. Now, he's inviting me to live with him, so that I can get out of my house. And you know what, guys? I'm gonna do it. I'm gonna move and live with Decker and his family."

# 37

## *Caitlin Decker*

"WHAT'S THE STORY with Decker's daughter?" Tisha asks. She sits with her back against the wall, her legs spread out on the bed. Mateo and I still sit on the floor, and Camila paces the bedroom. She looks at her phone a few times, then sets it down, disappointed.

"Like every freakin' old, straight dude, he freaked out at Caitlin's sexuality. She didn't come out until she was older. Like thirty. She hid it from her father, but she fell in love. She moved in with her girlfriend, and they couldn't hide it anymore." Camila pulls out Tisha's desk chair and takes a seat.

"Do you know her or something? Or is this what Decker told you?" Tisha asks, rolling over on her stomach, her heels kicked up toward her butt.

"Both," Camila says. "Decker said I reminded him of Caitlin. She took karate lessons with him as a little girl, only stopping when she went away to college."

"Did she and Mister Samuels train together?" I ask.

Camila shrugs. "We didn't talk about your teacher." She gives me an odd look, and I tell myself to not make it about me. "They were close for years until—"

"She came out," I mutter, and Mateo elbows me in the side to shut up.

"No, it's not about that," Camila says. "*Sensei* Decker said they got into a fight because her uncle hit on her."

I sit straight up. "Wait a minute. Wait a damn minute. Her uncle. That would be—"

"Coach Krake," Camila says. "Yep."

"What happened?" I ask, sitting on the edge of my seat.

"Caitlin told her father that Krake came on to her. This was when she graduated high school. So, she was an adult and all—"

"But freakin' gross and wrong," Tisha says.

"Yes," Camila agrees. "Krake was drunk and hit on Caitlin at a graduation party. She rejected him. When she rejected him, Krake accused her of being a lesbian."

Tisha shakes her head. "Of course. Straight man gets rejected, and straight man must blame anyone but himself."

"Well, *Sensei* Decker didn't believe his daughter. Krake told him he was drunk and made a stupid joke, and that Caitlin misinterpreted it."

"Wait a sec," I say, rubbing my temples, trying to understand this messed-up family tree. "Krake's wife is Decker's sister. So, Krake did this while married to Decker's sister? To Decker's daughter? And Decker believes... *Krake?* Why didn't he stand up for his sister or at least his freakin' daughter?"

Camila nods. "All that is why Caitlin and her father got in a huge fight. It wasn't long after that that she moved to college. Then she was an adult on her own. She rarely talked to her dad, and by the time he decided he wanted to be a better father, she was living with her girlfriend."

"How did Decker react to that?" Tisha asks.

"He says he was mad that she lied to him and didn't tell him about any of it. Never once was it about her being gay."

"I still call B.S.," I say. "You've seen him around us. He's not the guy who would show up at a pride parade to support his daughter or anything."

"Agreed," Camila says.

Which catches us all off guard. Mateo, Tisha, and I exchange confused looks. Finally, Tisha speaks up. "But you're moving in with this guy? I don't understand why you'd be around him."

Camila's phone lights up, and she looks at it. A brief smile flashes on her face, and she texts a quick response back to whoever messaged her. "I know. I know how it must look. But you don't see what I see. Decker wants to make things right with his daughter. He's regretful for not being in her life, and that's made him hard. But he looks out for me. He trained me to protect myself when my stepmother started abusing me."

"He's a cop," I say. "He should have arrested her."

"I begged him not to, Aiden. I want to fight for myself."

I can't argue with that.

"Decker was there when all my friends betrayed me. I mean— when it felt like that's what you all were doing," she follows up, reading our apologetic facial expressions. "And now, he's giving me a place to stay. Plus, he's talking to his daughter again."

"And giving my boyfriend black eyes, threatening us in parking lots, making kids fight each other for his own entertainment!" I argue.

Camila's phone goes off again.

"Who are you texting?" Tisha asks.

Camila smiles, and for a moment, I'm worried she's going to tell us that it's Logan or Jeff or some other creep she's dating who will make our lives hell. But that's not what she says.

"I'm texting Caitlin," she tells us.

"What for?" Tisha asks.

Camila gets up from the office chair and moves back to the bed. She sits on the mattress corner and nods, perhaps thinking about what to say. "Because I'm worried, too—worried about the black eyes, the crazy training we're going through. We're not joking when we say that Decker is training us for war."

"Mila's right," Mateo says. "Mister Samuels trains us for fun. For the sport and art of it all. Decker trains us like we're soldiers. He even invites the police force to join us. We fight adults, and we don't stop the fight until someone quits." Is that why all the cop cars were outside the wrestling room? They're all training together? "That's why my father insists on me training with him. And you know, this sucks to say, but I kinda sorta agree. If I have any chance of getting this scholarship money so that I don't have to move, this is how I must train. Not for fun, but for war."

"But what's all this have to do with Decker's daughter?" Tisha asks.

"Because I think she's the only one who might be able to talk some sense into him," Camila says. "If she can't, if he never changes…." She doesn't finish the sentence, looking down at the carpeted floor instead.

"If he doesn't change, then what?" I ask.

"As hard as we're training," Camila says, "I'm worried someone's gonna get seriously hurt. Or even die."

# 38

*Therapy*

"HI, DOCTOR KAUTZ," I greet my therapist at our weekly session. Although I've only had a few sessions, it's not what I expected. Maybe I've seen too many movies, but I thought I'd be lying down on a couch while talking about my childhood and absent father. It's not like that at all. It's a conversation, and I can talk about anything I want.

After I fill out my survey, that is. I begin by rating my mood, writing down any topics I want to discuss, and describing if I have any suicidal thoughts. That last part always gives me a strange feeling. On a scale of zero to ten, how likely am I to hurt myself? The first time, I rated myself low, a one, but Dr. Kautz made me talk about it.

It's weird to think about suicide and depression. I don't want to harm myself, but thinking about nothingness, non-existence—I admit sometimes I wonder what nothing feels like.

Dr. Kautz diagnosed me with general anxiety disorder and post-traumatic stress disorder. That's too many disorders, I think, but Dr. Kautz says it's perfectly natural, that almost everyone she sees has at minimum anxiety issues.

"And how are you and Mateo?" she asks. She's older, maybe mid-fifties, with super short hair. She wears a sweater and has a space heater in her office that blasts out heat no matter what the temperature is outside.

I catch her up to what's been going on and ask, "What would you do if you were me?"

"First, I'd stop thinking about Mateo in terms of what he's given up for me. We all make our own choices. We all must live with the choices we make. You are not responsible for his choices or anyone's choices."

"I guess," I mutter. "But, like, if he hadn't met me, he'd still be on the wrestling team, still in line to get all the college scholarships he could possibly need, ya know? He lost that to be with me."

"No, Aiden. He found himself. He chose to be himself. You helped him find much more than he lost. If you hadn't come along, do you think Mateo would spend his life in the closet, denying his identity?"

"I dunno."

"As you no doubt understand, sexuality is complicated. Many young people bury their identities to fit in with their peers. But guess what changes that?"

I shrug.

"Love," she says. "Romance. Or what if I said hormones instead?" I can't help but laugh, and Dr. Kautz smiles at me. "Yeah, eventually, Mateo would have had feelings for another boy and would have to make similar choices. It's not all about you."

"Oh."

She pauses for a long moment, letting me think.

Eventually, I tell her about the voice in my head when I kiss him. "What do I do? I want to kiss my boyfriend without that stupid voice in my head telling me it's all a lie."

"Do you trust Mateo?"

"Yeah. I think so, anyway."

"It is not your fault if you don't. It is his responsibility to earn your trust. Most relationships take a long time to develop trust. That's a big part of intimacy, more so than kissing. It's even harder for you, though, because your relationship was built on a shared history that turned out to be manipulative."

"He apologizes to me all the time."

"That's great. But actions speak much louder than words. What is he doing to create trust in your relationship?"

Waves of terrible thoughts flow through my mind. He's training with our opponent. He distrusts DeMarcus. He shuts down a lot. We never have any time to spend together anymore.

"Take your time," Dr. Kautz continues. "You can share anything you want."

My knee bounces for a minute, and I stare at it, not sure what else I want to share today. Some moments are like this—pensive, more questions than answers.

"I'm tired, Doctor Kautz," I finally say. "Why does our school have to be so crappy? Like if we weren't having to deal with the jerks here, maybe Mateo would be happier. He wouldn't have had to quit, if people just accepted him. Us."

Dr. Kautz listens, her eyes never leaving me, even though most of the time I'm looking down at the floor. I vent some more, and our hour comes to an end.

"Aiden, you shouldn't have to deal with so much, so young. What I want you to do is to spend time with those who make you feel good about yourself—your friends, your mom, your karate teacher. There will always be people who will bring you down and make you feel bad about yourself. We can't change that. What we can change is how we react to it and how we deal with it. I want you to think about what makes you happy. What brings you the most joy? What makes you smile the biggest? When do you feel safest, no worries about getting hurt or being lied to? Will you think about that?"

I nod instead of answering out loud. Dr. Kautz may not like my answer to most of those questions.

Mateo.

He brings me the most joy. He makes me smile the most. The problem, though, is that being with him also enhances the fear and anxiety I'm trying to eliminate. I love Mateo, and I don't want him to give up on me or us.

I think of Camila, too, and every friend or situation that I've given up on.

Like David, the friend I lost in middle school. I almost told Dr. Kautz about David a few times. Almost. Some doors are harder to open than others.

I'm tired of giving up on things, and I'm certainly not going to give up on the person I love the most.

Fall seven times. Rise eight.

# 39

## *The Best Date Night*

MAYBE THERAPY INSPIRED me. What would bring me joy right now? A special date night with Mateo, something just for the two of us. Maybe even something that might end with lots of kissing. I'm not ready for sex yet. Not that I don't think about it. Like all the time. But things are complicated enough without rushing anything there.

Who can I talk to about sex? Would my mom or Mr. Samuels understand gay sex? Like, how do I know if I'm a bottom or a top?

A voice laughs inside me. Oh, you know who you are.

Okay, but do I have to do that stuff? What if I don't want to do the stuff that, um, well, like the stuff in videos I've "accidentally" stumbled across on the internet? And do people just announce that to each other? *Hi, I'm Aiden, purple belt, bottom, loves tacos.* I don't know.

I'm standing outside of Mateo's front door, shaking my head, telling myself to stop thinking about sex. It's a daily struggle. I never had a dad to give me a sex talk. Maybe Mr. Samuels will be the one to do that, but it sure would be nice to have some gay mentors as well.

"What are you smiling at?" Mateo asks as he opens the front door.

I'm thinking about how Mr. Samuels would teach me about tops and bottoms, and how uncomfortably weird and funny it would be. I don't say that, though. "Just thinking about, you know, things I want to do tonight."

"I know where your mind goes," Mat says with his cheesy smile. I can tell when hormones get the best of him, too. He becomes laser-focused on my body, his eyes moving from my arms to my chest and sometimes I even catch him glancing below the belt. Maybe he thinks I don't know that he checks me out, but I certainly do. And I love it.

Mom sits in Mateo's driveway. She insisted on driving us tonight. She'll drop us off, and Mr. Samuels will pick us up. I'm happy avoiding Mateo's parents and not having to walk around the entire town. That's when we get into trouble, and Mom realizes that, too. She waves at Mateo as we approach.

"So, the trampoline park tonight?" she asks, and we nod. We thought a date there would be fun. We can practice jump kicks, too.

Mateo and I both sit in the backseat because I want to be close to him and hold his hand. Mom looks back at me in the rearview mirror a couple of times and smiles.

Mateo whispers in my ear. "I hear there's like a special tunnel at the trampoline park. A kissing tunnel."

My heart goes wild.

"I want to kiss you so bad, Aiden." He holds my hand tighter. I think back to the last few interactions I had with Mat. Things haven't been great, but is that his fault? I can't help but wonder how amazing things would be if people just left us alone.

"Me, too."

We spend the next few minutes holding hands and laughing randomly at everything. Yes, I know anyone who sees us like this might throw up, but these are my favorite moments. Happiness for the present mixed with excitement for what comes next. It doesn't get any better than this.

Mom pulls into the parking lot. "Text us when you're ready. Lloyd said he'll come get you, okay?"

We nod and race to the entrance. We put on special trampoline socks, pay, and get our wristbands. Then we jump, but it feels more like flying. Mateo can do all sorts of flips—back flips, front flips, it's amazing. I try to do a flip, but I keep falling on my butt.

"Fear is holding you back, *Aiden-San*," Mateo says in an Asian accent that's probably inappropriate, but I laugh.

I grab his ankles and pull him down. We lay side-by-side as a few children run around, ignoring us. I touch his hand. He gives it to me, no hesitation. There's a part of me that wonders if the kids here will laugh or say anything. They don't, though. Some parents give us a couple of dirty looks. That's the world we live in. These kids would grow up to be perfectly cool people if the adults in this town could get their crap together.

Mateo leans over toward me as if he's going to kiss me. My heart pounds, wondering if he'll do that in front of all these kids and parents. I open my mouth, but he just laughs, punches me gently on the arm, and pulls me back up.

"There's a place for that, remember?" he asks, his perfect white teeth shining through those lips I can't wait to kiss.

"Where is it?"

"Follow me." We bounce our way around various trampolines until we find swings over a foam pit. Kids swing and fly off, like Mateo and I did at the park, but they fall right into a foam pit instead. It looks awesome.

A rock-climbing wall catches our attention near the pit. Mateo leads me to another playground area adjacent to the rock-climbing wall, one silly hop at a time. We hop across a dodgeball area, where kids toss soft objects at each other. Mateo leads me to the center, where a padded tunnel connects two different trampolines.

We crawl inside. Mateo looks around, but there's no one else here. We move to the middle, where it gets darker.

"How many kids do you think have peed in here?" I ask, laughing.

"Shut up!" Mateo says. "That's not what I want to think about right now." He grabs me and kisses me. It's passionate and hot—his warm, soft lips press hard against mine. His tongue dances with mine, and Mateo moves and kisses my neck.

I kiss him harder than before. I push him down and crawl on top of him, loving the physical excitement of his body pressed against me.

While kissing him, my hands run up his shirt, pulling him closer against me. He spins me, and we make out like this for at least a song, if not two.

"Ewww!" It's a sound that makes me stop immediately. Mateo and I let go. A child coming from the same entrance as us sees us kissing. He points at us and laughs. He turns around, still giggling.

But it wasn't a mean laugh. It was a normal "eww" and giggle, one a child would say to anyone, any kind of couple he might catch kissing. It's a cool feeling to be teased in this way, instead of what I'm used to experiencing.

Still, it's a wake-up call that Mateo and I should take our make-out session elsewhere. We've still got some time on our wristbands that we bought, so we jump a bit more. We find a private corner and practice our jump kicks.

"Record me, will ya?" Mat asks. He hands me his phone, and I take a string of videos and pictures of his flips and kicks. Then he encourages me to do the same.

"You know I'm not that good."

"Oh, shut it. You're awesome, and this is just for fun. Maybe we'll share these pics later and make our opponents worry with your mad skills!" I laugh, but I give it a shot, trying jump front kicks, flying side kids, three-hundred-sixty-degree spin kicks, and even more.

What feels like two seconds turns out to be two hours, and our time is already up at the park.

But not for our date.

"Wanna go back to my house?" I ask. "Mom and Mister Samuels will give us some privacy."

"Yes," Mateo says. "Yes, please."

Thinking about all the kissing I want to do, I text Mr. Samuels and ask him to hurry.

# 40

*Making Out
is the Best*

WE RUN THROUGH my house laughing, not caring that Mom looks up at us from the couch like we're animals in the wild. She smiles, and her mouth opens—to tell me to keep the door cracked open, yes, I *know*, Mom!—but I don't give her time to talk.

"We gotta get online for a game that's about to start!" I shout over our footsteps. There's no game. I'm sure one day when I've adopted children with my future husband—or dogs, maybe I'm more of a dog person, I don't know—that Mom will forgive me if I decide to tell her I lied so I could make out with my boyfriend.

Make out with my boyfriend! What a delightful thought. We push my bedroom door open, still laughing with nervous excitement.

Mat's lips press against my mouth. We fall on my bed, and I hope Mom didn't hear any thump. Maybe she'd think we were wrestling? As we clumsily fool around on my bed, I reach for my phone, turn on my Bluetooth speaker, and play music. Loud enough I hope that no one hears us, but soft enough so I'd hear any footsteps approaching.

Mateo's hands run up my shirt. "Can I take it off?"

I gulp. I want to say yes. But I don't want to get in trouble. The last thing I need is to get grounded when I have such little time with Mateo already.

"Yes," I say, my mouth betraying logic, as mouths do.

He pulls my shirt off over my head.

"Look at you, Aiden. You aren't the skinny boy I fell in love with." I'm not sure which part of his sentence I like better.

I kiss him as passionately as I can, removing his shirt, too. My mouth moves to his neck. Mat hugs me tightly, moaning softly in my ear. I move down his body, kissing his chest, exploring every inch. My heart could freakin' jump out of my body. Here I am—with the hottest boy I know, making out, touching him, being touched. And he loves me.

I kiss Mateo's chest again, and he laughs. "What?" I ask, my heart leaping into my throat, like I did something wrong.

"It tickles."

"Oh. Is it okay?"

"Yes, but it's my turn." He kisses me again, harder, and I can't help but moan.

Mateo blushes, and it's the cutest thing in the world. We hear movement outside of my room, and both of us fall silent and still. I grab my T-shirt, moving faster than I ever have in my life.

"You guys want any snacks?" Mom shouts.

"No, thank you! Just playing a game, can't pause!"

"Clever," Mateo whispers.

I kiss him again. He pushes me toward my bed, his mouth so eager against mine, like my lips are the only source of oxygen.

It's pure heaven.

Until my stupid brain tortures me. With my eyes closed, a different image of Mateo appears. First, it's the version of Mateo when I initially kissed him. The Mateo who hit me and threw me out of his house. How is that the same person next to me now? Then the version of Mateo in the Chinese restaurant parking lot comes back. *"I lied. I'm not even your friend."*

My body shakes.

"Are you okay?" Mateo asks.

I take a deep breath. "Just cold."

"You sure?"

If I tell him, he'll feel terrible yet again, apologize, and reassure me about everything. I hate always making him feel bad, too. So, I keep it to myself.

"Wanna watch a movie?" I ask, not answering the subject. He flashes me that charming smile, and I wish I could say that it wiped away all my fears and anxieties.

But it doesn't.

Maybe one day I'll feel better, I hope, because right now I feel like I'm never going to be one hundred percent perfectly happy or even just okay. All I want is to enjoy these moments with my boyfriend without my brain or anxieties screwing everything. Maybe I'll always be a little screwed up.

And maybe that's okay. But I don't know.

DEMARCUS GRABS TONY and me after karate practice the following week. No Mateo—I hate that he must train at Decker's, especially after our fun date. I had all sorts of dreams, from innocent handholding jumps on trampolines to those of the kind I don't talk about with others.

"Hey, I know it's been like forever. But do you guys still want to spend the night? This weekend would be good. My parents are going out of town and putting my older sister in charge."

"Ooh, Carissa is hot," Tony says. DeMarcus slugs him on the arm in response, which makes me laugh.

"You have a girl!" DeMarcus says.

"Yep!"

"Congrats," I tell Tony. "Good for you." He blushes in such a charming way that I can't imagine anyone not being happy for him.

"Saturday night," DeMarcus says. "You both in?"

"Absolutely," Tony says, looking at me.

I nod and ask, "What about Mateo?"

"If he's not too busy hanging out with the jerks that want to kill us, then I suppose he can come too," DeMarcus snaps. Frustration lines his face. He's kept quiet about Mateo since the run-in with Decker. Although he may not have much to say out loud, his facial expressions say a thousand words. I don't challenge it, though. I get where DeMarcus is coming from, but he doesn't see Mateo the way I do.

No one does.

He's the love of *my* life.

"Cool. Thanks," I say, avoiding eye contact. "See you Saturday."

The rest of the week goes pretty much like every other week in my life. School sucks, and I miss having Mr. Samuels as an English teacher. He at least made the class entertaining. The rest of the staff sits on edge. They stick to pre-approved textbook lessons. Even the teachers with cool reputations have lost joy. Everyone tries to avoid additional controversies.

Some of our school's conflicts got picked up by national news sources. Apple News did an article on the school's "Don't Say Gay" rules, and rumors are that LGBTQ+ activists are planning a protest here. I can't wait to meet them! I even subscribed to news updates to make sure I don't miss a thing. The world needs to see what's going on here. What's happening here could happen anywhere.

Krake wins the award for the worst part of the week, to no one's surprise. Every day, he gets grumpier, if that's even possible. He's been doing daily pop quizzes for everyone except the wrestling team. He's even starting to piss off the other athletes. Football and basketball players are starting to turn on him, too. Well, basketball at this school is just a tier above the karate club, so they've been outcasts for years. But football? Wrestling may have the spotlight due to Krake's success, but this town prioritizes football over religion.

So, I take my quiz, and I pass it. As much as I hate to admit it, I've been studying harder for Krake's class, wanting to prove him wrong. And if nothing else, I figure if an asshole like him can learn this stuff, then so can I.

After school, the karate club practices, with doubles coming soon. Decker and Krake are already putting their students through double practices a few times a week, but Mr. Samuels says timing is everything. Too early, and we'll burn out.

The other recent change is Camila. She looks at me in the hallway again. I even got a hello the other day and almost a smile. Camila and Tisha have been hanging out more, and Tisha claims she's going to get Camila back on our side. It's complicated, though. Camila did move out and now lives with Decker. It's not legal, as Camila is a minor. Tisha says Camila's step-monster isn't pursuing anything, though. No crap—pretty sure child abuse is the worse crime here. Camila's bio father picked up a truck-driving job and isn't around. I'll never understand how a parent can simply not care about their child. Camila and I have more in common than either of us realized. It's also strange to despise Decker as much as I do but to respect this decision. He's helping Camila, but what might he turn her into?

One thing's for sure—there are no boring days here at Washington High.

When Saturday arrives, I remove my martial arts gi and equipment from my gym bag and replace it with extra clothes for the night at DeMarcus's place.

Mom drives. I didn't tell her that DeMarcus's parents were out of town. My heart pounds in my chest the entire way over, thinking about the possibilities of a parent-free night.

"There's something I want to talk to you about," Mom tells me.

*Uh-oh.*

"How would you feel if Mister Samuels moved in?"

Oh. Not what I was expecting. "I think that would be awesome."

Mom smiles. There's a beauty and peacefulness to her face that I haven't seen in… well, maybe never. She's in love. I'd like to think I know the feeling.

"Good, honey. I was hoping you'd say that."

"Mom, does this mean, um, I mean… do you think you two will get married?"

Mom smiles even wider. "How would that make you feel?"

I shrug. "I mean, of course, it's a little weird." Her smile vanishes, and I quickly follow up. "It would also be cool, though. He's the best guy I know."

Rosy colors wash through Mom's cheeks, and I think about Camila again. How can any kid grow up without a happy parent? Mom works so hard and had such a crappy relationship with my alcoholic father. She deserves joy, too.

"So, it's possible. We talked about it, and I'll be honest with you. I think he's going to propose. Maybe not super soon. But eventually."

"That would be amazing, Mom."

She parks outside of DeMarcus's house. "So, are you doing okay, kid? You and Mat? You and your friends?"

I remember calling Mom last year and sobbing into the phone when Mateo kicked me out of his house. She came for me instantly.

"I think so."

"Is therapy helping?"

"It is," I say. "As much as I may not want to admit it."

"Good. You deserve happiness, kiddo. You deserve to be loved. You do not deserve to live in fear. Do you understand?"

"Yes, Mom." At least I think I do.

"Good. I love you. Have fun, but not too much fun. You understand that?" She raises her eyebrows. This time, I completely understand what she means.

"Yes, Mom. I love you, too."

I jump out of the car and head to DeMarcus's front door.

My stomach flips around with every step like some part of me knows this could be the best night of my life.

But every time I have thought that, it turned out to be the worst.

# 41

## *Strip Tease*

DEMARCUS SWINGS THE door open and welcomes me with his charming smile. Tony cusses in the background, playing a video game.

A gorgeous girl shoves DeMarcus to the side and sizes me up. "So, you're the famous Aiden."

"Famous?"

"I think anyone who fights the toughest guy in school and then kisses him in front of everyone is famous in my book," she says, her eyes wide, her head moving up and down and she takes a close look at me. "Cute, too."

"This is my older sister, Carissa," DeMarcus tells me. "She graduated college a year ago so she could find her own place to live, you know."

"Ignore my stupid brother," she says. "I'm saving money because the cost of housing has tripled over the last few generations, while our salaries haven't even doubled. Pay attention in school and you'll learn something, dumbass. Anyway, nice to meet you, Aiden."

"Thank you. Nice to meet you, too."

"If you get bored with my brother, come down to the basement. I'm having a few girlfriends over, and I bet they'd love to meet you."

"Really?"

Carissa smiles. "Hmm. You really have no idea how many people admire you, do you?"

Shrugging, I say, "Well, honestly, it feels like everyone hates me most days."

Carissa bites her lip and adjusts the black-framed glasses on her round face. She has thick, beautiful hair, a thin physique, and wears a cute purple top. "Fascinating," she says. "You come say hi to my friends later. It's easy to get distracted by the haters, Aiden." She stares at me for a second longer, as if trying to figure me out, and then turns around and leaves the room.

Tony sits in their living room, still shouting at the screen and ignoring me, except for a quick wave, followed by a middle finger, which must be for the game he's playing. He makes me laugh. His hair keeps growing out, longer and darker. He wants to see how long it can get before the tournament.

DeMarcus puts his arm around me, and my heart rate instantly jumps. "My sister is cray but cool."

"She seems nice."

"She never invites my friends to hang out like that."

I'm not sure how to reply to that, so I don't say anything.

"Wanna play something?" he asks. "We'll kick Tony off."

The doorbell rings, and I jump again. That must be Mateo. Or Carissa's friends. DeMarcus opens the door, and yep—it's Mat. He wears a Dead Poet Society T-shirt, not the movie, but a cool rock band we both love. He smiles weakly at DeMarcus, but his lips stretch from ear-to-ear when he sees me. I can't help but return the same cheesy, happy grin.

"Hey," DeMarcus says. "Come on in." His tone borders on curt. More laconic than curt—that was a vocab word last week in English class, I think, proud of myself.

"*Gracias,*" Mateo says. He looks uncomfortable but loosens up when I jump over and put my arm around him.

"You *whores!*" Tony screams.

"Is he talking to us?" Mateo asks, a humorous expression on his face.

"Nah, some kids he's battling online," DeMarcus says.

"Oh," Mateo laughs. "Well, let's join him and cause some trouble."

The evening goes by smoothly, and it's a lot of fun, too. We play these Jackbox games where you make up lies about trivia questions to fool people. It's hilarious, especially because Tony keeps writing random things about poop for his answers.

We break to cook some frozen pizzas. Carissa's friends show up while we eat. They don't even knock. They just come in and go into the basement without looking our way. College students mixed with adult friends. Young adult, but adult enough, that they want nothing to do with high school students, I suppose.

Hyped up on too much caffeine, DeMarcus suggests a game of Truth or Dare.

"I've got nothing to hide," Tony says.

DeMarcus starts and picks me. "Um, dare," I tell him.

He thinks for a second. "I dare you to take your shirt off and run downstairs to scare the girls."

"Done!" I say. Taking my shirt off, I catch both Mateo and DeMarcus checking me out. It's a nice feeling. I'm not the same kid as last year, and I certainly don't have the same body.

I run into the basement, and the girls scream. They follow it up with lots of giggles, though. When I come back up, it's Mateo's turn.

"Truth or dare?" I ask. If he says truth, I may ask about the letter he wrote me. Tell me one thing in the letter, please, or tell me why I'm still waiting to open it!

"Dare."

Shoot. But okay. What can I do for a good laugh here? "Um, I dare you to do a strip tease for one minute!"

"I don't need to see that," Tony says, but he laughs.

"Me, neither," DeMarcus mumbles, but there's a little humor in his voice. And perhaps curiosity, too.

I choose the dirtiest song I can think of, hit play, and Mateo dances.

It's hot. He has rhythm and coordination—of course, he does. He takes off his Dead Poet T-shirt, revealing that body I can't get enough of.

Mateo starts to unbutton his shorts. He looks up at me, winks, and then says, "Okay, minute's up!" He laughs, buttons his shorts back up, and sits down.

Tony and DeMarcus both laugh, too, But I notice something about DeMarcus. Something I've never seen before.

Maybe it was the way his eyes lingered on Mateo's chest. Maybe it's the way his eyes look now—wide and extra alert, a biological trigger of attraction. Maybe it's the way he looked away—quickly, almost embarrassed, swallowing and clearing his throat.

But it's absolutely clear to me that DeMarcus was just checking out my boyfriend.

# 42

## *Truth or Dare Trouble*

WE PLAY THROUGH several cheesy dares—live-streaming dances on social media, lip-syncing fast songs, swapping clothes and trying to look like one another.

"Truth," Tony says when it's his turn. "Ask me anything."

"Um," Mateo starts, scratching his head. "Okay, how much have you done with Amanda? Are you a virgin?"

"That's two questions," Tony says, laughing. "You only get one."

"Tell us about you and Amanda, then," Mat says.

Tony smiles. The silliness of our evening aside, it's clear he's really into her. I know what that feeling looks like. "Um, well, I felt her boobs." He immediately blushes, like he's violated some kind of secret. "Please don't say anything to her, though. It was the outside of her shirt. It happened kinda by accident."

"It's cool, dude," DeMarcus says. "We won't say anything."

*"Arigato,"* Tony says. "I've got a truth question for Aiden."

I raise my eyebrows, curiously thinking what Tony would want to know about me.

"How do you know you're in love?"

Instantly turning red, I look at Mateo, who blushes, too. I reach for his hand, and he squeezes it.

"Um, I dunno. You just are."

"That's an unacceptable response," Tony says with a curious grin. "Seriously, how do you know?"

"Do you think you are in love with Amanda?" I ask.

"It's your turn, dummy," he tells me. "How do you know?"

"Because his name floats in my brain right before I wake up. Even then, I see his face, and I wake up smiling every time. He makes me happy."

Mateo's face softens, and for a second, I think he's about to wipe back a tear. With the hand that holds mine, he pulls me toward him and kisses me.

"Ew!" Tony says, making a fake gagging noise. "I didn't ask to watch a make-out session. Not again!"

"Again?" I say, pulling away.

"Oh, you think you two were quiet when we spent the night at your house?" He laughs, though, not an ounce of anger in his voice.

"Wait a sec," Mateo says. "Does that mean you watched us?" He doesn't give Tony a chance to respond. Instead, he picks up a pillow from the sofa and slams it across Tony's back. Tony dives into Mateo, and they roll on the carpeted floor, equal parts wrestling and laughing.

Mateo flips Tony and puts him easily in a chokehold. Tony taps. "You're too good. Not fair!"

DeMarcus looks away. He rubs the side of his head. Is that jealousy?

"Hey, losers!" It's Carissa, her head poking out from the basement door, yelling at us. "It sounds like you're gonna break the floor and crash on us!"

"You sound like Mom," DeMarcus tells her.

She flips him off, starts to shut the door, then catches my eye. "Don't forget to come say hi later, Aiden. With your shirt on this time. And *only* Aiden. The rest of you aren't nearly as cool." She shuts the door.

Tony and Mateo settle down and rejoin us. Tony struggles to catch his breath, while Mateo looks like he didn't even move a muscle.

"I've got a question for Mat," DeMarcus says. "Truth?"

Mateo looks at him curiously, hesitates, but nods.

"If the tournament came down to you and Aiden again, what would you do?"

Dammit, DeMarcus. It's a crappy question. Instantly, an image of Mateo from the tournament last year comes to him—not the shock from taking him down. The look that came next—pure persistence. Anything to win. A relentless determination to win. Mateo's more than an athlete—he's a fierce competitor. Proud. Persistent.

Mateo squeezes my hand gently. "We haven't talked about it. We'll talk about it first and figure that out."

"Like last year, when you both had a plan to pretend to fight? And then pretend turned out to be real?"

"Dude, stop," I say. "That's between us."

"Aren't we a team?" he challenges. "Don't we all deserve to know? We should talk about what would happen if we face each other."

"We give it our best," I answer. "Each of us gives it our best. Mateo wouldn't want to win any other way, and I wouldn't want to win by someone letting me. Right, Mat?"

Silent but with eyes that send a thousand messages, he glares at DeMarcus. Laser-focused, he lets go of my hand.

"I've got a question for you," Mateo tells DeMarcus.

"You never answered mine."

Mateo huffs. "Aiden's right. We'll fight. The best competitor wins."

I wish Mateo were still holding my hand. Just hold my hand and stop talking about fighting.

"That's what I thought," DeMarcus mumbles, almost inaudibly. Then louder, he says, "What's your question?"

"Do you like Aiden more than a friend?" Mateo asks, no hesitation. A brief shock flashes on DeMarcus's face.

He looks at me, the white in his eyes extra wide, the pulse in my throat exploding.

He opens his mouth. "If you want the truth, okay, I'll tell you."

# 43

## A Secret Crush

"I HAVE A crush that I've never told anyone about," DeMarcus says. He sits on the carpeted floor of his living room, his head now on a coffee table. After a long sigh, he continues. "Just promise it stays here, okay? Like, I wanna be the one to say this. I don't want a rumor going around."

My quickening pulse slows. His crush isn't me? The moments we've spent together in Krake's classroom always struck me as more than friendly, and he was all flirty at the grilled cheese place.

Has my perception of DeMarcus been wrong? Has it all been in my head? Well, okay. Good. I can focus on Mateo, my training, and our friendships. That would be better than DeMarcus telling my boyfriend that he has a crush on me.

"Of course," Tony says to DeMarcus. "So, who is it?"

"It's, um, it's…." DeMarcus lifts his head from the table and looks at me. The deep expression in his eyes captivates me. What's he thinking? "It's hard to say, sorry," he mumbles, looking away. "I haven't told my parents I'm bi. Just my sister and you guys."

"You can tell us anything," I say, smiling gently.

"Okay, boy or girl?" Tony asks.

DeMarcus's smile deepens, and he laughs.

"It's a—"

Before he can finish, Carissa pops upstairs, the basement door swinging open. "What did I walk into?" she asks, as the room falls to complete silence.

"Nothing," DeMarcus says. "What do you want?"

"We heard a noise," Carissa says. "From outside. We figure the big, strong karate boys can go check it out." She looks at the group of us, cocks her head to the side, and frowns. When none of us move, she says, "How about *now?* I'm serious. Someone's outside."

"Crap," Tony mutters while jumping up. "We got this. Let's go, ya'll." Perhaps caffeine fuels Tony's excitement, but fear pumps into my bloodstream. DeMarcus, Mateo, and I exchange a worried look. Who is after us now?

We open the front door slowly. DeMarcus sticks his neck out and shouts, "Hello? Anyone there?" We listen quietly. Carissa stands in front of the basement door, two of her friends' heads twisted around the door, eyes wide, taking in everything.

No one responds to DeMarcus. We take a careful step outside. It's pitch-black except for a sliver of the moon. The air cools, and for the first time in a long time, we see our breath. I put my hands in a fighting position. Tony does the same. DeMarcus and Mateo keep their hands by their sides, but they walk very gracefully, trying not to make any noise.

From behind, a scream pierces our ears. I spin, my guard up.

An object comes flying at my face from someone in the shadows, a few feet in front of me.

I yell, my heart rate spiking, every fear I've had over the past year rising quickly to the surface. We're getting attacked at one of our homes. This has gone too far.

And then—*splat!*

It's cool, creamy, and—is that laughter?

Crazy giggles rise around us. Mateo looks at me and cracks up, too. He takes a finger, runs it down my face, and then licks what must be whipped cream.

I took a pie in the face. Or, rather, a pie-shaped container full of whipped cream.

From behind the corner of DeMarcus's house, multiple shapes emerge, and the front porch light illuminates the mystery figures.

"Wow. Just wow," I say with a slight chuckle. "What are you all doing here?"

Tisha, Amanda, Camila, and Michelle walk toward us.

"Sorry if we scared you," Tisha says, grinning. "You all had a night without inviting us, you gender-discriminating jerks, so we thought we'd have our own night."

Camila pats me on the back. "You deserve that and more, just so you know. But I'd rather throw pies than punches." She holds out her fist for me to tap it. I can't believe it, and I look at Tisha for confirmation that I'm not being duped. She nods and smiles at me. What kind of miracles has Tisha been pulling off?

I fist-bump Camila. Amanda runs over to Tony and kisses him. Michelle's the only one who looks uncomfortable, and Tisha catches that, too.

"Okay," Tisha starts. "Let me give you the short of the long of it. We decided to have a truce. Not a truce in the ring or anything, but for tonight we all decided to put our past in the past. No punches, only pies. Deal?"

"We've been playing Truth or Dare," Tony says, coming up for breath after lip-locking with Amanda during Tisha's little speech.

"Can we join?" Tisha asks.

"Yeah," Mateo says. "DeMarcus was about to reveal a big secret to all of us. You're just in time."

DeMarcus gives Mateo a dirty look, but he smiles at the girls and says, "Yeah, okay. Come on in. Why not?"

"But instead of Truth or Dare, how about I Never?" Michelle asks.

"How about Spin the Bottle?" Tony suggests, kissing Amanda again.

She smacks him. "Is there someone else here you wanna kiss?"

"Ignore the love birds," Camila says. "All we heard about on the way here is how wonderful Tony is. Gag!" Camila sticks her finger down her throat, and we laugh.

"Spin the Bottle meets I Never!" Tisha says. "Whoever does the 'I never' spins the bottle. The person it lands on can choose whether to say an I Never or take a kiss. How about that?"

"I'm in," Michelle says.

DeMarcus holds the door open, and we go back inside. Carissa and her friends gather around the living room and peer out the windows.

"It's all good," DeMarcus shouts.

Carissa's eyes narrow, inspecting each of the girls as they come inside. She whispers something to DeMarcus, and he nods.

"Too many kids for us," Carissa says, revealing a beautiful smile as she nudges her brother gently in the ribs. "The adults will be downstairs."

"Adults? I don't see any adults," DeMarcus jokes. Carissa flips him off, and her friends follow her back into the basement. They're a bit strange if you ask me, but then again, I can't imagine what most people think about multiple groups of diverse feuding teenage martial artists.

"All right, I'll start," Camila says, sitting on the living room floor and grabbing the empty Mountain Dew bottle Tony previously threw. "Everyone got a drink?"

"I don't have any alcohol, sorry," DeMarcus says.

"No, that's cool. Anything works," Camila tells him. He grabs a couple of two liters out of the kitchen and some red party cups. We've got Sprite and Orange Crush, and I choose the latter.

"I've never been cheated on," Camila says. "Sorry, last time I'll bring it up tonight, I promise," she says, specifically to Tisha. Then to all of us, "If you've been cheated on, you drink."

Camila takes a sip, of course, avoiding my glances. I'm glad she's hanging out with us again, and maybe we need some fun to move beyond the past. What would Decker think of us all hanging out?

Michelle also takes a drink.

"Ooh, now you have to tell us," Tisha says. Michelle smiles sweetly, something I'm not used to seeing. She's so beautiful—long, dark hair, a strong, toned physique. Today she wears a Heidi 'N Closet T-shirt, a star from *RuPaul's Drag Race*.

"I don't think that's how this game really works," Michelle replies, winking.

"How about if you don't want to explain your I Never then you have to spin the bottle?" Camila asks. Camila also looks gorgeous. I love the freckles on her face, although they're fading. They come out mostly in the hot months, replaced by a smooth, brown tone the rest of the year.

"Deal," Michelle says. She takes the empty Mountain Dew bottle and spins it. We sit in a circle, watching it rotate. Just a few minutes ago, I worried I'd find myself in the middle of another brawl. And now we're playing Spin the Bottle. I wouldn't trade these strange, pie over punches nights for anything.

The bottle lands right on Tisha. She laughs, doesn't give the situation a second thought, and leans in to kiss Michelle. Michelle gives her a quick peck. We complain and laugh in equal parts.

"Okay, I'll go next," Tisha says. "I never… had a crush on someone who is the same gender as me."

Tisha immediately drinks.

"What?" I ask. "You never told me!"

Tisha shrugs and gestures at the rest of us to drink before offering any explanation. Even Tony drinks. My eyes bulge a bit at him, too. Then Amanda sips. What?!?

"I can explain this one," Tisha says. "I hate to lose my spin, but maybe you cisgender males need some mansplaining?" We laugh at her delightful sarcasm. "Here's a shocker. Most people are a little fluid."

"What's the difference between bi and fluid?" DeMarcus asks.

Tisha shrugs. "I dunno. I don't know if I wanna strictly define it, either. Just be who you are."

"I'd say fluid means you can find everyone hot," Tony says, kissing Amanda before she says anything.

"Whose turn is it?" Camila asks.

"I'll go," DeMarcus says. He spins the bottle, and we watch it make endless circles on the floor. The game has become a free-for-all, and my nerves spike again.

When the bottle stops, my stomach drops. It doesn't land on me.

It lands on Mateo.

# 44

## *Kisses I'll Never Forget*

MATEO'S FACE REDDENS, his eyes locked on mine. I don't know what to say, so I shrug. Maybe people in relationships shouldn't play this game.

"It's only a kiss," Michelle says, reading my body language. Her tone lacks judgment, but I'm not sure I trust her fully.

DeMarcus also shrugs but leans in, while Mateo rolls his eyes. Still, Mat mirrors DeMarcus's movement.

Stomach acid sprays inside me, burning through my throat. As their lips approach one another, my body shakes. I'm uncomfortable, nervous, and conflicted with an ounce of "Is this hot?"

DeMarcus opens his mouth first, his lips parting, and Mateo closes his eyes. DeMarcus kisses Mat's lips gently. Mateo doesn't return anything, remaining completely still. Right as DeMarcus almost pulls away, Mateo's lips move. He kisses DeMarcus back and both break apart.

"How about another I Never?" Tisha asks, breaking the awkwardness in the room. "Aiden, you go."

"Yeah, okay. Um, let me think," I say. "I never...." Watched my boyfriend kiss another boy? No, that's not what I want to say. My emotions are all over the place. One second, I want to lash out at Mat or DeMarcus. Then I want to insult Michelle. Why does she get to be with us after all the stuff she's said and done? Is she ever going to apologize or talk about that? She's hurt more than our feelings, but no, I don't want to start that fight tonight, either. "I never… I've never cried myself to sleep at night because… like, um, I thought my entire existence was wrong. Like never meant to be."

I lower my head and toss back a big drink.

I look up. Everyone else drinks, too.

"Way to bring the mood down, Aiden," Camila says, but she smiles warmly.

"You guys, this is why I always wanted us to stick together," Tisha says. "It's not about sexuality or gender, not *only* those things, anyway. We all know what it feels like to not matter. Aren't you all tired of that feeling?" She stretches out her legs. "I want us to remember that. That we have more in common than not. That we should be on the same team."

"Cheers to that, Tisha," Amanda says, raising her red party cup. "Now someone else spin the bottle and get this party going again."

"You brought the mood down, Aiden. You spin it," Camila insists.

I take a deep breath, and I spin the bottle. Mateo kissed DeMarcus, so maybe it's only fair that I get to kiss someone else. No, I push that thought away. Those thoughts get me into trouble.

The bottle lands on Tisha.

"This will be like kissing my brother. No offense."

"None taken!" I reach for her, pull her close, open my mouth, and lick her face from her lips to her nose and even her forehead.

She pushes me back. "Gross!"

We alternate between more I Never statements—much less serious—and spinning the bottle. In between, we listen to music and tell stories, laughing and enjoying every second now that the previous awkwardness has passed.

Michelle spins the bottle and this time it lands on DeMarcus.

He smiles at her.

Like really smiles at her. What's that about?

Michelle parts her lips, brushes the hair out of her eyes, turns her head to the side slightly, and kisses DeMarcus with a little more passion than the previous kisses here.

"All right, all right, maybe you two need to get a room!" Camila says, laughing.

DeMarcus pulls away, and he looks embarrassed and excited. My emotions and hormones wage war with my logic. I shouldn't care, but curiosity compels me. DeMarcus can like whoever he wants. I have a boyfriend. Who he kisses is none of my business. Why do people play these stupid games?

"When do you guys have to leave?" Tony asks.

"Trying to get rid of us?" Camila replies.

"No," Tony says with a grin that I understand. He looks coyly at Amanda, and I can tell he may want his own private make-out time with his girl.

"I don't wanna think about that," Camila says, smacking Tony with a pillow.

"We're crashing at Tisha's place," Amanda says.

"Yeah, and my parents are sound sleepers. We can sneak back in any time and we'll be fine," Tisha tells us.

Tony hops up, hand-in-hand with Amanda, and exaggeratedly tip-toes out of the living room. We laugh at them, but no judgment. Good for them.

I whisper in Mat's ear. "They've got a good idea. Wanna find some privacy?"

His enthusiastic kiss on my lips tells me everything I need to know.

I get up and pull Mateo with me.

"Not in my bedroom," DeMarcus says, rolling his eyes. "Or my parents' bedroom! Gross."

"Follow me," I say, pulling Mateo away. We find a guest bedroom, and Mateo pushes me on the bed and kisses me hard. His tongue plays with mine. He takes off my shirt, and I remove his. We're in familiar territory, and it becomes a bit of a dance. Kissing on the lips, kissing on the neck, even kissing on the chest. His body against mine—it's fireworks every time.

It doesn't go any further than that. As much as I want to see and do more, I'm scared. I have no idea what Mateo wants. Although I know I should talk to him about this, it's much easier said than done. Plus, I don't know what I'm truly comfortable doing. I want to do everything! But I also want to be safe.

We lay there, holding each other for a long time, chest to chest, arms wrapped around each other.

Eventually, we get up, remembering there's still a party going on, at least I think there is. After using the bathroom, sounds from DeMarcus's bedroom catch my attention.

I listen closer. Smacking lips, bodies moving, heavy breathing—woah! I recognize those sounds, but who is with DeMarcus?

I shouldn't be here listening, but the strong drug of curiosity engrosses me. Lingering a moment longer, I jump when footsteps approach the bedroom door. I hop in the bathroom but leave it open a crack so I can still see.

DeMarcus's bedroom door opens and closes.

Standing outside of his bedroom, Michelle adjusts her shirt. She smiles, and I know that look—it's joy and desire.

Michelle and DeMarcus. Really? Wow. I don't know what to think about that.

# 45

*Eye of the
Lusty Tiger*

AT KARATE PRACTICE, Mr. Samuels asks his highest-ranking students to run *Empi Sho* a billion times, or at least it feels like that. I've fallen into a trippy Russian doll loop, memories of last year coming back.

We run the *kata*, and Mr. Samuels asks, "What are the secrets? What do you see beyond the basics?"

Sweat.

It runs down my face. Secrets stay hidden. The study hall dojo captures all the school's heat like the furnace radiates fire right below us. Tisha takes off the top of her gi. She wears an athletic shirt underneath it. DeMarcus does the same, but he exposes his bare chest.

A defined, muscular, hot chest.

My eyes can't help but look at DeMarcus. Three hours of sweat-soaked training have every muscle and vein bulging in his body.

"What do you see, Aiden?"

*Muscles. Skin. DeMarcus kissing Michelle.* Are the two of them dating now? Or what's going on? And why do I care? When I shake the thoughts away, the peacock form flashes in my fatigued brain. *Kujaku.* That's an important form, too. Something tells me its secrets may be more helpful than I realize, if only I could discover what they were.

Clearing my throat, I make my best guess. "The elbow smash and drop are kinda weird in *Empi.* Could that be something else?" There's a move where one's elbow drives up into the opponent's spine and then drops right on the top of their skull. It's a complicated combo, very specific, but each martial arts form gets harder as we advance.

"What else do you see there?" *Sensei* asks. He rarely provides direct answers when discussing karate's secrets.

"Is it in the knife-hand blocks?" Tony asks.

"No, it's gotta be the jumps," Tisha says. "This *kata* is all about jumps and leaps. *Nihanchi Sho* kept us in a straight line against a wall. *Anaku* taught small hip thrusts. *Wansu* taught powerful thrusts. The secret must be in the jumps!"

"Run the *kata* again," Mr. Samuels says. The rest of the club—I almost snort at my thought, as we are smaller than ever—left after the first hour. We have a handful of white and yellow belts, but none of them have any interest in the tournament.

We bow and run the form for the trillionth time. What do I see? *Empi Sho* is *Wansu's* older sibling, so to speak. Mr. Samuels told us the same martial arts masters created both forms. They share similarities in their basic movements—low blocks, reverse punches, and even a movement that parallels the secret I found in *Wansu*. Instead of the ti-ger claw—the throat and crotch grab—and throw, *Empi Sho* features a mountain knife attack followed by a three-hundred-sixty-degree jump. In *Wansu*, I discovered the tiger claw attack could also be a defensive tactic to tie up someone's arms. If one's opponent is tied up, they can't strike. That's how I tied up Mateo at the tournament last year and found a throw hidden in the form, too. It shocked me as much as Mateo to find the secrets and use them.

*Empi Sho* must have a stronger secret. *Wansu's* secret couldn't keep Mateo down. But this form—it's so much more powerful. Something in these secrets has what it takes to knock someone down and keep them there, long enough for a victory.

I perform the mountain knife strike. Stepping forward with my right leg in a front stance, my left hand strikes the throat of my imaginary opponent while my right hand, directly underneath the left, strikes the opponent's gut. Left palm down, right palm up, both knife hands—they make a circle if they come together. After the strike, we jump and spin in the air and land with an augmented knife block. These aren't techniques we learned in *Wansu*. There's something much more advanced here, but I can't figure it out.

"What do you see, Amanda?" Mr. Samuels asks.

"I see my bed at the end of this long practice."

"Why can't you tell us the secrets?" Tony asks.

"It's one thing to be shown something and to mimic that. That's what we do as basic students. We repeat what our teachers tell us. The way to mastery is to discover things for oneself. Now, line up."

We bow out, and I head to the bathroom. Tony and Amanda sit on a staircase outside of the study hall. They launch right into an adorable conversation about their day.

In the bathroom, it's just me and DeMarcus. I haven't yet asked about Michelle, but today seems like a good day. I'm too tired to hide my curiosity, and maybe DeMarcus is too tired to say anything but the truth.

He washes his face in the sink, still shirtless, almost like he wants attention. He bends over to splash water on his face, and I can't help but stare at the shape of his butt in the karate pants. His butt looks like rounded eggshells, two perfect little ovals that pop in that white gi.

DeMarcus looks up, catches me checking him out, and grins in the mirror. "Hey."

I think fast... or try to. So, I ask the question that's been on my mind all week. "Hey, um, I had something I wanted to ask you."

"Yeah?" DeMarcus raises his eyebrows. With his right hand, he scratches his toned stomach. *Look up, Aiden, look in his eyes, not his abs!*

"At your house last weekend, um, you and Michelle?" I smile, my face feeling hot already. You're his friend. Friends ask about these things. *So why do I feel so weird talking about it right now?*

"What about me and Michelle?"

"I saw the two of you, um, you know?" I shrug and smile at him, hoping he'll fill in the blanks with his secrets.

"We made out," he says.

"Do you like her?"

He stares at me but doesn't say anything.

"Hey, we're friends," I say gently. "You never got to reveal your truth about your crush. Is it Michelle?" My heart beats crazy fast.

"The truth?" He takes a step closer to me, precariously close. My limbs feel like Jell-O, and my stomach twirls.

I gulp. "Just, um, curious."

DeMarcus looks around. "The truth is that I have more than one crush. But, yeah, I do like Michelle. She's cool. But she's not the only one I like, and I think that's okay. You ever have more than one crush at the same time?"

Butterflies wage war in my gut. Yeah, I might be able to relate.

DeMarcus puts the thumb of his left hand in the waistband of his karate pants. They lower a bit. My eyes catch his happy trail, the few hairs below his belly button. Warmth floods me.

"Can I ask you a question?" DeMarcus continues. "Would it be better to go after a crush who is on a different team that we have to face, or would it be better to go after a crush who is on the same team but has a boyfriend?"

Well, that's certainly direct.

I frown, shrugging slightly. "I don't wanna be that guy. You know, the guy who cheats. The bad guy. I've been the bad guy before. I don't ever want to be the bad guy again."

"Oh, man. Don't you see? I completely agree, and it's stuff like that that makes me want you even more."

We're exhausted from training, and DeMarcus's half-naked body certainly does not calm my hormones.

He moves toward me and puts his arms around me. At first, I gasp, surprised by his directness. But he smiles, and his body's so close to mine that I feel the heat coming off his bare chest.

His mouth, now only inches from mine, opens.

"Can I?" he asks. Consent. Consent is good. But I have a boyfriend. A boyfriend who also kissed DeMarcus.

*Don't say yes. Don't say yes. Don't say yes.*

No words come out. I can't talk. My body betrays logic, and my head nods slightly.

His lips press against mine.

He kisses me with such passion, and the warmth inside me turns into a full fire. I love it. No, I hate it. I'm not this person. But it feels amazing. I feel the heat rising off his body and my arms wrap around his shirtless back.

The door to the bathroom opens. We pull away quickly.

But not quickly enough.

Mateo enters the bathroom, an excited smile on his face, as if he came here in a hurry to tell me something.

He sees DeMarcus holding me.

How am I going to explain this? *Dammit, Aiden, kissing and hormones always get you in trouble!*

I pull away quickly, but not quickly enough. Mateo's previous excitement morphs into a heavy sadness. He wears it deeply in his eyes before he speaks.

"I just, um, actually had some extra time today and wanted to join you all. Guess you've gotten used to me not being here," he says. He looks hard at me, a mix of anger and profound sorrow in his eyes. Then he glares at DeMarcus.

My heart pounds against my chest. Mateo grips the bathroom door handle so hard that the white in his knuckles bursts from the skin.

"Mateo, it's not... Mat, please let me explain."

He responds by turning around, stepping out, and slamming the door.

## 46

### *Everything Changes*

MATEO DOESN'T RETURN my texts or calls. When I go directly to his house, no one answers the door. He's ghosting me, and I don't know what to do.

It's been three days since he walked in to the room and saw De-Marcus kissing me.

*You kissed him back!* It's not all DeMarcus's fault. Not by a long shot, and you know it.

*Shut up!*

I haven't been able to enjoy anything but angry music. No show can hook me on TV. I space out playing video games. I can't even get into karate.

Sitting in my room, I find a favorite album on my phone and play it on repeat.

*I wanna be underground. Cuz at least there I'll be safe and sound. And all my walls keep crumbling down. So just let it go and leave me alone.*

While Mateo ignores me, the lyrics soothe me. I also ignore De-Marcus. He's texted every day—sweet, curious texts.

*I'm not sorry I kissed you. But I am sorry for the problems it caused. Are you okay?*

*I'm here if you want to talk.*

*I never meant to screw up what you and Mat have. I just like you.*

*I'm sorry.*

And when I didn't respond to any of the above, he texted, *Are we still friends? I'm sorry, Aiden.*

I don't know how to answer any of his messages because I don't know how I feel. I like DeMarcus—he's hot, fun, stands up for himself, isn't afraid of what others think, and really seems to like me, but he also has a crush on Michelle!

And I'm in love with Mateo. At least I think I am. Twenty-four-seven obsessions with checking messages, social media updates, sleeping with the ringer to max volume in case he calls. What about the fact that I see Mateo's smile when I close my eyes? That I hear his obnoxious laugh whenever I want to cheer up?

I spend the weekend alone. For the first time in a long time—and I have not missed this—I cry myself to sleep, all the while holding the unopened letter from Mat sent me last summer in my hands.

This continues for another week. The letter remains unopened. It's like another layer of self-torture, but maybe it's what I deserve.

Do I even have a boyfriend anymore? How many days of ghosting does it take to realize one terribly hard truth—I've been dumped.

*Dumped!* Right?

I can't focus on class. I don't doodle fight scenes. I even skip a week's karate practices, not caring about secrets or tournaments.

One evening—how many nights later, I don't know, everything has blurred together—Mr. Samuels knocks on my bedroom door.

"Can I come in?" he asks.

"Kay."

After he opens it, he stands in the door frame for a moment, looking around my room. It's messy—laundry on the floor, unopened textbooks, and incomplete homework scattered about, too.

"Aiden, I know you know your mom is here for you. She tries to talk to you every day and night."

*I know. I hear her but I don't have the energy to reply.*

I realize I'm not even saying these words out loud.

"I also want you to know that I'm here for you. Not just for karate, and I know you needed some time off practice while you're hurting. But I am here for you, for anything. Do you understand that?" Mr. Samuels says. I muster some energy to nod at him. "You know, Aiden, let me tell you a secret. Not a karate secret. A different kind of secret."

He sits on the corner of my bed and rests his arm on my knee.

"The first secret I want to tell you is this. No amount of words or talking will heal the pain you feel. Still, we want you to talk. It's a way of processing the pain. I'd like you to try and give your mother more than one-syllable responses when she talks to you. She loves and cares for you so much, Aiden."

He takes a deep breath and adjusts his seat on my bed.

"The second secret is this, but perhaps it's not so much of a secret." He clears his throat. "I love you, Aiden. I love you like you are my own son. I want you to let me be here for you when you need it. All right?"

A warmth consumes me. It doesn't erase the pain, but it's nice to feel something else.

"All right?" he asks again when I don't respond.

I manage to smile. "Yes, sir."

"Still one-syllable words, but at least that was more than one. I'll take it. For now." He takes a deep breath. "Now, I have to ask because you took some time off practice, which I understand. Do you still want to do the tournament? There's no reason to fight. You can walk away. That's a perfectly reasonable response, given everything you've experienced."

I roll and sit up next to him, still on the edge of my bed.

"No, *Sensei*. Let me fight."

"But why?"

"Because I'm trying to teach myself that nothing will ever hold me back. That I will always get up after losing." He smiles approvingly, and I put my arm around his shoulders. "Everything does hurt right now. But if there's anything I learned from last year, it's that the hurt won't last forever. I'll get back up. It's just taking some time."

"I will always be by your side," Mr. Samuels says. "Strong people know it takes time to process pain. You take the time you need."

I choke back a flood of emotions. "If words or talking won't heal pain, can anything?"

"The cheesy answer is time," he tells me. "But that's not the exact answer. Not really. What will heal you is having other experiences. Think of it this way." He looks around the room, sees an empty water glass on my desk, and points at it. "Look at the glass. Think of that as your life right now. The pain you feel takes up most if not all the room you have in your glass. As time passes, you will have other experiences. Your glass gets bigger. It has too—how do you think old people like me hold on to a lifetime of experiences like you've been through?" He nudges me gently, and I smile.

"You're not old."

"*Arigato.*" He laughs a little and continues. "Does that make sense? I lost my mother a few years ago. That was the hardest experience of my life. I didn't think I'd ever feel good again. Any little memory made me cry."

"You cried?"

"Oh, Aiden. Crying, grief—that's a sign of our love. It's terrible that society has made some people think such things are signs of weakness. In reality, they are signs of strength. Weak people don't cry, and that pain eats them inside, turning them into—"

Is he thinking about Krake? Or Decker? Something made them the way they are. Perhaps it was pain or an inability to process pain.

"Anyway," Mr. Samuels continues, "when my mother died, it consumed me. It was the only thing in my glass. It took over my life at that time. But as time passed, and as I allowed myself to grieve, my glass collected new experiences. In time, my glass got bigger. The pain from losing my mother is still very much with me. The difference, though, is that I allowed myself to collect other experiences. It allowed me to grow in a way that I could manage the pain. Does that make sense?"

"I think so."

"Good. You think about that. And Aiden?"

"Yeah?"

"If you want to win this tournament, you have to get your butt back in practice."

"Yes, sir. Tomorrow. I'll be there."

"Good." He pats me on the back.

"*Sensei*? Do you think I can win? Should I even win? This whole thing seems to be for Mateo to get scholarship money. If anyone else wins, he loses everything."

"Let's be perfectly clear. This scholarship money could change anyone's life. I love how much you care for others, but this could change your life. Have you thought about that?"

"Not really."

"Well, you should. You're a smart kid. What do you want to do after high school? Where do you want to go? You should start dreaming about that because the world is full of possibilities."

"You really think I could beat Mateo if I had to? Or Michelle?"

Mr. Samuels smiles. "Absolutely! If you figure out the secrets." He smiles in the charming, mischievous way that I've grown to love. "Look how close you came last year. You're much better now, much stronger. And your karate is much more advanced. Believe in yourself, Aiden, because I do."

He stands and walks toward my bedroom door. I feel better for the first time in days.

"Mister Samuels?" I ask before he leaves my room.

"Yes, Aiden?"

"I love you, too."

# 47

## *Cheaters and Chants*

"POP QUIZ," COACH Krake says in his ridiculous health class.

What have I learned about health this year? That we need teachers who support the mental health of their students as well as the physical. That we need a school that understands sexual and gender identity are important and worthy of proper education. Not that they'd ever ask my opinion, but here's my biggest problem with our school's "logical" thinking. If not talking about sexuality was a good thing, then the generations before us wouldn't have been so homophobic and, in some cases, just plain hateful or even violent.

Not teaching about things is not an education. But what do I know?

Nothing, at least for this quiz and the last seven. Coach Krake has been giving us a pop quiz every day for seven school days in a row, but guess who doesn't have to take them? The wrestlers, of course. "They're busy training with certified, state-recognized programs," he says. "If you want to waste your day dancing in the study hall room, that's your choice." He smirks, and I can't wait to see Mr. Samuels knock the snot out of his face. If there's ever been a human being who deserves an ass-kicking, it's Krake.

I'm barely passing his class, and another bad grade may bring my average down to an F. I've never failed a class before, but I've never had a teacher like Krake before, either.

"This is bull," DeMarcus snaps behind me. We haven't talked since the kiss in the bathroom, and we avoid eye contact at karate practice.

"Detention, Mister Freeman," Krake tells DeMarcus. "How many is that now? You're going for a class record."

"Have you ever treated students like this before?" DeMarcus says, undeterred. "You've never had anyone quit your precious state-winning team until us, have you? I may be half your age, but you are ignorant. But you want a real shocker? Every person in this class, even your precious wrestlers, knows you're an asshole."

Krake turns red as blood. "Out!" His nostrils flare, and I want to high-five DeMarcus and march right out with him. At the same time, I'm mad at him. He never should have kissed me. I never should have kissed him back, either. I lost a boyfriend and a good friend all at the same time.

It doesn't have to be this way. What would Mr. Samuels do? What would Mom do?

DeMarcus grabs his bookbag and hustles out of the room. At the door, he turns and says, "You know, Coach. It must make you feel so big, bad, and powerful to rule over the lives of teenagers for a couple hours a day. I can't wait to see you get what you deserve when Mister Samuels beats you at the tournament."

Krake lunges at him and grabs DeMarcus's shirt with his left hand. Veins pulse in his neck, and if he didn't have twenty-some witnesses, Krake may have slugged DeMarcus right there. Instead, he lets go, takes a step back, and smiles.

"Ahh, the tournament. Class, anyone who attends our Mixed Martial Arts tournament will be exempt from quizzes for the week. I want you all to attend. Bring your family. Your friends. Your neighbors. We're going to make this the biggest event possible, and you won't want to miss it." He crosses his arms and glares at DeMarcus. "And let me tell you this about that loser of an English teacher. You're gonna be terribly disappointed when you see how weak he truly is. Now, get out."

DeMarcus glances at me before he leaves the room. It's the first time we've held eye contact since the kiss. I'm proud of him, but I don't know what to say or do right now. He frowns at me and leaves.

"Anyone else got something to say?" Krake says. Even if I did, his arms shake and his veins pulse, and I don't want to walk into that hornets' nest. I keep my head down and my mouth shut.

But noise erupts elsewhere. People yell from outside the classroom, and the class jumps out of their seats to look out the windows. Our classroom faces the town's Main Street. We're on the second floor, and the main entrance is about four rooms to the right.

"Settle down!" Krake yells, but there's power in numbers as intense curiosity beats the threat of authority.

It's about twenty adults, holding signs, marching. I can't read any of the signs, but their words coalesce into a chant.

"Who cares what your school says!" It's mostly women outside, with a few men mixed in. I don't recognize anyone.

"It is okay be you!" The words are louder now, and the group marches around the main entrance.

"If you are bigoted or anti-gay, it's time for YOU to go away!"

The chant repeats from the top. My stomach performs somersaults. I look around the class for a friend—DeMarcus would love this. Krake claps his hands at the front of the classroom, trying to capture our attention.

"Ignore those snowflakes and sit down!" Krake yells. He walks right up to me, and, directly in front of the entire class, he asks, "I suppose this was your doing? You set this up? You are always looking for attention, always causing distractions. I'm so sick of it. Get out of my classroom. Join that fa—"

Krake catches himself. *What* was he going to say? As if I should even be surprised.

He clears his throat. "Go join that boyfriend of yours and get out of my classroom."

I stand without speaking, thrilled to leave. I don't know if I've ever hated a human being more than I hate Coach Krake. The intensity of my hatred scares me.

Oh, Mr. Samuels. *Please* kick the ignorant crap out of this turd at the tournament.

"What are you smiling about?" Krake asks.

I look around the room. "Can't you feel it?" I ask, speaking more to my classmates than to Krake. "Hate. Bigotry. That's, like, so 2020." I stare at a room full of students, who physically lean forward, hanging on my every word, as the chants continue outside.

"I told you to get out, Miss Rothe," Krake shouts.

*"Miss?* You hear him?" I ask the class. "You've heard every insult, every unfair policy now for months. And what have you all done? Think about that the next time you wonder who is strong and who is weak. Your silence is weak. Your *compliance* is weak!" I shake my head, thinking of something I've heard said before. "If you don't stand for something, you'll fall for anything. And right now, you're falling for this guy's BS!"

I do something I've been wanting to do for a long time.

I give Krake the middle finger and march out of his classroom.

# 48

*Hidden Kisses*

I RACE TO the counselor's office. The administrative staff runs around the school like chickens with their heads cut off, trying to figure out what to do about the protests outside. Who are these wonderful people, and how do I make friends with them?

DeMarcus stands outside the counselor's office, also looking out the window at the protests. Casually, I walk over to him and look out again.

"No surprise, but guess who showed up right after the protestors started chanting?" DeMarcus asks. It's the first time we've spoken in person since our kiss.

"Yeah, I'm all too familiar with his squad car." Decker stands outside the school, shouting at the adult protestors. To my absolute joy, the adults don't care about the police captain. Decker even yells into a megaphone, but the protestors simply increase the volume of their words.

"Do you know why they're here?" DeMarcus asks. "I mean, obviously, I get this school is stupid, but how did they hear about it?"

Chaos erupts in the hallways as some students leave their classrooms before the end of the period. I'm not surprised by the first face I see running down the hallway.

"Yes! Outside, everyone, outside!" Tisha yells, racing toward the main entrance. She doesn't see DeMarcus and me in the counselor's office. DeMarcus and I both laugh, and it feels good to relax around him.

"She's the baddest of us all," he says, smiling.

"I completely agree. I love Tisha."

"Me, too. We're lucky to have a friend like her. Maybe she even organized this?"

I shrug, remembering the viral story we saw on socials about our school not that long ago.

"Hey, Aiden," DeMarcus says, grabbing my arm gently. "I wanted to tell you something, but, you know, it's um, hard."

His soft, warm face contrasts wildly with the current raucous moment. "Yeah?"

"I really am sorry. I didn't mean to create drama or anything. I certainly didn't mean for you and Mateo to break up."

I wipe at an itch on my nose.

"I mean, oh, I dunno," he says. "I mean—why is it so hard to say what I mean? You do something to me, Aiden. I feel like I can stand up to Krake and anyone else, but around you? I lose my words. If you and Mateo breaking up might lead to my chance at happiness, my chance to have what you guys had, then sorry, not sorry at all." He smiles gently, bracing himself for my response.

"What about Michelle?"

"She's not the one I'm telling all this to." He reaches for my arm again. One of the counselors runs out of her office without even looking at us. She speaks quickly on her phone and storms off. I glance outside the window. Tisha, Amanda, and Tony join the protestors, along with a small group of other students. Decker continues to shout, and I catch one thing that bothers me—Camila and Michelle walk outside, but they stand by Decker.

"We should be out there," I tell DeMarcus.

"We will be. I just wanted to finish what I wanted to tell you."

"What about Mateo?"

He sighs heavily. "What about him? He lied to you last year. You forgave him, and ironically, it's one of the things I adore about you. You get stronger and stronger, but your heart… I dunno, it's like still always in the right place. Always believing or hoping for the best in people."

I swallow hard, uncomfortably flattered.

"Then this year, he trains with Decker, and he's never here. *I'm* here, Aiden."

DeMarcus looks around, but there is no one to be found. The noise outside gets louder, and he pulls me into one of the empty counseling offices and shuts the door.

"It's not fair, you know?" DeMarcus says.

"What's not fair?" I ask.

"That you get a great love story, and that Mateo gets a great love story, and here I am just sitting on the side, waiting for you to see me."

"What about Michelle?" I ask again.

"She's out there standing by Decker, and I'm standing in front of you waiting to be seen."

His poetic words capture me in a spell, and even with the chants outside, everything falls silent, just for a moment.

"I see you," I tell him, my heart pounding.

"I'm gonna ask this time, but please don't say no." He wipes his mouth and takes a deep breath. "Can I kiss you?"

I hesitate. Do I want this? Or do I want to fight for Mateo? But what else can I do? I've shown up at his house, I've texted and called daily, and he ghosts me. That's not cool either.

Blinking several times, I take in the cute, confident boy in front of me.

"Yes."

His lips press against mine. It's different than kissing Mat. Not better. Not worse, not exactly, but my mind's distracted here, too—thoughts of Mateo and Michelle, not to mention protestors.

"You ready to go out there?" I ask, forcing myself to break away.

"I'm ready," he says, and I can't help but think he's talking about us as well.

"Okay." He takes my hand, and we walk out of the office. I let him hold it even as Mat walks down the hallway. He's in front of us, so he doesn't see DeMarcus and me holding hands. A question comes to mind, and I decide to hold on a little more tightly to DeMarcus's hand.

Where will Mateo stand outside? With Decker? Or with us?

Maybe the answer will help me determine whose hand I should be holding right now.

# 49

*Taking Sides*

ADULT PROTESTORS WITH both humorous and important signs march outside the school, while Captain Decker and a few of his police buddies shout into megaphones.

"People!" Decker yells. "This is a school where children learn. You are disrupting the peace."

"Screw you! Arrest us then," one adult yells.

My eyes about pop out of my head. I love it. DeMarcus and I beeline right to Tisha.

"Isn't this amazing?" she asks.

"It's something," I say, feeling in shock. This group of adults isn't what I'd expect here at Washington High, and I wish we had more people like them in this town.

Who is on whose side, though? Camila and Michelle stand by Decker, but that doesn't mean they disagree with this protest. Camila, in fact, smiles and waves at me when we make eye contact. Tisha gestures enthusiastically for Camila and Michelle to join us. Camila nods at Decker, shrugs, and frowns. She and Michelle aren't going anywhere, I guess.

Most of the school has spilled out onto the streets now. There are several entrances on all sides of the high school, and students swarm the front of the building like bees to a flower. The wrestling team stands behind Decker, no surprise there. Coach Krake crosses his arms and glares out into the crowd, right by Decker's side, like he's part of the police. It makes me gag.

A strong hand grips my shoulder from behind, and I spin, hoping it's Mateo. He wouldn't stand next to Krake and the wrestlers, would he?

"Mat—" I start to say until I realize it's Mr. Samuels behind me.

"Some exciting drama today, eh?" he asks.

"Just another day in high school."

He smiles, patting my shoulder. "You all stay back here. If Decker tries to do anything to the protestors, you stay out of it, all right?"

"What are you gonna do?"

Mr. Samuels's lips stretch across his face in a delightful expression. "I'm going to join them, of course." He winks at me, moves to the circle of the twenty-plus protestors, and talks to one of them carrying multiple signs. A person hands Mr. Samuels her extra sign, and he joins them, marching and chanting in rhythm.

"He's got like tenure or whatever it is, right?" DeMarcus asks.

I don't know. All I know is that he's the bravest, coolest man I know, and if anyone tries to take his job away, then Mom and I might have to burn down the entire school.

I keep looking for Mateo. Krake talks to Logan, Jeff, and other wrestlers. They run back inside the school in a hurry. What are they up to? Michelle and Camila take a few steps away from the wrestling team. When Logan, Jeff, and the wrestlers return, they carry a large speaker and a microphone. It's a PA system, and Decker and Krake set it up quickly.

Decker takes the mic. When he speaks this time, his voice projects loudly through the portable speaker, drowning the chatter of students and the chants of the protestors. For a moment, there's quiet, as everyone turns their attention to Decker.

*"Ladies and gentlemen, we all appreciate passion and standing up for what you believe in. Let me introduce myself. I am Captain Claude*

*Decker. I'm also the owner of Decker's Mixed Martial Arts Academy."* He pauses like he's expecting cheers, but this isn't a halftime show. Scanning the audience, he puts on a fake smile I hate—that arrogant, I'm-the-king-of-this-town grin. The entire high school must now be outside, with hundreds of students in the streets. Media vans from nearby towns pull up, and news crews race to capture video footage of the protestors and Decker.

"*Look,*" he says, forcing his smile to widen, "*we have mixed passions. On one side, we have parents who want the best education possible for their children, with no outside distractions, whether it be a protest or a discussion on topics that aren't part of a rigorous educational curriculum.*" He pauses, and the protestors boo at his words.

I laugh out loud at the boos.

"*Now, wait!*" Decker says quickly. "*Let me finish. That's one side. On the other side, we have parents who care about the safety, identity, and the physical and mental health of their children. Now, I do believe one of these sides is misguided—*" Boos erupt again, making me laugh once more—"*but no matter what I think, I also want us to listen to each other. To have a place where we can express our passions and frustrations. And that's why I'm asking you all to pause this protest today. Let there be peace and learning at school. Instead of fighting today, join our fight. Our second annual MMA tournament will once again be held on the first of March. Show up and show us that you are made of more than words.*"

The protestors look at each other incredulously. I'm sure they've never had an event quite like this—one where they're invited to compete in a martial arts tournament.

"*I realize,*" Decker continues, "*that not everyone has the experience and training to compete. That's not exactly what I am offering you. Let me offer you our stage. Last year, we had a full gymnasium of people, and this year, I'd expect ten times that. Our hometown UFC hero Tanner Mc-Queen will also be present for pictures and autographs.*"

"Is this all just a marketing gimmick?" Tisha asks.

I chuckle. Decker sure knows how to be a politician.

*"What I'm trying to tell you all,"* Decker says, *"is that instead of you yelling nonsense outside a school in the middle of the day, I'll give you the biggest stage in our community. I'll give you a microphone and an audience to express your concerns. Would that satisfy you for today?"*

"What does that mean?" DeMarcus asks.

"There's no way Decker would let LGBTQ+ advocates speak publicly at his tournament. Would he?" Tisha asks.

"It feels like a setup," Amanda says.

"Yeah. A trap," Tony adds.

While listening to their conversation, I continue to scan the crowds for Mat. When DeMarcus and I walked out of the high school, Mateo was right in front of us. Where is he now?

*"Before you leave, don't just listen to me. I want you to listen to my top two students."* Decker's eyes find Mr. Samuels, and Decker flashes a terrible grin. *"They're the two best students I've ever had. Mateo? Michelle? Come here."*

I don't know where Mateo had been standing, but he appears from behind Decker. He knew this was happening, then. I could scream! Michelle wears a stoic expression. She and Mateo stand side-by-side with Decker.

*"Ladies and gentlemen, my top two students—both members of the LGBTQ+ community. Both competing in our tournament. There's another team that has said a lot of awful hate about people like me. Cops, you know? But I am the least bigoted person here. Just look at my top two athletes for proof."* Decker again finds Mr. Samuels in the crowd, locks eye contact, and grins. *"They and the hundreds you see right in front of you will be at our tournament. Come and speak your mind. We'll listen."*

He sets down the microphone—I was honestly waiting for a mic drop—and puts his arms around both Michelle and Mateo.

They smile and wave to the crowd.

Mateo avoids looking at me, and I think I'm going to throw up.

# 50

## *A Surprise Sensei*

OUR KARATE PRACTICES mirror that of a circus.

The first week, reporters were outside the high school after every karate and wrestling practice. Although our small town has one newspaper no one reads, we're surrounded by lots of other communities, and news media from even a hundred miles away have shown up here.

"Do you feel a tournament like this, where kids fight each other, helps or hurts your cause?"

"What message do you hope to send at the tournament?"

"Isn't it inspiring to have a police captain who gives a voice to all in his community?"

The last question makes me gag. The reporters don't know the context, although it surprises me that someone hasn't dug up history on all the drama last year. I would hope someone in the media can connect the dots, but right now, they're making Decker look like a hero. Thankfully, after a couple of weeks, the media frenzy died off, but they'll be back for the tournament, which is right around the corner.

Before practice today, I scroll through socials, and a local story catches my attention.

***Police Captain and Karate Sensei: A Local Hero Hosts Unique MMA Tournament.***

It's a video story, and I press play. Footage from Decker's school, featuring Camila, Michelle, and—much to the ache in my heart—Mateo plays in the background. *"After LGBTQ+ advocates disrupted a school day—adults swarming on our high school, which recently made several efforts to prioritize learning and minimize other drama such as this—local police Captain Claude Decker saved the day. He uses his passion for martial arts and competition to bring together diverse voices."*

It's a few minutes before practice, and the students gather in the study hall room. Tony, Amanda, DeMarcus, and Tisha look over my shoulder, watching with me.

*"Martial arts has always been about balance,"* Decker says. *He wears his karate uniform, stands tall, and for once even looks like he brushed his teeth.* *"Yin and yang. Blocks and attacks. Defense and offense. I've witnessed the division in our town first-hand. Confused kids, misguided adults, everyone thinking they know what is right and what is wrong. This year's tournament shines a spotlight on those voices. We invite you, the media and the public, to attend. Teams will be available for interviews, and that will be their opportunity to share their important perspectives with the world. We will fight—this is a competition with a great prize. But we will also listen to each other. Never in the history of martial arts competitions has there ever been an event like this."*

*"Speaking of the great prize, we also have breaking news that we want you to deliver first-hand to our viewers. Tell us about that."*

*"Initially,"* Decker says with a sly grin, *"we wanted a scholarship prize. We've been raising money, and I've been reaching out to several generous donors that I know. We now have two prizes. First-place will receive twenty-five thousand dollars of scholarship money. That's life-changing for someone. Second place will receive five thousand dollars."*

*"Tell us about the mixed gender divisions, girls and boys competing against each other."*

*"It's about equality and strength,"* Decker says. *"Some people say the equality means—"*

"Oh, turn it off!" Tisha snaps. "I've heard it all before. Gag."

"How do Michelle and Camila put *up* with him?" Amanda asks.

Tisha shakes her head. "I can think of twenty-five thousand reasons, right?" She sticks out her tongue. "And Camila's living with him. She says he's been amazing. Cooks meals, gives her privacy, lots of extra training time, too. It's weird. I hate him so much, but Camila's happy for the first time in a long—"

"Line up!" Mr. Samuels shouts.

We form a single file line in the study hall room, kicking abandoned pencils and forgotten-about worksheets as we move. As we do, a woman enters our study hall room, someone I've never seen before. She sports a traditional gi with a black belt. Probably right about Mom's age, she has short, black hair, a round face, thick but strong-looking arms and legs.

"Class, allow me to introduce you to a special guest instructor, *Sensei* Denise Rivera."

She bows then flashes a bright, cheery smile and waves. "I go by Niecy. *Sensei* Niecy or Miss Niecy, please."

"Wait a minute," DeMarcus whispers to me. "Isn't she—"

Mr. Samuels, overhearing DeMarcus, nods his head. "You may have heard of her name before as *Sempai* Denise. At that time, Miss Niecy was a student of Decker's—a higher rank than me, too. I believe Captain Decker asked you all to ask me about my relationship with her, yes?"

Tisha and Amanda glance over at me, and we exchange some WTF glances.

"I'll tell you that story today, but first, we train," Mr. Samuels says. "We must focus on the MMA rules Decker and Krake are using for the tournament. Are you ready?"

We nod.

"What kind of response is that?" Mr. Samuels asks. "Are you ready?"

"Yes, *Sensei!*"

"Good. Because these practices are going to be harder and more challenging than you've ever experienced. Are you ready?"

*"Hai, Sensei!"*

"Good. Aiden, you're up first," Mr. Samuels says.

I walk forward, admittedly a bit nervous. "First for what?"

Mr. Samuels grins, but it's not the cheesy, happy smile I've grown to love. It's the smile of six a.m. workouts. The mischievous, "good trouble" smile he wears when the stakes rise.

"You'll fight first."

"Oh, okay. Who?"

"Every single person in this room. One at a time. Starting with the lowest-ranking student. No matter whether you win or lose, you'll fight every person. Including *Sensei* Niecy." His grin widens. "Including me. And we aren't holding back. This is how we must train. Do you consent?"

I gulp. My arms shake. That means I'll fight, in this order—Tony, Amanda, DeMarcus, Tisha, *Sensei* Niecy, and finally Mr. Samuels.

"I do," I say, trying to project confidence. Still, I hope Mr. Samuels has paramedics on standby.

To say that I get my ass kicked is an understatement. I'm exhausted after my first match with Tony. We're the same rank, and although I might have a couple of months more experience than him, Tony's improved wildly. The moment the match begins, he performs a quick take-down with mind-blowing speed. I've underestimated him. Shit, and I mean no offense to Tony, but if I can't beat him, what chance do I have to take first place?

At last, I beat Tony with a rear choke hold, making him submit, but just barely. Before I can catch my breath, Mr. Samuels signals for Amanda to enter the ring. And by ring, I mean the rectangle we made with masking tape on the carpeted floor.

"The carpet will hurt," Mr. Samuels says, "but it will give you a tougher advantage. Everyone else is practicing on mats."

In other words, the school would never give us any money to help fund our club.

Amanda acts like she's going to dive at me like Tony, but it's a fake. I pull back, and she executes a roundhouse kick to my head. I fall, and she rushes in for a pin. I use her momentum against her, roll, and land on top of her. Managing to grab her arm as we roll, I put it in an arm bar. Amanda taps out.

"Well done, Aiden," Mr. Samuels says with pride in his eyes. It gives me hope. Maybe I can be a champion. "DeMarcus, it's your turn."

DeMarcus lunges at my legs, but I move, performing a sweep right out of our last *kata* that makes him stumble. DeMarcus is tough, though, and I'm already fatigued. He steadies himself, and I strike with one of my favorite combos—back fist to the head, reverse punch to the body. DeMarcus knows I love this combo, and he's ready for it. He blocks both and performs a one-arm shoulder throw. I fall hard, and he grips my arm as I hit the floor, putting me in the same arm bar that made Amanda tap.

This time it's my turn. I submit, terribly disappointed in myself.

"All right, Tisha, you're up," *Sensei* says.

"No break?" I barely have the energy to get the words out.

"Doesn't matter if you win or lose. You keep going," *Sensei* says. "We're watching you, especially because you're tired. This will give us insight into each of your strengths and weaknesses. Now, enough talking. Go!"

Tisha fakes a jab to my head, but I block. With my arms up, she punches my gut, kicks the back of my thigh, and I fall. She rushes in for a scarf-hold pin. Mr. Samuels counts, and although I do my best to escape, Tisha's form is perfect. It's impressive. I'm honestly not sure Mateo could have kicked out.

Having beat me, Tisha smiles, extends an arm, and pulls me up. "Fall seven times, rise eight," she says. I don't have the strength to smile, let alone reply.

"*Sensei* Niecy," Mr. Samuels says. "Your turn against Aiden."

"What?" I ask. Yes, my brain understands what's happening, but my body remains incredulous.

"Everyone faces everyone."

All right. Get creative. Have some fun with this. There's no way I can win, so take a giant risk.

I set up in my tiger stance, the infamous position from *Wansu* that I performed on Mateo at last year's tournament. *Sensei* Niecy smiles knowingly at me. Certainly, she knows the form, but does she know all the secrets we discovered?

She charges at me with rapid punches, and I spin my arms in a circular fashion, blocking them, tying her up, just like I did Mateo. I must wear a dubious look on my face because the others laugh and then cheer.

"Go, Aiden!" DeMarcus yells. "You got this!" His voice is pure joy. Mateo should be here with us. Mateo should be training with us and cheering me on. He should also understand—if he's never here, how can he be mad if I fall for someone else?

Am I falling for DeMarcus? Is that what my brain is telling me?

*Sensei* Niecy takes a step back. "Well done, Aiden. Try that again." This time, she fires off rapid techniques without pausing. She took it easy on me before—a few basic punches that I managed to block. But in seconds now, she throws at least a dozen punches. I've never seen such speed. It's beautiful.

She also strikes me multiple times—head, stomach, chest, ribs, back—and before I know it, I'm on the ground. *Sensei* Niecy puts me in a chokehold, and I have no choice but to tap.

"One more match," Mr. Samuels says. He rolls his neck and cracks his knuckles. My stomach drops—at least this match won't last long.

I bow to Mr. Samuels. Then I try to surprise him, taking another risk. I run at him, jump in the air, and attempt a flying sidekick right at his head. With his height and my lack of jumping talent, my foot flies about at his chest level. He steps to the side like he's holding the door open for a senior citizen. I try *Sensei* Niecy's approach—rapid punches. Mr. Samuels blocks them all, pulls me toward him with his arms, sweeps my leg, and knocks me down. He goes for a pinfall, with *Sensei* Niecy counting.

"Nice work for your first time, Aiden," Mr. Samuels says, not even out of breath. I feel like I'm dying. Everything hurts. "I want you all to know that I'm gonna be extra tough so that you all have a chance to win this tournament. This is anyone's game. Don't forget that. I am rooting for each one of you. My goal is that first and second place comes down to two of you." He reaches for his water bottle and motions for us to get a drink, too. "Quick water break, and then it's Tisha's turn to face everyone."

Tisha beats Tony, Amanda, and me. She loses only to DeMarcus and our teachers. She's incredible.

"Let's take a quick break, and I'll tell you a story about *Sensei* Niecy and me," Mr. Samuels says.

We gather in a circle, grateful for a break. Everyone sits except for Mr. Samuels, who paces around the carpeted study hall room while he talks. "Long ago, I asked out a beautiful and talented girl, Niecy." She smiles warmly at him, and my stomach turns. I don't like him talking that way about anyone except Mom. "She rejected me, though." I immediately relax. "*Sensei*, do you want to tell them why?"

"Sure," she says, standing and walking over toward him. "Class, I'm a queer woman. I wasn't out at that time, and I didn't tell Lloyd why I didn't want to date him, not specifically. I just said he wasn't my type."

"Captain Decker told you to ask about my story, so here it is," Mr. Samuels says. "I was a teenager at the time, and I didn't take rejection well. I accused her of being a lesbian only because she wasn't interested in dating me. I was ignorant and arrogant. I've since apologized many times, but that doesn't make up for the harm I caused then. Niecy, again, I'm very sorry."

*Sensei* Niecy nods.

"But it started a big conflict. At the time, she was next in line for black belt. Every time we entered the sparring ring, it was like a world championship match. And I have to tell you, she won most of those." Mr. Samuels puts his hands on his hips and laughs gently. "The point is that I was a real ignorant jerk. Decker saw it then, and probably saw himself in me. He wants to use that against you all. Class—you need to know that none of us is perfect. I have great regret for some of the things I've done, but I've learned that regrets are reminders to do better today. Eventually, I realized I was only lashing out because my ego was hurt. I used my martial arts training to discipline myself to learn more about those who were different from me." He walks around us and stops right behind me. "Want to know another secret? When I met Aiden, it was like the universe had given me a second chance. A chance to make right what I did so poorly with Niecy. And Aiden—getting to know you—it's changed my life. I will always be on your side." He looks up at all of us. "All of your sides. I wanted you to know the truth from me directly, and it's okay to be mad or upset at me. Just take it out on me in the ring. Okay?"

Honestly, part of me hates that I know this about Mr. Samuels. It shatters that perfect hero impression. But perfect heroes are a fallacy. Perfection doesn't exist. But progress does, and we should celebrate the progress that anyone makes, be it a hero or villain.

Perhaps the best heroes are the ones who acknowledge their mistakes and learn from them. Heroes apologize. I can't imagine ever hearing the words "I'm sorry" from someone like Decker or Krake.

I think about the mistakes I've made, both with Mateo and De-Marcus. And I think about how I want to move forward. The tournament is only one day of our lives, but relationships last much longer.

Too bad there's not a karate secret to help me understand that.

*Sensei* Niecy stands, and Mr. Samuels nods at her.

"Class, I'd like to teach you one of my favorite techniques, a Brazilian Jujitsu move that might come in handy against big wrestlers. I need a volunteer."

DeMarcus raises his hand.

"Now—charge at me like you want to tackle me or take me down," she says.

DeMarcus smiles and does as he is told. *Sensei* Niecy puts her foot in the middle of DeMarcus's chest, falls backward like she's sacrificing herself, and somehow with her foot in the center of his chest, she throws DeMarcus completely over.

"Remember this class. The bigger they are, the harder they fall. Who wants to try this move?"

We all enthusiastically raise our hands.

# 51

## *The Worst Phone Call of My Life*

MR. SAMUELS REQUIRES double practices now—endurance training in the morning for sparring, and then he focuses more on *kata*, specific techniques, and strategies in the evening. We practice twice a day Monday through Thursday, only once on Fridays and Saturdays, and he gives us Sundays off.

But our small group also gets together, just the five of us, every Sunday for our own private training.

"Any news about Mat? Have you tried inviting him here?" Tisha asks as we warm up.

"I texted him a hundred times, and then he blocked me," I say, and that's the truth. I've been blocked. Completely locked out from the love of my life, or who I used to think was the love of my life.

"I'm sorry, Aiden. That must really suck," she says, putting an arm around my shoulder.

"So, let me get this straight," Amanda says. "Mateo saw you and DeMarcus kissing, and now he won't talk to you at all. Not even a chance to explain?"

I nod. "Sadly, that is one hundred percent correct. I've tried everything—calls, texts, emails, and I've even shown up at his house. He won't give me even a second of his time."

Amanda glances over at DeMarcus and Tony, who have started

some partner exercises. We're training in my basement dojo. It's not that big, but they're busy enough that they can't hear us. "And how do you feel about DeMarcus?" Amanda asks.

I shrug.

"C'mon, you can do better than that," Tisha says.

I sigh. "I don't know, okay!" DeMarcus and Tony look over at us, so I lower my voice. "I mean, I do like DeMarcus. But my heart is broken right now. I can't think about dating anyone else, not with the tournament coming up. Not without closure with Mateo."

"Maybe we need a different kind of practice today," Tisha says. "If our minds aren't focused right, we're all gonna suck. So, Aiden, I think we need to hash stuff out with Mat, for better or for worse."

"You've always got a plan," I mumble with a half-hearted smile. "What are you thinking?"

"He's not answering your calls. So, let me try. And if that doesn't work, I'll get Camila to help."

"How is she?" Amanda asks.

"Busy, like us. She spends a lot of time training or hanging with Michelle. I dunno. I hope when this tournament is over that we can all go back to just being friends and hanging out more." Tisha takes out her phone, finds Mateo in her contacts, and calls him.

He answers the video call on the second ring, and my heart leaps into my throat.

*"Bueno,"* he says, his friendly voice making my heart hurt even more. *"What's up, Tish?"*

"Don't hang up," she says and hands me the phone.

I stare into Mateo's eyes for the first time in... days? No, weeks! I've stressed about this forever, and Tisha gets him on the phone in seconds.

"What Tisha said," I say. "Please."

*"What do you want?"* Mateo asks, his voice cold.

"Mat, I'm so sorry. Please let me explain."

He stares at me through his phone, but he doesn't say anything. I look up, and everyone watches me closely. I can't have this conversation with DeMarcus here.

I take Tisha's phone and run upstairs to my bedroom, shutting the door behind me.

*"What are you doing?"* Mateo asks. Even such a mundane question sends little bursts of joy through me. It's his voice. It's like hearing a favorite song for the first time in forever.

"Practicing. It's all we do, it seems."

*"I know the feeling."*

We stare at each other through our screens, and I take several deep breaths, trying to think about what to say to break the awkward silence right now.

"Can I see you?" I ask. "In person? Can I talk to you like that, please?"

*"Aiden, you broke my heart."*

"It was just a kiss."

*"Was it? Can you tell me he doesn't have any feelings for you?"*

I don't say anything at all.

Mateo shakes his head. *"Can you tell me you don't have any feelings for him?"*

I keep quiet again.

*"Then what's left to even talk about?"*

"I never want to lie to you," I say. "I'll never lie to you. Certainly never in the ways you've lied to me."

Adrenaline rushes through me like I'm about to jump out of an airplane. My heart pounds so hard it scares me. But there are some things that I'm pissed about, that I never bring up because I love this boy so much and I'm always scared of saying the wrong thing.

*"That's not fair,"* he says. *"I apologized to you more times than I can remember. And Aiden—it was my fault. Everything that happened. Everything that I let happen. It was my fault, and I will always be sorry for that. I don't know how else to convince you of that. But that does not excuse what you did!"*

Walking over to my bedroom desk, I pick up the gemstone craft that looks like a red bonsai tree, the one Mateo brought me back from Brazil. It's such a beautiful crystal. He told me it reminded him of my strength, that I was the stronger one for being able to be honest with myself and with the world about who I am. I squeeze it in my hand, hoping for some of that strength right now.

"I never meant to hurt you," I say.

*"Do you think you can ever fully trust me? And never worry that I'd do something to hurt you again?"*

"I don't know."

Awkward silence again. He scratches his forehead and sighs. *"And you can't even tell me that you don't have feelings for DeMarcus?"*

I squeeze the gemstone so hard that it cracks open the skin of my palm and I bleed.

Shaking my head, I say, "It's not the same. I don't wanna lie to you because I know how much it hurt me when you lied. I can't say I've never thought about DeMarcus or anything. But, Mat, you're the only one I love."

*"I love you, too, Aiden."*

My eyes turn instantly wet. "So, can you forgive me? Can we be together?"

He doesn't answer right away. *"I don't think love is enough."*

"What do you mean?"

*"I hate the way I feel when I'm jealous. I hate that you like him, even if it's just a little. I hate that you can't ever fully forgive me or fully trust me. I love you, but I hate the way all this makes me feel."*

"So, what do we do?" I ask.

He doesn't answer.

"What do we do, Mat?"

He still doesn't respond.

"Why won't you answer me?"

*"Because I don't want to say it!"*

"Say what?"

He shakes his head. *"You're forcing me to say this. We're not good for each other. I make you feel like crap. That's the last thing I want to do to someone I love. And you make me feel bad, too. You want a truth? I didn't know it was possible to cry and hurt so much over one other person, but you broke my heart."* His face vanishes from the screen. Deep, sad breaths come through the speaker. Is he crying? *"You know what else? There's a good chance I'm not winning this tournament. You have no idea how incredibly talented Michelle is. I know you think you do, but you haven't seen half her talent. I'm gonna lose, Aiden. I'm gonna lose, and then I'm gonna have to move. So, you breaking my heart—it's, well, I dunno."* A soft cry comes through the phone. *"I'm gonna have to move anyway, Aiden. So, it's best to break up now, yeah? A clean break."*

"Mat, no! Please. There's always hope. Hope you can win. Hope for you and me. Isn't there?"

*"I've cried so many nights recently. I wake up to nightmares where I see the boy I love kissing someone else, and it makes me just wanna die."*

"Me, too! I fall asleep holding your letter, the one I'm still waiting for you to tell me I can read. Mat, please. It's you I love. It was only a kiss." I wish I could see him.

*"This town, our school, Decker and Krake—it's all poisonous. And our love story? Our love story starts with me hurting you and ends with you hurting me. I honestly just wanna start over somewhere else. Some place where I can be trusted again."*

"Stop talking like that! Weren't you happy with me?"

*"I was in love. It was the happiest I've ever been in my entire life."*

*Was?*

Tears run down my face.

"Why would you give that up?" I ask.

*"Because my heart is broken! I don't feel happy. I feel terrible!"*

More tears spill down my face, and I don't bother wiping them. "What does this mean for us?"

*"I'm sorry."* He takes a deep breath and a long pause. *"It's best if we break up. I'll see you at the tournament. I'll be rooting for you. I really will be. I hope you win. I hope you find a secret that somehow takes down Mi-chelle. Because you'll need a big one to do so."* More cries come through the phone. *"And I'll miss you more than you'll ever know. I love you so much it hurts."*

He hangs up right after that before I can respond.

I'm left alone in my bedroom. I fall to the floor and sob. At some point, Mom comes in to check on me, takes Tisha's phone and returns it to her, and tells me my friends went home.

All I can do is cry.

# 52

## *The Night Before the Tournament*

PANIC SWELLS INSIDE me, making every limb feel heavy. I can barely walk right now. How am I going to fight tomorrow?

Tomorrow! The weeks flew by, my time consumed with either sadness or training to distract myself from the sadness.

I sit on my bed and stare into a small mirror that hangs on the back of my closet door. My T-shirts used to wear me—everything always seemed extra baggy. I've grown into them now, and not just with growth spurts, but with muscle. It's nice to see. It's why I joined that stupid wrestling team in the first place. Such a simple goal—just to be stronger.

Still, I haven't found myself, not yet. Opening my top dresser drawer, I smile at the eyeliner and nail polish that I want to experiment with much more. If karate can have hidden meaning in its movements, then I can have hidden meaning in how I express myself, too. A fun idea springs to mind, and I smile for the first time in days.

But the smile vanishes quickly. I've lost Mateo. I'm heartbroken. I still haven't opened his letter, and I consider throwing it away or burning it instead almost daily.

I don't care about fighting. If I have to face Mateo in this tournament, I'm bowing out. Seriously. It's not worth a fight anymore. I'd rather cheer for any of my friends. Let Tony, Tisha, or Amanda take a big win.

Or DeMarcus.

DeMarcus inspires me. He likes me, and I like him, too. But I can't get Mateo out of my head. It doesn't feel right to move on.

Last year, I fought for myself. To stand up for myself and against the hate and homophobia from the Logans, the Tanners, the Krakes, and the Deckers of the world. I stood up to them, but they're all still here. If anything, they've gotten stronger and bigger, too. Is anything ever going to change? And if not, why fight?

Earlier this year, my relationship with Mateo inspired me to fight—to fight for us, to show the world we exist, that we want happiness and love like everyone else, and that we won't back down. And now?

A text alert takes me away from my thoughts.

"Here," is all it says.

I had some ideas as to how I wanted to spend the night before the tournament. The first part begins now. I wanted a "date." No, nothing romantic, and not even with a boy.

Tonight, I want to do something nice for Camila.

She waves goodbye to Captain Decker in the driveway, and I'm surprised she was honest with him and that he'd be willing to drive her over to my house. He doesn't look at me as he backs out of the driveway, and that's perfectly fine with me.

"How's it going, living with him?" I ask. Our garage door opens, and Mom backs out with her car. She's going to drop us off at a restaurant so Camila and I can eat and talk.

"Good," she says. "I know you can't stand him, but he's not so bad. Especially once you get to know him, and when he's inside the privacy of his own house. When he drops his guard, he can be cool."

I don't get it. I probably never will. But if Camila is both safe and happy, then that's all that matters.

"It's weird, if you think about it," I say. "You and I—we're like the same in a lot of ways. My dad hasn't tried to call me in years. I don't know what I'd do without Mister Samuels in my life, you know?"

"Exactly." She smiles, her dimples deep and cute. It's a real smile, too, and it brings out a beautiful sea green in her eyes. "I guess we both needed father figures, huh? And to think that yours is Decker's student. Weird."

"Former student," I correct her. "They have some disagreements about values and how to teach, I think."

She laughs gently. "That is true." I open the backseat door for her, and she slides in. Mom smiles and says hello in the rear-view mirror. I hop in next to Mila.

"Camila, it's good to see you," Mom says. "How are you?"

"Okay, thanks. Better than before."

"So, what will happen if you two have to fight each other tomorrow?"

I laugh. "She'll kick my butt."

"You may have it coming." Camila elbows me gently in the ribs. "But you better give me your best if we do. I don't want anyone letting me win."

"I don't even wanna fight anymore."

"What? For twenty-five grand? That could change our lives."

"So does beating up all your friends," I say.

"Are you really not wanting to fight?" Mom asks.

"I dunno. No, what a waste of all that training, I suppose. My heart isn't in it is all."

"Lloyd says you're very close to discovering the secrets of your current *kata*," Mom says. "I'm not even sure if I understand the sentence I just said." She laughs, and Camila joins in.

"What about Mister Samuels and Krake?" I ask.

Camila's facial expression turns dark.

"What is it?" I ask.

"Nothing," she says.

"No, that look wasn't nothing. What do you know?"

She shakes her head.

"Um, kids," Mom says, slowing the vehicle down. "I'm doing my best to support this martial arts feud here, but if you know something that might affect Lloyd, you better tell me."

Camila and Mom exchange a look in the rear-view mirror.

"No, it's nothing," Camila says. "I just think Decker wants to open with that match, and we thought it would also be better to end with it."

"Is that all?" Mom stares hard into the rearview mirror.

"Yes," Camila says, nodding. I don't believe her, but I'll ask her at dinner. She's holding something back, something she doesn't want my mom to know.

Mom drops us off at the restaurant. "All right, text me when you're ready, and I'll come get you. Have fun."

"Thanks, Mom," I say, and we hop out of the car.

Once inside the restaurant, we order our food and get through some more awkward small talk. Then I get to why I wanted to see Camila tonight.

"So, hey," I start. "I dunno how to do this, but I just wanted to say I'm sorry. Like *really* sorry. I've been thinking a lot about last year and everything that's leading up to, you know, the tournament tomorrow. No matter what happens, I want us to be friends again."

"It's been nice hanging with Tisha again."

"And me?" I flash my cutest puppy eyes and cheesiest grin.

"It's been okay, I guess," she says returns my smile. "Thank you."

"Yeah. No problem," I say. "I've owed you a real apology for a long time. I just want you to know that I never meant to be a liar or a jerk. I was just in love. Or super hormonal. Who knows? But that's all over now, too."

"Mateo's heartbroken, too, you know."

I gulp. I told myself I wasn't going to ask about Mateo. That I was going to focus solely on Camila.

"What about you? You dating anyone?" I ask.

She shakes her head. "No. Maybe after the tournament. All I do is train."

"Same," I say. "And there's the spring fling dance around the corner. We should all relax after the tournament and just have fun."

"Yeah," she says. "I like that. So, you and DeMarcus? What's going on there?"

"Nothing."

"Do you want something to happen?"

"I dunno."

"You have to go after what you want," she says. "That's one thing I've learned, dealing with my stepmonster and all. You can't wait for good things to come to you. You have to get the life you want."

I laugh. "I thought you were about to say, 'Only you can prevent forest fires.'"

She laughs and throws a napkin at me. "Yeah, well. Look in the mirror, Aiden. You're cuter, smarter, and stronger every day. You deserve to have fun and be with whoever you want."

"So do you," I say.

She raises her water glass. "Cheers to that."

"So, what do you know about Mister Samuels and Krake that you weren't telling my mother?"

She lowers her head. "I overheard something. You're not gonna like it, but I'll tell you. Only because we're friends again, and because I, well, I kinda want our friendship to continue."

"Me, too," I say. "If fighting has taught me anything, it's that I'm tired of fighting."

"Okay, well, here's what I know."

# 53

## *All Caps Emergency*

"WAIT, WHAT?" I ask, a mix of anger and incredulity swelling inside of me.

"That's what I overheard," Camila says. "Decker was on the phone with Samuels. So, I didn't hear how Samuels responded. Just what Decker told him. But yeah, it sounded like they made a deal and Samuels agreed to lose."

I raise my hand to get the server's attention. "Check, please."

This tournament will be a disaster if I don't act quickly.

"What are you doing?" Camila asks.

"Do you think that's right? What your teaching is doing?"

"No, but—"

"No buts," I interrupt quickly. "I don't care anymore about 'sides,' all right? We stand up for what's wrong. They should have a fair fight or no fight at all." The server hands me the bill, and I hand him my debit card right away. "Sorry, in a hurry."

He rolls his eyes, and for a moment I admire the obliviousness of the people around us.

"How would you even stop it?" Camila asks.

Hitting the table with closed fists, I almost scream. "I dunno. But if Michelle and Mateo knew about this…. This can't happen." I scream, not super loudly, but enough to get some wildly strange looks from around the restaurant. The server rushes back with my debit card, now anxious to get rid of me. I sign, tip twenty percent—Mom's rule is if you can't tip twenty percent, then stay home—grab Camila's hand, and race out of the place like it is on fire.

"You text Michelle and Mateo. Get them to meet us," I say. "I'll message Tisha and get our group together, too."

"Where should we meet?"

I look around, standing in the middle of the parking lot outside the restaurant. Mom will be pissed that I didn't text her to get us, but she'll understand. She'll likely blow up the entire gymnasium tomorrow if we can't fix this first.

"Let's meet at the park off Monroe Avenue," I say. "At the swing set." Mateo will know the exact spot. My heart aches at the memories we created there, but right now I have more important things to deal with than my romantic life.

Camila and I speed walk to the park after sending out the texts.

"I'm sorry, Aiden. About all this." She holds my hand as we walk.

"So, this call you overheard…. This morning was the first time you heard it?"

"Yeah. I would have called you right away, but I knew I'd see you tonight." She squeezes my hand. "To be honest, I had to think about it. Decker's been good to me. But he has problems. Don't get me wrong. He's got stuff to work on, and this is something I don't agree with. I just don't know how to convince an adult who happens to be my teacher, our police captain, and now my landlord—"

"I know, Mila. I don't blame you. We have to stop blaming each other for the stuff other people do, you know?"

"It's been a long time since you called me Mila and I liked it." We pick up our pace, anxious to get to the park. "You know, just listening to you—you've grown a lot in the last year."

I smile, appreciating the compliment. "Mister Samuels has been a good influence. I don't know what I'd do without him." I scream again, this time louder since we're outside. I don't care who looks out the window and sees us.

"It'll be okay."

But I don't believe her. Once darkness consumes someone's heart, what's left for hope?

When we arrive at the park, everyone's already here. Even though it's cold, some rode bikes. Others got quick rides. If you text in all caps *EMERGENCY,* you can get someone's attention.

"Tell us now. Everything," Tisha says, the first to speak. Michelle and Mateo stand next to each other, near the sandpit where Mat and I had jumped before, where we had swung, rolled, and laughed. Is he thinking about any of that?

Camila repeats the story she told me in the restaurant.

"In short, Decker made Mister Samuels promise to lose. Otherwise, he won't award the scholarship money if one of his students wins." I watch everyone's reactions. Tisha, DeMarcus, Amanda, and Tony wear appropriately horrified facial expressions.

Michelle and Mateo show only poker faces. It pisses me off. I don't care who their teacher is. Some things are just plain wrong, and if they can't see that, then—

"Wow, this is crazy," Michelle says, interrupting my thoughts. Every muscle in my body relaxes, thankful that even our opponents know when their team goes too far.

"And what about you, Mat?" DeMarcus speaks up. "What do you think about all this?" My arms shake again, worried how Mat will respond. There's a good guy inside of him. I know that better than anyone. But there's also an ego inside of him, an ego that may want to beat the crap out of DeMarcus if he gets the chance. I nervously wait to see which part of Mateo will respond.

"I think, um…." Mateo fails to form a coherent sentence. The color runs from his face, and his expression tells me that he's just as shocked by this news as anyone else.

*Stand up, Mat! Stand up for what's right. Please, show me you can do that.*

"I can't believe Mister Samuels would do that for, well, uh, for any of us."

"Yeah, yeah, there's a lot of money at stake here, but I'm asking what you think about Decker—"

"Hey, kids," a voice calls out from behind us, interrupting De-Marcus before he can finish his thought. It's a voice I haven't heard in some time.

But it's a voice I'll never ever be able to forget.

"Feels like *deja vu*," Tanner McQueen, the UFC star, says. Logan, Jeff, and some other guys follow him. "Didn't we have a fun meet-up before last year's tournament? I'd hate to break tradition." Tanner cracks his knuckles.

"Get out of here, asshole!" Tisha shouts. "This is an important and private matter, and you are not welcome."

Tanner laughs. "We heard there was some kind of breaking news, and we didn't want to miss out on that."

Tisha stares at him with her mouth so wide open in anger that I think she's about to attack him.

"But you know I didn't come to talk. I came to play," he says.

I open my mouth, but there's no time to speak.

Tanner snarls. "Get them!"

The boys charge at us.

Logan aims for DeMarcus. DeMarcus grabs Logan, and Logan elbows him in the ribs, then tosses DeMarcus over his shoulder with a wrestling throw. They're here to show off, I realize. To send a statement that we shouldn't underestimate them either. We've focused so much on Michelle and Decker that we forget there's an entire wrestling team to defeat, too.

Suddenly, everything blurs—Jeff jumps on me, literally, and I fall on the ground. He gets the better position, and he starts slugging me in my stomach and ribs. Tasting blood and losing hope, I look over my shoulder. Logan pushes DeMarcus to the side and now attacks Tony, punching him in the face. Amanda tries to pull Logan off Tony, and then Logan grabs Amanda's hair with his left hand and punches her in the face with his right.

That's Decker's definition of equality in action.

Tony yelps like an animal at the sight of it. He throws Logan off, kicks him hard right in the balls, and rushes to see if Amanda's okay.

My vision blurs as Jeff strikes me in the face with a closed fist. Sand, dust, and dirt fill the air.

Tisha and Camilla act quickly, and seeing that Amanda is okay, they charge right at Logan. Good. Let Logan get what he deserves.

Standing up, I glance at Mateo and Michelle. Why aren't they doing anything? They choose not to get involved, perhaps not wanting to take a side, but that angers me even more.

Before I can say any of that, a car approaches quickly, tires squealing. Then a door slams, and I wish…. Please don't let it be Decker or Krake! Please don't let this get worse.

"What is happening here?" It's a loud, powerful voice that makes everyone freeze.

"Go away, old man," Tanner says. "This isn't for you."

"Mister McQueen. So, you chose to attack teenagers? And you recruited a few of Krake's bullies to help? It's a shame such talent is wasted on you."

"Let me ask you this honestly, Teach," Tanner replies. "You think spending all day in a high school classroom will prepare you for someone like me? I've been training with real pros all year long. It's time I show you what I've learned."

Tanner growls and charges right at Mr. Samuels.

# 54

## *Mr. UFC*
## *vs. Mr. Samuels*

TANNER DIVES AT Mr. Samuels's legs. There's no way I'd engage in a striking contest with a karate expert, so it makes sense to take him right to the ground. Why is my brain thinking about strategy when my teacher is in trouble? Nausea rises in my throat, and I look around at everyone else—is anyone going to stop this? A real MMA athlete just attacked a high school teacher right here in public with witnesses. This is what happens when the Deckers and Krakes of the world get to be in charge.

Mr. Samuels's movements are magical, though. Tanner grabs at his legs, and as graceful as a Broadway dancer, Mr. Samuels spins, jumps, and maneuvers right out of Tanner's grip. I saw something else, too— something so fast, if anyone blinked, they'd have missed it.

It was a series of short attacks to the back of Tanner's head, neck, and back. As fast as bullets from a gun, Mr. Samuels's open hands strike Tanner rapidly.

Tanner looks around the playground, his body swaying like he chugged a twelve-pack of beer. He rubs the back of his head, and then he looks at Logan, Jeff, and the other dude that came with them that I don't know. "Get him! Do something!"

Mr. Samuels glances quickly over to me and smiles. *Don't take your eyes off these jerks, Sensei!*

Logan and Jeff grab *Sensei*'s arms, and *Sensei* drops right into a familiar but mysterious movement. The peacock.

He drops low into what we call a jungle stance, his hands dropping low and then shifting into an incredibly wide, circular motion—the wings of a peacock. The secret reveals itself, or at least part of it. The peacock movements remove the threats without hurting them. It's a defensive tangling and then shoving to the side. The other boy takes one look at *Sensei*, turns, and runs away.

*Sensei* rushes over to us. "Are you kids okay? Is anyone hurt?"

No one answers, and Tanner screams. "What did you do to me?" He remains on the ground, embarrassed, unable to stand.

"Is anyone hurt?" Mr. Samuels asks again. We're bruised, our egos more so than our bodies right now. *Sensei* runs from one person to the next to check on them, including Camila, Mateo, and Michelle.

Tanner manages to stand and stumbles over to Mr. Samuels. Tanner grabs his arm.

Mr. Samuels spins, puts him in a simple arm bar, and Tanner screams in pain. "Mister UFC. What is it going to take for you to stop? I'm a simple high school teacher. These are high school students. Grow up." Mr. Samuels twists Tanner's arm more, and the professional athlete cries.

Tanner taps out, slapping his other hand repeatedly against his leg.

"Think, Tanner," Mr. Samuels says, releasing him. "It's not too late for you, but you have to grow up. These are minors. You are an adult. In any other town, you'd be arrested and would have just ruined your entire professional career. Do you understand that?"

Tanner spits. "You're a fool. You've agreed to let these kids enter the tournament. You think anyone on your team is walking away with money or a championship, old man? Think again."

"If you're so confident," Mr. Samuels says, "then why did you come here to scare them?"

"Screw you!"

"Want a free punch, Mister UFC. Take a swing at me. Right now. I promise you. I won't even block." Mr. Samuels extends his chin in an exaggerated fashion. He even clasps his hands behind his back. "What not enough? I'll close my eyes then. Free shot for the big shot!"

Mr. Samuels shuts his eyes. Tanner tries to raise his right arm, but he can't. He tries to swing his arm at our teacher's chin, but his arm flops in the air like a fish out of water.

I burst out with uncontrollable laughter.

"What did you do to me?" Tanner cries again, and my laughter spreads throughout the others.

Tanner can't even lift his right arm.

"Let's get out of here," he tells Logan and Jeff. The three of them leave—the other dude they came with long gone—to the sound of our laughter. Somehow this terrible night provided a silver lining. I blink several times, memorizing the look on Tanner's face when Mr. Samuels defended himself. I may have to recall that anytime I want to get out of a sad mood.

"Gather around," Mr. Samuels calls. "Everyone." He locks eyes with Mateo and Michelle, too.

"What did you do, *Sensei*?" Tony asks. "Why was Tanner acting like that?"

"Secrets," Mr. Samuels says. "It's all in *Empi Sho*. Strikes that if timed and targeted properly can render limbs useless, or even leave someone unconscious."

"Can you show us that, like, now?" Tisha says, smiling. "Sounds like something we could use before the tournament."

Mr. Samuels nods his head several times. "Many lessons have crossed my mind," he starts. "But some require… more thought than others. I don't want to teach you things you're not ready to handle. I don't mean that you can't do the techniques." He takes a deep breath. "Some lessons shouldn't be taught for winning tournaments. Some lessons are only for life and death situations and must be carefully considered."

"Can you show us now, please?" Tony asks.

"Everyone up. We practice *kata* now. Together."

"What?" Camila asks.

"Is now really the time to train?" Amanda asks, holding her face.

Mr. Samuels smiles empathetically at her. He didn't see Logan slug her. Oh, Logan's got it coming in the tournament, that's for sure.

"Can you think of a better time to train than right now? Line up. Now." The smile is gone, and it's replaced by the seriousness of someone preparing for battle. "Camila, Michelle, and Mateo—join us."

"What? Why?" DeMarcus asks.

"We're all a team right now," Mr. Samuels says. "Maybe you train at a different school. But you are friends. You are students who love martial arts. You have more that unites you than divides you. I need you to see that and remember that. Right now and forever."

It's a strange time to train—having just been in a fight. And let's not forget what Camila told us about Mr. Samuels. *Sensei* absolutely cannot lose to Krake.

"Mister Samuels," I start, raising my hand. "There's something we need to ask you."

I swear he can read me. For a second, he looks like he wants me to continue, but he sees something in my eyes and shakes his head. "Not now. Now, we train. Class—see the secrets. See what the *kata* is trying to teach you. Follow my lead."

He begins running through all the katas he's taught us. He includes *Kujaku*, too, the peacock. The way he looked at me when he performed *Kujaku* against Logan and Jeff…. There's something he's trying to show me. What did he do to Logan and Jeff? He used their energy somehow, and then he faced the other boy. No—the other boy ran away. I don't understand the hidden meaning.

I search for secrets, but other mysteries compete for my attention.

I need to figure out how to stop Mr. Samuels from letting Krake win. Michelle, DeMarcus, Mateo distract me, too. Who will win the tournament? Will Mateo move? Will we all still be friends after this tournament, or will the fighting create more enemies?

For now, I run the katas and follow Mr. Samuels because when I wake up tomorrow, it's time to fight.

Someone will win. But way too many people will lose.

# 55

## *The Green Mile*

IT'S A BIZARRE night, restless, sleepless, full of vivid dreams. De-Marcus fights me, and he changes—no longer the cute, confident boy I know but a nightmare who wants to hurt me. DeMarcus morphs into Mateo in my nightmare, and Mat puts me in an armbar and breaks me. He wins, takes the money, and goes away to college, never to talk to me again.

I wake up screaming. The sun has risen, and it's time to get ready.

"You okay?" It's Mr. Samuels from outside my bedroom door. He knocks gently, then pushes it open.

"Night terrors. I have a bad feeling."

Mr. Samuels sits on the edge of my bed. "Sometimes bad things pave the way for good." He's not himself this morning, either. His gaze makes me think he's picturing his match with Krake. I know what's going to happen, and I must stop him.

"Mister Samuels?" I start. "Camila told us she overheard Decker talking about your match with Krake. I just wanted to say—"

"No, Aiden. Don't you worry about me. I can handle myself." He forces a half-smile, making me miss his genuine one. "My focus is on each of you. Any of you could win this tournament."

"Do you really believe that?"

"Everyone is scared today," he says. "Trust me—Decker and

Krake's teams are scared, too. They wouldn't be trying to intimidate us if they weren't."

He doesn't address my primary concern.

"Come downstairs. Eat something. We need our energy today." He pats my legs and stands, moving toward my bedroom door.

*"Sensei?"*

"Yeah?" He turns around, one arm pressed against my doorframe.

"Tell me a secret. Tell me something I can use to win. I know I'm like the last person who stands a chance today. But I need something. Please?" I sit up in bed, staring at him, hoping to avoid turning my nightmares into reality.

"Stand." He motions for me to rise.

Wearing a white T-shirt and my boxers, I clumsily get out of bed.

"Run *Empi Sho* with me again. Picture the knife hand sequence at the end. Visualize your attacker coming in for any kind of grapple, and then perform those moves on them."

We run the *kata* together in my bedroom, walking through the moves, nothing too intense. I visualize what he tells me. Am I tying up their arms again, like I did with the tiger moves in *Wansu* last year?

"What am I missing? I don't get it."

"Let me tell you another secret," he says. "The secrets aren't the same for everyone. That's why you must discover it for yourself." He pats me on the head, but frustration and lack of sleep put me in a bad mood.

"That doesn't help. I'm just gonna get my ass kicked again. Thanks for nothing." Immediately, I regret it. Mr. Samuels looks at me with terrible disappointment.

"Come get something to eat and get ready," he replies, ignoring my disrespect with his words, but the way he looks at me—that fatherly disappointment—hurts my soul.

When he leaves, I run the *kata* again, begging my subconscious to figure out the hidden meanings. After no revelations, I sit at my desk.

There's one more thing I want to do today for the tournament.

Opening a drawer, I take out eye liner and nail polish I had hidden.

MOM DRIVES US to the tournament. It's a silent, uncomfortable ride, like we're driving to a funeral. Or to an execution, like a dead man walking the green mile to the electric chair.

Decker reserved the high school gymnasium but rented it out under his MMA school's name. "He signed waivers and paid a fee for the gym. This way the school's off the hook, in case, well, you know," Mr. Samuels tells Mom, as I fidget in the back seat.

"Lloyd, just promise me two things. Keep Aiden safe. Keep yourself safe. I don't know what I'd do if either one of you got hurt." Mom wipes away some tears in her eyes. To be honest, I'm surprised she's letting me compete. Mr. Samuels must have worked some magic with her. Mom wears a business suit, and she looks exceptionally professional for a karate tournament.

"I'll do my best," he tells her.

She breathes hard through her nose, and the white in her knuckles intensifies as she grips the steering wheel hard. "That's not the response I want."

He flashes her a sad smile.

My stomach sinks. Is it too late to turn around? Does Mom even know what arrangement he's made with Decker today? She'd be furious! Should I tell her? Or would that be betraying Mr. Samuels?

"Mom—" I start, determined to help my teacher even if he gets mad at me.

"Here," she says, pulling up to the high school far too quickly before I can tell her. She parks and turns around to face me.

"Aiden," she says with a deep breath. "Be safe today. I know this is important to you, and I know it's more than just fighting or karate. You're standing up for yourself, and you're representing every LGBTQ+

kid who can't stand up for him or herself. That's so meaningful, and I am very proud of you for that. You have inspired me. Do you know that?" She takes my hand and squeezes it. "I may have my own surprise for you today. Oh, by the way, Aiden?"

"Yeah?"

"You look very nice today."

I blush. For the first time this school year, I did something I've been wanting to do all year. Something simple, I know. But it feels big, too.

I painted my nails in pride colors, and I even tried a little eyeliner. Although I don't feel very artistic, I like the way it looks. It's an extra layer of confidence that I need today.

"Thanks, Mom."

"And you," she says, turning to Mr. Samuels. "So help anyone if you get hurt or let these kids get hurt—you're no match for me, no matter how good you think you are." She leans in and kisses him. I turn away, staring out the window.

Mateo and his parents arrive and step out of their vehicle, walking toward the entrance of the gymnasium.

*Last year, you came out and kissed me in front of everyone.*

Any chance this year you'll forgive me for kissing DeMarcus and kiss me again? Make it all right? One more happy ending?

I open the backseat car door and throw up in the parking lot, the nerves in my stomach overwhelming me.

"WELCOME, LADIES AND *gentlemen, to our second annual mixed martial arts tournament,*" Decker announces from the center of the gym, speaking loudly into a microphone. The gymnasium is packed. A thousand people must be here, a huge event for our small community, ten times the size of the event last year.

Half of the gym came out in pride colors, too—bright clothes, rainbow apparel, "love is love" accessories. The other half of the gym looks so plain and boring.

*"This year's tournament is extra special. First, the winner will receive a twenty-five-thousand-dollar college scholarship prize! We are also thrilled to have a special guest, our own hometown-proud UFC star, Tanner Mc-Queen!"* Tanner walks onto the gym floor, waving and smiling at the crowd. I want to puke again. *"He's even agreed to be a special referee for us today. How about that?"* He laughs and glares at us, watching to see our reactions. We should have seen that one coming. Of course, even the referees will suck. *"That's not all for tonight! We also have a special Sensei versus Sensei match—our own Coach Krake against English teacher Lloyd Samuels."*

"Ugh, Decker's such an asshole," Tisha whispers.

*"Coach Krake is so kind that he's put his beautiful wrestling practice rooms on the line. If Mister Samuels wins, his martial arts club will have priority use of the practice rooms and mats for their club for the rest of the school year."* Decker covers his eyes like he's blocking out the sun, looking for Mr. Samuels. We're inside, but he's ridiculous. *"There are you, Lloyd. That sure would be better than practicing in a study hall room, right?"* Decker laughs and shakes his head. *"Plus, for the first time, we are mixing the genders—that's true equality, and only the strongest will win!"* The pride side of the gym doesn't cheer, but some applause comes from the other side. *"Finally, let's not forget all the controversy we've had over the past year. I believe in the principles of martial arts—that they can heal divisions and make the world a better place. Today, the media will be interviewing competitors at various times to feature their voices on local news stations. If you want to change the world, it takes more than a sign and a chant. I'm happy to offer a spotlight to our passionate youth, so that their voices can be heard by tens of thousands."* He laughs again, and my stomach rolls.

He passes the microphone over to Coach Krake, who's dressed in a full suit instead of a wrestling singlet. Oh, boy—am I going to have to see that body in a singlet later? Yuck.

*"Thank you all for coming,"* Krake says. *"It has been an honor to train my wrestlers. It's not just for sport, although we love the sport. It's about life. We train them to be strong, to overcome weaknesses, and to be the strongest version of themselves. Today, you'll see what progress we've made in just a year. Let us now rise for the singing of our great country's national anthem."*

Krake gestures, and our school's choir comes out to sing the anthem.

"Boy, they went all out this year," Amanda says. "By the way, Aiden? You look hot." She looks at my nails and then back at my eyes. The rest of the team smiles and nods, too.

Blushing, I say, "Thanks."

"Seriously, this looks great on you," Tisha says, holding my hand and looking at the color of my nails. "Nice eyeliner, too. It makes you shine brighter. You should always do what makes you shine brighter."

My face burns, but I smile.

We stand in one single line. Decker's MMA school stands on the opposite side of the gym. I look at Mateo and Michelle, as well as Camila, Alyssa, and the other competitors. They're strong and focused. Next to them stand Krake's wrestling team—Logan, Jeff, Wyatt, and a dozen other boys I'd be happy never to see again in my lifetime.

Although Decker said this event was an open tournament, it looks like it's only the three groups again—Decker's school, Krake's wrestlers, and us. No surprise. He wouldn't want an outsider winning. He's got one purpose in mind, and that's to make sure he wins, and we lose.

*"Round one,"* Krake says. *"Competitors to your rings!"*

Mr. Samuels gathers us around. "Okay, team. The gym is divided into multiple rings. Ring one is Amanda versus Alyssa. Ring two is Tisha versus Caitlin. Ring three is Tony versus Jeff. Ring four, DeMarcus versus Riley. Ring five, Aiden versus Jonathan."

I'm grateful not to have to face Mateo at least. I was worried Decker would destroy us right away by making us face their best in round one.

"Looks like they're gonna make us earn it," DeMarcus says.

"Huh?" I ask.

"Look—Mateo, Camila, Michelle, Logan, all their best competitors aren't even fighting in round one?"

"That's bull. So, we need to earn a shot to even face them, and we'll already be tired," Tony says. "Assuming we even win."

"Enough!" Mr. Samuels shouts loud enough that the entire gym silences for a minute. We have one more guest who joins our circle who clearly has been rushing.

"Flat tire," she whispers to Mr. Samuels, but she says it loud enough that I overhear. He shakes his head knowingly. Did someone intentionally damage *Sensei* Niecy's vehicle? She joins us in our circle, and Mr. Samuels claps his hands to focus our attention.

"I've heard enough excuses. I've heard enough worry. We trained all year for this. Karate-ka, you are ready. It starts by believing in yourself. Nothing good will ever happen if you don't first believe that you can do good. Now you go show that you all have what it takes to be champions. Can you do that?"

"Yes, *Sensei!*" we shout.

"Good." Mr. Samuels wears the first genuine smile I've seen all day. "You are stronger than you realize. You have more talent than you know. Go show them that. Show the world that. I believe in all of you." He puts an arm around *Sensei* Niecy, and they both turn around until they make eye contact with Decker.

*Sensei* Niecy waves at her old teacher. Mr. Samuels tries to resist grinning, but he can't help it. He's trying to get under Decker's skin, and we have our own surprises today, including an extra *Sensei* to help coach our students.

"*Sensei* Niecy, any words of encouragement for our team?" Mr. Samuels asks.

"Yes," she says. "Like that look on Decker's face right now? Go kick some ass, and you'll get to see that look all day long!"

# 56

*Fight!*

WITH MULTIPLE MATCHES happening at once, the gym transforms into a cacophonous rumble. I face one of Krake's wrestlers who wears that stupid singlet that got me in trouble last year. Before we enter our specific rings, we remove our current belts. For the tournament, we bring out our red and black special uniforms that Mr. Samuels got us last year. We all had to order new ones this year, thanks to growth spurts, but he had them embroidered on the back. It's a simple rising sun to represent Japan, with Japanese *kanji* spread over it that translates roughly into, *"True strength lies in character."*

I remember thinking that the blue belts last year clashed with our uniforms. So do our current purple belts, but we don't wear them, either. We take out the pride belts Sensei got us for the high school football demonstration, which feels like decades ago. My opponent scoffs at the belt, dramatically rolling his eyes.

Mr. Samuels grabs my shoulder before I step into the ring. "They want to humiliate us in round one, Aiden. You can do this. You can go all the way to the finals. Show them the strength that's inside you."

I nod, and Tanner motions for us get into position. Of course, that douche referees my ring. My teammates spread out through the gym. We're all fighting at once, so there's no time to cheer for them. Oh, please let us all survive round one!

When Tanner blows the whistle, Jonathan, my opponent, dives for my legs. I'm ready for him and his basic wrestling—as he comes in, I execute an inside crescent kick, smacking him on the face with the bottom of my foot. When my foot connects with his face, I jump on his back. His momentum causes him to drop hard on the floor, and I easily shift into a chokehold. The dude taps out right away.

I jump, my arms high in the air. Mr. Samuels raises his right fist and cheers. Mom screams.

That's right, jerks. This queer karate kid isn't taking any shit today.

Even better news—Tisha, Tony, Amanda, and DeMarcus win their first matches, too! Sensei Niecy runs back and forth between the rings, cheering on as many as she can. Her passion and excitement energize us. The pride section of the gym stands on their feet and applauds.

My heart explodes. The tournament is only beginning, and we're getting a standing ovation. Maybe this is all I needed—a reminder that there are more people fighting with us and for us than there are people fighting against us. "Enjoy it," Mr. Samuels tells us. "This is about so much more than martial arts today. You're fighting for them, too."

The expressions on Decker and Krake's faces right now pretty much make an entire year of training and heartbreaks worth it. They are pissed! They exchange angry words. My neck stretches in their direction, as I'm dying to hear what they say.

"Sonofamotherfu—" Krake snarls through gritted teeth.

Mateo makes eye contact with me, and he almost smiles.

Almost. The corners of his lips nearly curled up, but he looked away quickly from me. We should be celebrating together. He should be with our team. On our side. Holding my hand. But he made his choice.

Seeing Mateo look at me, DeMarcus puts his arm around my shoulder. "We got this, Aiden. We can do this."

"Yeah, thanks," I say, my gaze not leaving Mat. Mat's gaze also doesn't leave mine. I wish I could read his thoughts. Does he hate me? What will he do to win? Would he hurt any of us?

"Man, you know what?" DeMarcus asks. "Let's give ourselves an extra challenge. If I win my next match, will you go on a date with me? Just us. One date. What do you think about that?"

DeMarcus looks extra cute in his uniform. I could cuddle in his strong arms. And why shouldn't I? Maybe I need to stop holding out for a relationship that may never work.

"Okay. Deal," I say, determined to find as many good moments in today as I can. "And if I win my next match, you have to pay."

"It's a deal," DeMarcus says. He glances at Mateo, who still hasn't taken his gaze off us, and then DeMarcus kisses me on the cheek. "Forget anyone who doesn't stand by your side, Aiden," he whispers in my ear. "Let's make sure it's you and me in the final two."

"I like that plan."

"Round two," Decker says into the microphone. "Competitors, please go to your assigned rings. Ring one, Amanda versus Camila. Ring two, Tisha versus Logan. Ring three, Tony versus Wyatt. Ring four, DeMarcus versus Damien. Ring five, Aiden versus Jason."

"Hell yes," Tisha says, cracking her knuckles and looking for her homophobic ex-boyfriend in the crowd. "I cannot wait to kick this jerk's ass."

Tony puts his arm around Amanda. "You can do this. You got this!" Amanda nods, but her eyes are wide and worried. I'm too familiar with that feeling.

"You too," she tells Tony.

"I get Coach Krake's kid," Tony says. "I'm gonna put that family where they belong. In the losing column."

"Yeah!" DeMarcus cheers and turns to me, putting his arm around me again the second Mateo glances our way.

Mateo's skin turns red as lava.

I'M DETERMINED NOT only to win but to win my match quickly so I can cheer for the others.

It's another one of Krake's wrestlers, who snarls at me. He'd be a cute kid if it weren't for the anger plastered across his face. When the match begins, he rushes at me like my last opponent. I'm trying to recognize patterns. They do what they've been taught, and they've been taught to attack quickly.

It's a good thing karate is about self-defense. Jason fakes a jab to my face only to throw himself at my legs. I take my defense straight from *Empi Sho*. A strong low block drives his arms away and even spins him around. All blocks are also strikes. I haven't forgotten that lesson. Dizzy, Jason tries to refocus. He's not used to strikes in his wrestling matches, and I use that to my advantage. Following up the low block, I attack with a reverse punch. It hits Jason right in his solar plexus, and he spits out his mouthguard. Jason grabs it, and then he repeats the same move, diving at my legs.

I'm beginning to think Krake isn't as good of a coach as everyone makes him out to be. Why is their strategy so repetitive?

This time, I counter with a series of punches. With his arms protecting his head, I perform a sidekick to his stomach. He drops his guard. I execute a roundhouse, smacking the side of his face. Jason falls, and the match is over. I got a knockout! Throwing my arms in the air, I celebrate. Mom and Mr. Samuels applaud and cheer for me, too. My smile stretches even wider at the look on Krake's face.

DeMarcus also won his match quickly. We high-five and spread out to watch the other matches. Tony and Wyatt, Krake's son, grapple hard. Wyatt's on top of Tony, but Tony knows how to reverse this—it's the cool Brazilian Jujitsu move *Sensei* Niecy taught us. Speaking of Niecy, she's cheering excitedly for Tony, joy plastered across her face. We've been taught well. We might win this whole thing after all.

Tony swings his hips to the right, enough to change Wyatt's momentum, and then Tony moves quickly to the left. He swings his legs around Wyatt's neck. Holy crap! Tony slams Wyatt on the mat, his strong legs now choking Wyatt. Wyatt goes from pink to red to dark purple, and then he slams his hand on the mat to tap out.

"Yeah, Tony!" *Sensei* Niecy, DeMarcus, and I cheer.

Two other matches begin, and I'm torn because I want to watch both. Tisha faces Logan in the first mixed-gendered match of the day. And Amanda faces Camila.

Krake throws a clipboard on the gym floor and kicks at an empty chair. It's such a delightful sight that I find myself snorting. DeMarcus looks at me curiously, and I point to what makes me laugh. Krake storms out of the gym, kicking a garbage can as he goes. DeMarcus laughs and puts his arm around me. Each time he does, his eyes search for Mateo. I know he's trying to get under Mat's skin, and it's a good strategy. Still, it makes me uneasy, and I subtly pull away.

DeMarcus doesn't have time to react. Tisha and Logan are now fighting. Logan yells and tackles Tisha, scooping her up in a bear hug and slamming her on the mat.

The crowd groans. "Tisha!" DeMarcus and I yell. "C'mon, Tisha!"

Logan swings at her with his right fist and it hits her in the stomach. The crowd groans again.

Logan hits her in the face with his left fist. The crowd realizes instantly that this is why we don't have mixed-gender fighting. No matter what one's opinions are on strength, gender, or athleticism, it's terribly uncomfortable to see a cisgender male punch a cisgender female. Of course, Krake and Decker might choke on the word cisgender. Ignorance is dangerous.

Logan hits her again, and the crowd is aghast. He punches her in the face, in the stomach, and back in the face again. Part of me is mad at the audience too—*You wanted to see this, that's why you're here, isn't it?*

"Get up, Tisha!" Our Pride side of the gym cheers for her, and it's contagious. Soon, the entire gymnasium roots for the underdog. Decker crosses his arms and glares angrily at the audience.

Tisha tries a move like what Tony did earlier, a variation on the jujitsu technique *Sensei* Niecy taught us. She gets her legs around Logan, but Logan stands up tall, gripping and holding Tisha in his arms.

He slams her down on the mat so hard it must knock her unconscious. Logan pins Tisha.

Logan wins. He stands up, nothing but smiles, arms in the air, but the crowd is quiet. Tisha lost the match, but Logan lost the crowd.

Sadness. Pain. Regret. Confusion. Tears run down my face as I rush to Tisha. "Are you okay?" She blinks, and tears stream down her cheek.

Mateo races toward us.

"You okay?" he asks Tisha, not looking at me once.

Tisha still lays on the mat, confused, hurt, and surprised. She's one of our best. She could have gone all the way, but Logan had revenge on his mind.

Logan steps up to Mateo. "Why are you talking to her?"

"You didn't have to do that," Mat says.

"Do what?" Logan asks. "Win? Because that's what I plan on doing, no matter who I face. You, any of your homo friends, Michelle, I don't care. I'm winning." He walks past Mateo, hitting him hard with his shoulder as he does.

Mat finally looks up at me, deep concern in his eyes. That's the boy I fell in love with. The boy with a big heart. But also the boy with one hell of an ego and an even tougher punch.

DeMarcus steps next to me and throws his arm over my shoulders. "Nice people you hang with," he says to Mat.

"You should save your energy for the ring," Mateo snaps.

"Oh, I've got plenty saved up for you. Like two years' worth." DeMarcus replies, standing his ground.

Mateo glances over at me, but I can't read his expression. He walks away quickly, and I'm at least grateful that he stopped engaging with DeMarcus. I also wish DeMarcus would take it a little easier on Mat.

I have so many thoughts running through my mind, but there's no time to think. Camila and Amanda scream, currently in the middle of a brawl. Both girls *kiai* in the ring.

As the audience refocuses on the current match, I watch Tisha quietly slip out of the gymnasium.

## 57

## *MMA-Mania*

RIGHT AS CAMILA and Amanda fight, reporters gather around a stage Decker set up for interviews, all part of today's event.

They interview our town's mayoral candidate first, which makes me gag. Liam McCarthy. Logan's father—running for mayor of this town. Gross. Like father like son, I can only imagine the manipulative lies coming out of his mouth. But I only see them from the corner of my eye, as I return my focus to the match at hand.

Camila and Amanda exchange a series of blows. First, Amanda gets the advantage with some low kicks. Samuels always said, "Kick high in practice, kick low in defense." Amanda knows how to apply it.

Smart and quick, Camila adapts to Amanda's strategy. She grabs one of Amanda's legs and sweeps her, turning the tables. They roll, moving from judo techniques to strikes. Amanda uses her speed with lightning-fast punches to Camila's ribs. Camila falls, and Amanda goes in for a choke. She gets it! Camila turns pink and gasps for air.

"Don't hold this against me, but I don't know who to root for," I whisper to DeMarcus, still looking around for Tisha, wondering where she went. I see Mom and Tisha's mom talking and walking out together, so I assume they are checking on her.

When I look back at the ring, the positions have reversed again. Camila flips Amanda over with a powerful hip throw and applies a choke. Amanda taps out. And yet—I cheer for Camila, too. They shake hands and smile. It's such a low bar, but we finally see respect after the conclusion of a match. When Amanda approaches, DeMarcus and I leap in and hug her.

"Don't say a word," she says. "I know. I know."

"What is there to say?" DeMarcus asks. "You are amazing."

"I agree," Mr. Samuels adds, his loud voice projecting from behind us. "I couldn't possibly be prouder of you. You did a wonderful job. Keep your head high and be proud."

*"Domo arigato,"* she replies.

The media continue to take small groups of competitors for interviews, and Wannabe-Mayor McCarthy—*puke!*—helps by escorting them.

Decker takes the mic, and we immediately enter the next round. We watch Mateo and Michelle win easily. They beat their opponents so quickly that if we had blinked, we may have missed their matches.

No reporter has asked us a question yet. It's strange that they aren't talking to us. Considering, though, that Daddy McCarthy is helping with the interviews—well, maybe he's keeping us away from the media, controlling the message.

When the next round ends, Decker announces the new matchups. *"We've made it to our semi-finals, ladies and gentlemen! Ring one—DeMarcus versus Mateo."*

I gulp, anxiety lodged in my esophagus. I knew this would happen, but I can't help but dread it. DeMarcus looks at me, his usual positive and animated face now indifferent and focused.

"You can do it."

"You bet I can. So far, you owe me a date. And maybe after this match, a kiss?"

A kiss? A kiss in front of everyone... like when Mateo came out, apologized, said he loved me, and kissed me?

*"In ring two,"* Decker continues, and I'm somewhat grateful I do

not have to answer DeMarcus about the kiss, *"Aiden versus Camila. In ring three, Logan versus Tony. In ring four, Michelle versus Billy…."*

He continues talking, but I can't hear anything. All I heard was *Aiden versus Camila.*

I can't fight Camila. No way. I don't want to. Not going to happen.

Camila looks at me from across the gym, and she frowns. I make a hopeless gesture. "Mister Samuels, what do I do?"

"It's like the secrets in our karate, Aiden. Sometimes it seems like there is only one choice or one option. That's rarely ever the case, but often we can't see it."

"I should be saying the same to you about your match."

He gives me a very adult look at the comment but manages a small smile. "You know, adults like me are probably the worst at accepting criticism." He pauses. "I care for you so very much." His tone shifts—gentle, fatherly. "Please do not judge me for what I have to do today."

Mom, Tisha, and her mom walk back into the gym. It's obvious Tisha's been crying, but they comfort her and return to the bleachers.

*"Competitors—to your rings!"* Decker says.

I don't know what to do.

"Good luck," I tell DeMarcus.

"Any last-minute advice?"

"Do the tiger moves from *Wansu.*"

DeMarcus smiles energetically. "Got it."

"What about me? What do I do?"

"I dunno, man. I just dunno."

Neither do I, but my feet move to my assigned ring. Camila enters and faces me. We bow to each other and get into our positions.

When the referee starts the match—and of course I get Tanner again—I freeze. Since my brain isn't helping, I hope my body knows what to do.

Camila and I stare at each other. She fakes an attack to see what I'll do. I stay still. I'm not fighting Camila. No prize or amount of money is worth this.

Camila grabs me gently. We move around the ring, but we don't attack. "What are you doing?" she whispers in my ear.

"I don't wanna fight you."

"I don't wanna fight you, either. But Decker would be very disappointed if I don't try to win."

We shuffle side-to-side like we're in a practice session. "I'm tired of being worried about disappointing others, especially for doing the right thing."

"Decker has my best interests in mind. I can tell you twenty-five thousand reasons why he'd want me to fight you."

"Yeah," I say, pulling on her *gi* to pretend like I'm about to make a move. "But what happens when you face Mat? Or Michelle?"

"It's a long shot. Is it worth giving up, though, just because the odds are hard?"

"No. But it's worth giving up if we want to make a different kind of statement." I let go of her and drop my guard.

"What are you doing now?"

"Take a swing at me or take a stand with me."

Tanner gives us a WTF gesture. Camila drops her guard and takes my hand. We walk out of the ring together, and reporters immediately swarm us.

"What's your message to the school and the community, kids?"

"Why aren't you fighting?"

More questions come from other reporters. I take the mic and a deep breath, focusing my thoughts while ignoring the harsh glare from Wannabe-Mayor McCarthy, who stands next to the reporters. My mind may have been in a thousand places these last few days, but I also thought long and hard about what I wanted to tell everyone if I had the chance.

Clearing my throat, I begin. "Fighting is always a choice. My team chose to fight here today because we want to stand up against our school's anti-LGBTQ+ policies. This school and town aren't just hurting us. They're making our lives feel shameful, and that's what we must defeat today."

"So, why don't you two fight?" a reporter asks.

"Some people here wanted to see boys and girls attack each other," I say. "We believe in equality, but we never wanted this to happen."

"Why did you agree to it? Why enter?" the reporter asks.

Camila steps up and speaks. "Why don't you ask the adults who made these rules?"

Decker steps up to the stage and takes the mic. If looks could kill, we'd already be ashes.

"What is your message, Captain Decker?" another reporter asks.

"In the real world, there is no equality. You are stronger than your opponent, or you are not. No one on the street is going to say, 'Oh, I won't mug you because you weigh less than me. Oh, I won't harm you because you are a different gender or sexuality and that's not fair.' Nope. Trust me. I've been protecting and serving for longer than these kids have been alive. Today, we show them that there is no equality. You are strong or not. Now, what do you say we get back to the competition? I have a feeling this next match will be one to watch." He walks off stage, even as multiple reporters shout questions.

"It's DeMarcus and Mateo," I say to Camila. "I've got so much I want to say, but thank you. Thank you for standing with me."

I am tired of fighting for the wrong reasons. I'm not tired of fighting, though. Whether it's karate secrets or life secrets, a fight doesn't always have to include punches. We fight for others when we lead by example. We show up, we stand up, and we never back down. But like karate teaches, we don't have to throw the first punch or any punch. There are other ways to defend oneself.

"I've got a lot of thinking to do. I hope I made the right choice."

I'm incredibly proud of Camila, but I'm torn, too. Did I cost her a life-changing scholarship? I know the odds of either of us winning were low, but low doesn't mean impossible. Still, there's something else happening here.

Change. Change and hope. Camila did what she thought was right even in the face of others like Decker who wanted her to fight. When we find our voice, we don't have to only listen to others. We need to truly start listening to ourselves.

I hug her. "You did. That was the bravest thing that's happened all day."

When the match begins, Mateo wastes no time. Clearly, both Krake and Decker have been teaching an aggressive strategy, but it's the one thing that has become predictable. DeMarcus jumps to the side and lands in the tiger position from *Wansu*. His stance is deep, and his hands turn to claws, one protecting his head, one covering low.

Mateo shakes his head and snarls. He kicks at DeMarcus's legs, but DeMarcus shows strong athleticism. He performs a jump kick, dodging Mateo's attack, and smacks him in the face at the same time with a right front jump kick.

Mat's head snaps back, and DeMarcus flies at him with a series of punches. Two hit Mat's stomach, another his head.

I wince at every strike. I don't know who to root for. At this point, I just don't want either getting hurt.

Blood streams from Mateo's mouth, but he wipes it away without even flinching. DeMarcus dives at Mateo's midsection, trying for a takedown. He should have stuck with strikes. Wrestling is Mateo's greatest strength. When DeMarcus hits Mat, Mat scoops him up in the air. He spins DeMarcus around and drops him hard on the ground. Instead of going for a pin or submission, Mateo picks DeMarcus back up. He's not done yet.

He should be done. He could finish this match. But he wants more. I know that side of Mat—the competitive, egotistical side.

With DeMarcus back on his feet, Mateo leaps into the tiger position. He glances over at me, but I can't read his face. DeMarcus charges at Mateo, but Mateo knows the secrets to this technique.

I'm the one who showed him.

Mateo tangles DeMarcus up easily. He picks him back up, one arm under DeMarcus's legs, the other around his neck. Mateo spins around several times and then slams DeMarcus hard on the Mat. He grabs DeMarcus's arm, pulls him up, and smacks him in the face with the opposite arm.

DeMarcus falls hard, and it's an immediate knock out.

Mateo raises his arms at the victory, and the crowd cheers.

But I don't. That was an ugly attack and an ugly match, and I didn't like one thing about it.

It takes a moment for him to regain consciousness, but DeMarcus stands shakily, looks first at Mateo, then to me, trying to understand what happened. Mateo turns to face the other side of the gym, his hands still up, his back now turned to DeMarcus.

Losing his temper, DeMarcus throws a sidekick at the back of Mateo's leg. It makes contact right under the knee, and Mat buckles over instantly.

DeMarcus looks at me, his face turning from anger to regret in a heartbeat. He shakes his head, turns around, and runs out of the gym.

My stomach completely sinks. Not a single of us, not one of Mr. Samuels's students, will make it to the finals. Every time I think we're "winning," like with Camila and I choosing not to fight, I doubt myself again.

How will we ever feel like champions if none of us ever becomes one? Mateo and DeMarcus aren't helping either. We'll never make progress when people who should be friends keep attacking each other.

*"You need to teach your students to control their emotions, Sensei,"* Decker says into the microphone. *"But right now is an extra special match, just for all of you who took time out of your day to attend and support our students. It's karate against wrestling—Mister Samuels versus*

*Coach Krake! And then it's time for our semi-finals. Mateo, Logan, and Michelle all advance to the next level! Who will be crowned our tournament champion? Stick around."*

# 58

## *Mr. Samuels vs. Coach Krake*

MR. SAMUELS SHOULD be prepping for his match, but instead he chases after DeMarcus. The rest of our team follows.

"DeMarcus, you okay?" Tony asks.

He mumbles something incoherent in reply.

"DeMarcus," Mr. Samuels says gently. "Tell me why we learn how to fall?"

DeMarcus buries his face in his hands and cries. "I'm sorry, *Sensei.* I'm sorry to everyone. I messed up!"

Mr. Samuels puts his arm around DeMarcus and repeats the question. "Why do we learn how to fall?"

"Do I have to talk about this now?"

"It's more important now than ever," *Sensei* replies. "Why?"

DeMarcus sighs deeply. "We learn how to fall so that we learn how to get back up."

"Good. We are all more than our worst moments. But DeMarcus, we're going to be practicing falls a lot more, you realize that?"

DeMarcus manages a small smile. "Are you mad at me?"

"You know how much I'd like to kick Krake like that?" Mr. Samuels asks. "We can all be more than one thing. I can be disappointed and also be understanding at the same time. We'll talk more about this later, okay?"

Mr. Samuels takes a deep breath and addresses all of us. "You all know that this entire mixed-gender situation made me very uncomfortable, but I didn't realize just how uncomfortable it would be until we saw it in action. What Logan did to you," he says to Tisha, pushing her hair back to examine her face, "is unacceptable. I should have stopped it. I shouldn't have allowed it in the first place. I hope you all can forgive me. I don't have all the answers either. Not by a long shot, but I shouldn't have let you get into this mess."

"Mister Samuels," Tisha starts, "you should also know that I'm stubborn enough to not have listened to you. I wanted to fight Logan. I still do."

*Sensei* Niecy speaks up. "Decker's biggest opponent is his ego. When one has a big ego, there will always be another challenge. The way to end this is to do what Aiden did. To choose not to fight."

Reluctantly, we nod in agreement. But what choices do we have left? Our team is out of the tournament.

Mr. Samuels smiles warmly at *Sensei* Niecy. "Now, you all may not like what you see in my match," he says. "I ask all of you not to judge me. What I am doing—it's all for you kids. I hope you understand that."

"If the solution is to stop fighting, then why would you fight, sir?" I ask.

"Sadly, peace often requires a sacrifice." He turns and heads straight to his ring. DeMarcus's parents take him to the side, and the rest of us race to the ringside.

Coach Krake looks like a semi-truck wrapped in spandex.

Mr. Samuels, in his full gi and black belt, enters the ring. Hesitantly, he bows to Tanner, the referee for this match, too. He also bows to Coach Krake, who of course doesn't return the gesture of respect.

Like he teaches his athletes, Krake follows the same strategy—a quick dive and take down. For his size, he's surprisingly fast, a giant truck with a fast and furious engine. Mr. Samuels goes down hard.

"C'mon, *Sensei!*" Tisha screams.

Yeah, he could win if he would only choose to do so.

Instead, Krake hits him in the stomach, back and forth, a dozen strikes. Mr. Samuels takes them all, blocking only high strikes that would have hit his face. Krake hops off and mockingly bows at Mr. Samuels. He laughs and faces the audience. He bows again, trying to do so in an extra effeminate way, like a curtsy. Krake even bends his wrist and winks at me. Oh, how I despise him!

"*Sensei*, stop this! Get up and fight!" I yell.

Mr. Samuels gets up on one knee. Krake scoops him up and throws him back down, a one-arm shoulder throw. He picks Samuels back up and slams him again, this time with a hip throw. He repeats it twice more. Then he leaves Samuels on the mat and prances around, mocking every gay stereotype there is. He blows kisses at me. Tanner, as unprofessional as ever, laughs hysterically. If Mr. Samuels doesn't get up and fight, I'm going to have to enter and face Krake myself.

"Why would he agree to this?" Amanda asks. "I can't watch."

"Me, neither," Tony says, looking away.

I know this is the only way Decker would promise to award the scholarship money, but it makes me sick. People in power or privilege—they are always getting away with things like this at Washington High. How dare Krake hurt Mr. Samuels and mock us!

"This is so not cool," Tony says. "Mister Samuels didn't have to do this."

Something snaps in me. "No. He did. He wasn't thinking about himself. He just wanted to make sure one of us would get that money." I hate seeing him take this beating, but the last thing we need to do is add disappointment.

Krake picks Samuels up and throws him again. And again. Half of the crowd cheers as Krake dances around the ring. Our section boos. Wannabe-Mayor McCarthy stands in the front row, riling up the audience, standing and screaming for Krake.

I want to throw up. This crowd—this school! It makes me sick.

This isn't sport. It's brutal entertainment at the expense of the people I care most about in the world.

I search for Mom in the stands, but I can't find her. Mr. Samuels must have asked her not to watch. It's a good thing, too, or Mom would be in there crane-kicking the snot out of Krake.

The match continues for another minute. Krake makes ridiculous karate moves, obviously mocking everything we do.

Finally—what feels like forever—Krake moves to pin Samuels. Mr. Samuels doesn't even try to kick out. He takes the loss.

I guess it's a good thing our team is out of the tournament now. I can't imagine having to fight after watching this. Of course, that was a part of Decker's strategy too, no doubt—to destroy our morale before the final matches in case one of us made it to the end.

My fingernails dig into the palms of my hand until blood seeps out.

I need to find Mom and figure out how we're going to burn down this gymnasium today. Because contrary to what I may have thought earlier today, now is not the time to sit down.

Now is the time to fight, and I've never felt more fired up.

# 59

## *The Finals*

"MOM, HOW COULD you let him do this?" I shout outside of the gymnasium.

"Oh, Aiden. You think I *wanted* this to happen?" Mom wipes at her eyes, and her face reddens. "Lloyd talked to me about everything. You have no idea how much it pained him. You also have no idea how much he cares about you and all his students. He did this for you all."

"Bull. He did it for Mateo," I snap, my heart racing.

Mom's eyes narrow.

"It's the truth. Mat's the only one who has a chance to win. We all knew that even if we chose to believe in miracles. Mister Samuels could have said no!" Even with my anger, I realize I was mad at Tony for feeling the same way moments ago. Maybe I didn't like Tony's words because they mirrored thoughts I didn't want to have.

"Son, look at me," she commands as my eyes glue themselves to the floor. "Look at me. Now."

I curse the pain and the tears in my eyes, but I look up at my mother.

"He would do anything for any one of you. That's the person he is. And isn't that amazing? He did this not for you or Mateo, but for all of you. To make sure whoever won would be guaranteed the scholarship money. Don't make this any harder for him. Do you hear me?"

Reluctantly, I nod.

"No. Do you really hear me?"

"Yes."

"Good. Because Mister Samuels isn't the only one with secrets. I have a surprise for you, too"

"What is it?"

"When I said you inspired me by how you are literally fighting back at hate, I wasn't exaggerating. Just wait. Let's have one happy moment at this stupid tournament. Oh, and by the way, no more tournaments after this. I can't take it."

When we return to the gym, Krake speaks with the media, no doubt bragging about himself and his program. I can't stand this. If all we do is lose everything, how will our message be heard? The bad guys win again. And when they don't, all they do is claim the other side cheated or had an unfair advantage. Then they change the rules on us based on those lies, which in turn makes it even harder for us to win next time.

I want to break this cycle, but I don't know how.

*"Ladies and gentlemen,"* Decker announces from the center of the gym, *"we now enter the semi-finals! The winners of the next two matches will face each other for a twenty-five-thousand-dollar prize."* The crowd breaks into applause. *"Not bad for high school competition, eh? So, semi-final match one is Logan versus Mateo. Semi-final match two is Michelle versus…? Oh, right. We had no winner from the match that would have faced her, so she will automatically move to the finals!"*

Mom and I join the rest of my team and sit in the front row of the bleachers. Tisha sits next to Mom, and Mr. Samuels is on my right. On my left, it's Amanda, Tony, and DeMarcus. Everyone is silent. Across the gym, Camila and Michelle talk to Decker.

"I can't even get excited about Mateo kicking Logan's ass," I tell Tony.

DeMarcus and his parents join us ringside. He looks terribly sad, and it breaks my heart.

Logan and Mateo step into their ring. Mateo looks over at me and, for just a second, it looks like he might smile or wave, but he doesn't.

Coach Krake cheers for Logan, and Logan does the same stupid move every single one of Krake's wrestlers has done today—a simple dive to take down their opponent.

Mateo lets it happen.

He rolls back with Logan, using Logan's momentum against him.

He flips right on top of Logan and puts him in a hold. Mat looks up, searches for me again—no, that's not quite right. His eyes land on Tisha. I glance over at her, and she stands. Mateo points at her, a this-is-for-you message. Then he punches Logan in the face. Not once. Not twice. But like a dozen fast punches, just as quick as anyone I've ever seen. He picks Logan up and this time makes eye contact with Mr. Samuels. Then Mat glances at Krake. Mateo throws Logan while never once looking away from Coach Krake. He picks Logan up and throws him again. And again. It's the same pattern Krake used on Mr. Samuels, and Mateo and Krake both know it. A deadly glare exchanges between Mateo and Coach Krake.

Wow. I don't know if I'm falling more in love with Mateo or if he's terrifying me.

Finally, Mateo pins Logan and easily wins. Mat gets up, brushes himself off, and walks away like he hasn't broken a sweat. He moves to the side of the ring and sits alone, away from his team, away from us.

"Well, that was something," Tony says.

"Like a screw-you to both Logan and Krake," Amanda says.

*"All right. This is it! For the grand prize—twenty-five thousand big ones! Michelle, Mateo. Center ring. Let's go,"* Decker chirps into the mic.

This is what I've been wanting to see.

It all comes down to this match. If Mateo loses, he moves away from Washington. If he wins, what will happen to us? Two years of ignoring and avoiding me until we graduate?

Michelle and Mateo bow to Referee Tanner and to each other.

The tension in the gym is palpable, and the crowd goes silent once the match begins.

Michelle attacks first, using her long legs to kick at Mat. She performs a front kick to his stomach, which Mat blocks. She doesn't even set her foot down and uses the same one to throw a roundhouse at Mat's head. But he blocks that, too. Michelle bounces several times on the balls of her feet and throws a spinning hook heel kick at his head. Mat ducks, but Michelle spins again, executing a second kick. Mat blocks, taking the kick on the arm.

Then he charges at Michelle.

He knocks her down.

It's the first time I've seen Michelle fall. The crowd cheers for Mateo. No, they cheer for Michelle. They cheer for both!

I've never felt so much energy before, as we all focus on two of the best athletes at Washington High. And one is gay and one is trans, and we should be celebrating that! But no, Decker set this up so....

Decker set this up so no matter what, his side would win. And then he gets to control the message, make it about his program, and completely ignore the history being made between two incredible queer athletes. How did we not see this coming?

I don't know what to think or who to root for... but that's not true. No matter how much anger or frustration I've felt recently, I know that there's one person I will always cheer for.

There's one person I will always love.

*C'mon, Mateo. You can do it!*

Michelle's agility is incredible. She falls like a cat, landing gracefully, kicking Mateo even as she falls, her foot planted right in his midsection. When she hits the mat, she pushes him off her, and Mateo dive rolls over her. They spring into a guards-up position, a beautiful display of talent.

Mateo breathes hard. He's covered in sweat for once. His competition, also for once, may be more talented.

Mateo jabs high and throws a low reverse punch. Michelle blocks the jab and leaps in the air—a full, three-hundred-sixty-degree jump spinning crescent kick. It's absolutely beautiful, but Mateo sees it coming. He ducks, but Michelle executes a quick sidekick. The blade of her foot hits Mateo's ribs. He collapses.

"Mat!" I call out. DeMarcus looks sharply over at me. Mat's holding his ribs with one hand, but he gets back up.

"They should stop the match," Mr. Samuels says. "The way Mateo is holding his ribs—that kick may have broken them."

Mateo yelps and charges at Michelle. She kicks him in the gut, in the face, spins yet again—that super-fast hook heel kick lands right on Mat's temple. He stumbles but throws a front kick with his left leg. That's the one DeMarcus attacked from behind. Michelle grabs his leg and strikes it several times. Mat loses his balance and wobbles. Michelle jumps higher than before, completing a tornado kick that lands right on the other side of Mat's head.

He's down.

The crowd leaps to their feet, eager to see what's happening.

Tanner checks on Mateo. He shakes his head and signals that the match is over. It's a knock-out.

Michelle is the victor.

The crowd cheers for her, and I run to Mateo with Mr. Samuels right by my side. Mat's parents race down to us from the stands, too.

"Mateo, are you okay?" I yell when we get to him. He lies on the floor with his eyes closed. Tears run down my face, and I look up at Michelle. Decker shakes her hand and already holds a gigantic trophy. I bet he can't wait to give that prize money to anyone that's not on our team.

The bad guys win again. I hate it so much.

"*Mi hijo! Mi hijo,* are you okay?" Mrs. Hernandez asks. His dad stands right next to her.

"This is your fault!" I shout at his father. "Why do you have to pressure him so much?"

"*Our* fault?" His father blushes deeply, anger rising to the surface. "None of this would be happening if not for you! Our son would still be on the wrestling team. We wouldn't have protestors and school rules to embarrass our family. You are the cause of all of this, you little son-of-a—"

"Oh, you shut your mouth right now," my mother yells at Mat's dad. "You want to see another knockout, keep talking."

"I see now where Aiden gets his terrible manners," Mrs. Hernandez says.

We're about to start a new brawl when Decker shouts on the mic. *"What a fight! We have a champion to crown!"*

Mateo blinks several times. I grab his hand. "Are you okay?"

"No," he mutters. "But maybe this is what I deserve." I've never seen him look so defeated. I grab Mr. Samuels and run toward Decker.

"Aiden, what are you—"

"No time to explain," I tell Mr. Samuels. "I need your support. You sacrificed yourself earlier. I won't let it be for nothing."

We race to the center, and Decker gives us a dirty look. I talk quickly, explaining my idea to both Decker and Samuels. Decker doesn't react at first, but then he smiles. "It's your death wish, kid. Be careful what you ask for."

Mr. Samuels grabs me. "Aiden, you don't have to fight anymore."

"After what you did for us, I want to do something, too. For all of us. Win or lose, I'm facing my fears and doing this for us."

What are we fighting for if not for each other? It's why I wanted to enter this damn tournament in the first place.

Decker speaks into the mic. *"Well, well, well. Ladies and gents, we have another surprise for you. We have had a competitor make a special request. Because he was never officially eliminated, Aiden has asked for an opportunity to face Michelle. Michelle, do you consent?"*

She shrugs like beating me will be no more difficult than making a cup of coffee. She's probably right.

*"Very well. The trophy and the check will wait. Aiden Rothe is going to fight after all. Center ring. Let's go!"*

Mom grabs my arm hard. "Oh, son. You saw what she did to Mateo. You can't honestly want to fight Michelle, do you?"

"Yes."

"I don't want you doing this."

"I'm sorry, Mom. You can ground me tonight. Today, I fight."

DeMarcus runs to me next, reaching for my hand. "You are… I have no words. Just be careful."

I enter the ring. Michelle glances at me and yawns.

Mr. Samuels approaches. "Aiden, now is the time to figure out *Empi Sho's* secrets."

"Sir, I can't think about riddles right now."

"Close your eyes." Mr. Samuels gets close and whispers in my ear. "Do you remember when Tanner attacked me? Do you remember what I did to defend myself?"

I picture the fight. Tanner had dived at Mr. Samuels like every other wrestler has today. Mr. Samuels performed a series of strikes on Tanner's neck, back, and head.

"Yeah, I remember."

"Good. Now, picture what I did and overlap those techniques with the final sequence of the *kata*. Run it with me. Right now." I open my eyes and see that Mr. Samuels is serious. We bow and run the *kata*. Michelle rolls her eyes, and Tanner laughs at us from inside the ring. Krake dances mockingly to the side, making a section of his stupid audience laugh. When we get to the open-knife blocks and attacks, I overlap the movements with what I remember from Mr. Samuels's defense.

"Do you see the secrets?"

I smile bigger than I have all day. "I see something. Maybe several new things."

"Good. You'll need to use every single one."

# 60

## *Pride and Persistence*

MICHELLE WHISPERS TO me before the match begins. "Do you really think *kata* can help you win right now?"

Rolling my shoulders, I warm up and focus on the moment. "You know what I don't like? People who know all the answers to everything. I'd rather keep an open mind and see what I can learn."

Michelle stares at me curiously, as though she doesn't know whether to fight me or befriend me.

The match starts, and I leap to the side. She's got such fast, strong kicks, so I rush at her with high and low strikes, trying to close her off so she can't use her legs.

Michelle blocks my strikes easily, hops backward to get some space, and kicks me in the stomach with a hard front kick. It lands right above my belly button, and I can barely breathe. She knows it, too.

"Want me to make this quick and put you out of your misery?" she yells through her mouthguard.

I must get her to dive at me like Tanner charged at Mr. Samuels, like all the wrestlers here have done today. "Yeah, yeah, you can kick. Bet you can't beat me without kicking."

"Oh, please," she says, rolling her eyes. "I'm happy to oblige."

She lifts her right knee high, like she's going to kick me in the head, but retracts it quickly. Instead, she dives at me for a takedown.

That's what I wanted!

In *Empi Sho,* we perform a high open-handed knife block with one hand and a low open-handed knife block with the opposite hand. The center point of the *kata* consists of an elbow to the spine. But the secrets—what Mr. Samuels did to Tanner—layer the techniques together. All blocks morph into strikes. Mr. Samuels knew how the wrestlers would attack us. He's been preparing us for this all year.

When Michelle dives at me, I use a knife-hand block to strike her head, right below the ear at a pressure point behind the jaw. Then I pull her head closer, and my elbow strikes her spine. Pressure point strike under the ear, attack the spine, and then repeat—get the opposite ear's pressure point and hit the spine again. If done correctly, it creates temporary paralysis. Not long—I'm not nearly as precise or as powerful as Mr. Samuels—but long enough for a good attack or two before she can defend, and that may be all I need.

After I strike Michelle, she freezes in front of me, bent over, her head near my stomach. With Michelle on pause, I switch my stance and execute an ax kick—aiming for the back of her head. It's a sweet kick right out of Michelle's Tae Kwon Do playbook.

The kick swings high and comes down even harder. If I make contact where the spine meets the skull, it should be an instant knockout. That's another pressure point, and if done in combination with these others, it could send her straight to dreamland while I collect twenty-five grand.

I yell, a spirited *kiai,* and my foot comes down hard.

I miss by an inch, hitting closer to her shoulders than her head. Still, she falls hard, and I move in for a pin.

One, two—no, Michelle rolls me over! She locks my elbow. I scream, twist, turn, pull, but I can't do anything.

She applies even more pressure.

My arm will break. It's seconds away from breaking. I try to hold on. I kick, yell, cry, and—

Tap out.

*Dammit!*

I tap out. I lose again. I have no choice if I want to keep my arm.

The crowd goes wild, and my teammates stand, cheering and applauding. They're applauding for me even though I lost. I guess I'm good at losing.

Even Mateo smiles at me and claps, but I sure don't feel like celebrating. I wipe at my eyes, hoping anyone who sees my wet face will think it's just sweat. I'm tired of losing. I'm tired of coming so close. So close to winning, so close to having a happy relationship with Mateo. So close. But never succeeding. Michelle remains the winner. Mateo will move. This completely sucks.

I failed. What was even the point?

Decker gets the trophy and walks to the mic to announce Michelle as the winner for a second time. Camila races over to Decker, too, her eyes wide with excitement.

Limping, I make my way over to Decker so I can hear what my ex-girlfriend says to him.

"If Aiden can fight, so can I. Remember—neither one of us lost. So, if he was eligible, I better be eligible. Sir, I want to fight. I deserve the chance."

Decker nods. He takes the microphone and speaks again to the crowd. *"Aren't you all glad you came out for this event? What fighting! What competition! Michelle has won her final match twice."* He laughs, clapping for her, and the rest of the crowd joins in on another round of applause. *"But Michelle—are you up for a third final match? And everyone, listen, this is the last time I will make an exception. Is that clear?"*

Michelle looks at her competitor and nods consentingly. "Everyone deserves a chance. I don't want to win any other way then by defeating everyone who wants a chance."

*"I'm proud of you,"* Decker says. *"And this is a special one close to my*

*heart. I don't want to deny the dreams of any of my students. So, ladies and gents—one last time. Let's get your attention to the center ring for a special, final, final match. Michelle versus… Camila!"*

# 61

## *Not the Final Match We Expected*

CAMILA AND MICHELLE enter the ring and shake hands.

"Go, Camila!" Tisha and I cheer. Mom whistles and applauds, too, after giving me one heck of a quick, we-will-talk-about-this-later-medical examination. It might be the scariest expression I've seen all day.

"That was an amazing fight," DeMarcus says.

"Thanks."

"Seriously," Tony says. "You were awesome. Those were the secrets?"

"Some of them, anyway."

"So cool," Tony says.

Michelle begins the fight with her trademark kicks. Camila ducks and dodges. They spend some time moving around the ring, trying to find the perfect opening. Camila fakes a front kick. Michelle drops her guard, and Camila runs in, jabbing her twice in the face. Then she grabs Michelle's midsection and performs a hip throw. Camila has Michelle on the ground!

They roll back and forth, each getting the other in a pin or submission hold, but neither being able to hold on to it for long.

When they break, they jump back up on their feet. Michelle throws a backfist, and Camila blocks from the outside and attempts to lock the elbow. Michelle breaks the lock and spins with a sidekick, hitting Camila right in the stomach.

Camila barrels over, and Michelle rushes in, putting Camila in a headlock and taking her to the ground. Michelle goes for pin, but Camila rolls out.

Michelle's just too good. From the pin, Michelle locks in a chokehold. Camila turns pink, and it looks like she's going to tap out.

"C'mon, Camila!" Mr. Samuels cheers. From across the ring, Decker gives him a strange look. Mom whistles and our team starts a chant.

"Ca-mil-*ah*. Ca-mil-*ah*." We clap and chant, getting the crowd into it. Everyone loves an underdog. With Michelle's incredible talent, we manage to get the crowd behind Camila.

She elbows Michelle in the ribs and breaks the choke. She throws a ridge-hand strike at Michelle's solar plexus, and it makes perfect contact. Michelle's eyes widen as the wind gets knocked out of her.

Camila moves quickly. After the ridge hand, she spins and sweeps Michelle, knocking her on the ground. Michelle grabs Camila's leg. But Camila jumps with her one standing leg, locks both legs around Michelle's body, and purposely falls hard on the mat.

She has Michelle in an armbar, and it's a beautiful lock! The same lock Michelle put on me that made me submit.

Camila grins so wide her mouthguard pops out. Michelle squiggles left and right but can't escape. She performs a bridge with her lower body, but Camila has the armbar locked in perfectly.

There's no escaping it. I know the feeling all too well. Michelle's arm will break, or she will submit. Knowing Michelle, she might let it break before giving up.

With her other arm, Michelle tries several times to hit Camila, but Camila never loses focus. She puts all her strength and weight into the lock, her teeth clenched hard, her eyes closed, her face covered in sweat.

Michelle lowers her other hand and then slams it repeatedly on the mat.

"Yes!" I scream.

Michelle taps out.

Camila wins. Holy shit, *Mila wins!*

We rush the ring, our entire team. Tisha hugs Camila and screams. Amanda joins in, as do DeMarcus and me. We pick Camila up and almost drop her the first time. Mateo sees us struggling and rushes in. He helps us hold Camila up on our shoulders.

She cheers and cries, and I couldn't be happier for her. Camila is our champion!

When we put her down, Decker walks over to the mic, but Mr. Samuels stops him. They exchange some words, and Decker hands the mic over to Mr. Samuels.

*"Thank you, everyone,"* Mr. Samuels says into the mic. *"My name is Lloyd Samuels, and I want to congratulate everyone who competed today. But I also need to share a compliment when one is due. Congratulations to our own Captain Decker, whose two top students, Michelle and Camila, put on one heck of a fight. Congratulations, Camila, on being our ultimate champion today!"*

The crowd cheers, and Decker presents Camila with a trophy and a check.

Camila doesn't even have a home of her own and just earned twenty-five thousand dollars to help with her future. Honestly, I can't imagine anyone who needs it more. Mateo's tough. I feel terrible for him, but this is Camila's moment.

All the competitors and their family and friends gather on the gym floor.

*"While we have the reporters here, we have one more announcement to make,"* Mr. Samuels says. *"Susan?"*

He's calling out to my mom. Wait, what's happening? She walks to the center of the gymnasium and takes the mic.

*"I don't want to give a long speech, but I want to say a few things, please."* She speaks calmly and looks powerfully beautiful in her business suit. *"This year started with the school trying to implement homophobic policies. Today, we saw a few exceptional things. I want to*

*make sure those things aren't overlooked. You had multiple queer students compete. You had queer high school athletes competing wonderfully in front of this amazing crowd. Isn't that something worth celebrating?"* Mom smiles, and the gymnasium applauds. *"But we also witnessed something tragic. Something disgusting. You sat here and watched a grown adult try to humiliate another adult simply because he doesn't agree with him. You sat here and watched a grown adult who works at this school as an educator mock the queer community in front of your very eyes."* Mom finds Coach Krake and glares at him. *"I have two last things to say. First, I'm calling on all parents to ask for Coach Krake's resignation due to his awful behavior."* Then she finds Wannabe-Mayor McCarthy in the audience and locks eye contact with him. *"Lastly, I want you all to know that I, Susan Gardner, have officially filed the necessary paperwork to run for mayor of Washington. I am throwing my name in the hat to face Mister McCarthy. The wonderful students we watched today—they have inspired me to want to fight, too. And this is my way of fighting for actual freedom and true justice. We pride ourselves on freedom, don't we? But that means freedom for our gay and trans students, too. It means freedom for everyone. And I'm going to make sure this town and school move in a positive direction. If you feel the same way, I hope to have your vote in the election."* She smiles at Mr. McCarthy and Coach Krake, hands the mic over to Captain Decker, and walks over to me, putting her arm around my shoulder.

"Mom, you're amazing!" My heart skips a dozen beats. Goosebumps pop up all over my arms and legs. I don't just have a mom who accepts me and fights for me. I have a superhero for a mother who wants to fight for everyone like me, for any outsider this town has picked on.

It's the best feeling in the world, and I'm filled with unbelievable hope. Hope for a future without bullies. Hope for a future filled with nothing but love.

DeMarcus taps me on the shoulder from behind.

"I hope we still have a date? And that you won't hate me for what I did today?" DeMarcus asks.

But even as DeMarcus asks the question, my eyes find Mateo.

Mat's looking at me, too.

I feel pulled in multiple directions, and then I discover one final secret. Something else I think Mr. Samuels may have been trying to teach me all year that didn't make sense until now.

*Kujaku.* The peacock form offers another surprise.

# 62

*Heartbreak*

I DON'T ANSWER DeMarcus. At least not yet. I'm thinking about the peacock form, and its secrets, but everyone wants to shake Mom's hand. Many also want to talk or shake hands with Mr. Samuels and Captain Decker. Plus, the rush of people onto the gym floor distracts me from answering DeMarcus. Almost everyone leaves Krake alone or ignores him.

Good. He did that to himself, and I can only hope that Coach Krake truly gets fired.

"You know what that tells me?" Mom asks. "People here recognize good people. Krake's a total jerk, and they know it. Lloyd knew what he was doing. He didn't just lose to make sure Decker followed through with the money. He did what he did to show this school and town who Krake is."

Chills run through me. Like our karate, not everything is what it seems, and there are always more secrets below the surface. "Do you think it will make a difference?"

Mom and I study Krake, who gathers all his wrestlers in an opposite corner of the gym. Logan, Jeff, and Wyatt sit in the front. Krake berates his entire team, yelling, spitting, and cursing.

"For those with hate in their hearts, maybe not. But you changed some people today, Aiden." Mom speaks up, talking to all of us. "You all changed some hearts today. Not just with your words, but with your behavior."

"Susan is right," Mr. Samuels says, taking her hand. "True champions know that real victory comes from making a difference for others, not just making a difference for oneself."

Camila races over to our team, glowing with joy.

"Oh, Camila! You were the best!" Tisha says.

"Thank you. I'm sorry I was a jerk to you guys for so long."

"No apologies needed," I say. "We deserved it. It's crazy. It's too easy to think we are always doing the right thing, even when someone else is getting hurt. I'm sorry, too."

"Thank you, Aiden," Camila says. Mom smiles proudly at me, and Camila and I both find our attention momentarily distracted. A young woman enters the gym. She approaches Decker. When Decker sees her, he immediately runs to her and hugs her.

"Rebecca," Camila mouths at me. "His daughter."

Captain Decker and his daughter hug on the gym floor. I have that funny feeling again inside me—hope for the future. Hope and healing for anyone who chooses to get back up after falling down.

"Excuse me," DeMarcus says, taking my hand and pulling me away from the group and closer to him. I still haven't answered his question about a date, and he'd hate to know I'm thinking more about the secrets in the peacock form than I am about him. "I really am sorry for how I acted with Mat. My temper got the best of me."

"You fought well today," Michelle says, approaching DeMarcus and me, raising a closed fist for me to bump. Hesitantly, I tap it.

"Thanks."

"There's a lot I want to tell you," she says. "You and Camila—you both really, I dunno, inspired me today. I'm sorry if I didn't understand you at first, and I'm sorry for not trying harder to understand."

"I'd just like to be friends, Michelle," I say. "Especially now that I know how hard you can kick."

She laughs gently. "You know, I had a very bad year last year. From the stories I've heard, you and I had very similar experiences. It's the main reason why my parents moved. I threw myself into my training because I never knew when I would have to defend myself again for real. And then, I get to this place, and maybe I haven't made the best choices here, right? But I chose what I chose because… I thought it was the right thing to do for me. But I'd like to be real friends with you all, too. If you'll give me a chance?"

"Always," I say, raising my fist again. Michelle smiles and bumps it.

From my left, Mateo approaches.

DeMarcus on my right, Michelle in front of me, Mateo on my left. Three forces. Not all that different from three attackers.

"What are you smiling at?" Michelle asks.

"I'm thinking about peacocks, actually."

She raises her eyebrows curiously.

*Kujaku* provided a secret—a defense against multiple attackers. But it's more than that. If multiple people grab you and pull at you, what do you do?

*Kujaku* teaches that you use the strongest opponent's momentum against them. It surprises any other attackers, and it off-balances the strongest. But there's something else in the form, too, another secret. It's a compass. A way of helping figure out which direction to choose when you're unsure.

Direction. Picturing multiple forces—parents, school, friends—I realize how difficult it is to be one's authentic self. We're pulled in so many directions. Mr. Samuels used *kujaku* to show us a real secret— we have the power and the right to choose our own path.

When defending against Logan and Jeff, Mr. Samuels didn't want to hurt them. So, he used their momentum against them and refocused on what mattered most to him. *Us.*

DeMarcus whispers in my ear, "I'll give you guys some space. You don't have to answer now. But talk later?"

After I nod, DeMarcus leaves, still avoiding eye contact with Mateo, and Michells finds Camila and celebrates with her.

Out of everyone, out of all the "attackers" so to speak, my heart learns from *kujaku,* as well. If pulled in multiple directions, choose the one the heart wants most.

"Mateo," I say, my heart again leaping from my chest to my throat.

"So, um. You and DeMarcus like official now?" he asks.

I shrug. "We never were official, you know."

He looks down, frowning. "This means I have to move."

"There's always more than one option."

"Tell that to my father."

"Yeah. Sorry." I kick at the gym floor. "I am sorry, Mat. About everything. I never should have kissed DeMarcus."

"I was really hurt when I saw you and DeMarcus together. And every time I wanted to try and talk to you, you two were always together. Even today. *Especially* today."

"You were never around. And when you were..." I shrug.

"When I was around, you didn't know if you could trust me."

"Something like that."

"Well, I'm moving now, nothing matters, anyway."

"Is that how you feel? Honestly?" I ask, a mix of emotions attacking my gut like a punching bag.

He looks around nervously. "No. That's not how I feel. Not at all."

"Then tell me how you feel." *Tell me you love me one more time. Don't let this be goodbye.*

"There's so much I want to say, but I won't even be here."

"You don't know that for sure," I say. "Do you?"

He shrugs. "Before I go, will you spend one more day with me? Like at the swing set? Just one goodbye before I go?"

I don't answer. Of course, I'd love to do that with Mat, but would it hurt too much?

"We don't even have to talk," Mateo continues. "Maybe you'll just hold my hand. Hold my hand one more time before I leave." He blushes. "Maybe it's silly, but I never felt safer or happier than when you used to hold my hand. Just tell me everything will be okay even though I know everything will suck so much." He swallows hard. "Aiden, all I want is for you to say that you don't like DeMarcus and that you love me."

"I love you," I say right away. "And all I want is for you to say that you love me, too, and that you won't lie or leave me."

Tears well in his eyes. He wipes his nose, trying to cover it up. "I love you, too. If I could promise that I'd never leave, I would. I would promise that in a heartbeat."

"So, promise." My heart pounds so hard that my chest may explode. My eyes turn wet, too.

"You know I can't promise that... I don't know what to do."

"What can you promise then?"

"I promise that... no matter what you may think, or how much my emotions got the best of me, that I... that I always have loved you. And I always will." Tears roll down Mat's face, but he ignores them. "You holding my hand is all I ever needed to feel okay. That the haters don't matter. That nothing matters except you. Except us. When you hold my hand, it makes me think we could be together forever. Like you and I were always meant to be. If only you take my hand?" The last few words come out in between tears, which causes me to cry, too.

He extends his shaky arm and opens his hand, palm up, offering it to me.

I take a long, deep breath. I look hard into Mateo's dark, beautiful eyes, still trying to figure out the secrets below his surface.

"Lots of guys are going to like you," he continues, sighing deeply, wiping at the tears on his face. "And what you're doing—" he wipes at my eye with one finger, and then holds my hand, looking closely at the pride-colored nails—"this is beautiful. It really suits you." He smiles gently. "Oh, man. I promise you no one will love you like I love you.

No matter where I move or what becomes of us, I will always love you more than any of them can. That I can promise."

His trembling hand floats in front of me, waiting to be held, wanting to be loved.

I glance over my shoulders. DeMarcus has left. Mr. Samuels and Mom hold hands, talking to some other parents. The media has packed up, and I wonder what kind of stories they will share about today.

I turn back to Mateo, my first love, who still waits anxiously with his open hand.

Who knows what comes next? Maybe the wrestlers will still bully us, or maybe they'll grow up and leave us alone. Maybe Mom will win the mayoral election and change this town. Maybe I'll watch Coach Krake pack up his office and leave Washington High forever.

I smile at Mateo. I don't know what tomorrow will bring, but I know what I feel right now.

I take his hand and squeeze hard. I love the way it feels in my hand. We have such different hands—skin color, size, strength. But when they come together, they fit perfectly.

"Will you meet me at our swings at the park? Tomorrow? And bring that letter I mailed you."

I nod.

Tomorrow. As long as there is a tomorrow when I get to see Mateo, then everything will be okay.

Please just don't let me lose those tomorrows.

# Epilogue

WE MEET AT the swing set at noon. Mateo brings a picnic. We eat, talk about the tournament, try to joke a little here and there. It's familiar yet uncomfortable territory.

But he's here. And so am I.

I take his hand, and he lights up.

"It's time. Open the letter." His face darkens, and his arms shake, nervousness consuming him, which in turn makes me nervous, too. "Just read it. Silently. Please."

*Dear Aiden,*

*We took a day to go to the beach. It's so boring here. I don't have my phone. My parents won't let me use it here. I'm going to have to get a burner phone to message you, I swear, lol.*

*So, I watched this old couple talk, like, all afternoon. They must have been like a hundred years old, who knows. But I watched them and then something made me just want to cry.*

*The woman said, "I'm so happy I've been able to spend my life with you."*

*The man replied, "I wish I had another lifetime to spend all over again with you. I'd do it all over again and again, if I could."*

*They had like, what? Decades? Several decades. They were*

*old, dude! But they were so in love. So happy, just watching the waves and lying on the beach next to each other.*

*It made me realize how much more time I want with you.*

*But I'm so very scared, Aiden. My parents keep talking about moving. My dad is worried about his job. This international trip was like some kind of last-minute effort to save his job. My mom cries at night. She's so worried about money and bills.*

*I don't want to become my parents. I want to become the old couple, just happy with one another, not worrying about a thing.*

*So, I wanted to write you this letter and tell you something. And yeah, I'm asking you not to open it until I tell you. If you are reading this letter, then my family has decided to move. No joke. No exceptions. No alternatives.*

*I have to move.*

*They're so mad at me, too. I overheard them talking about how they have to save money now for my college education, and that I blew it all because of hormones.*

*It's not hormones, Aiden. I love you.*

*But the world won't let us be together, will it? Doesn't it seem like that? Like, why should our relationship affect anything? If I had kissed a girl at the tournament, it wouldn't even be an issue.*

*But here's the thing and here's why I am writing this letter now. I am scared I will have to move. I am scared I will have to somehow say goodbye to you. Like goodbye forever.*

*If that happens, I want you to know that I love you. That for a moment in time, you have been perfectly loved. That someone fell in love with you.*

*That someone sees an old couple on the beach and wishes that could be our end game.*

*So, Aiden Rothe, mi novio, I love you. I will always love you. You will be the boy I remember forever, my first love, my first kiss. And probably my first heartbreak.*

*I am mailing this as soon as I am done with a note asking you not to open until I tell you so. Because I hope we can throw away this letter and that I will stay with you forever.*

*But sadly, if you are reading this, it means that I am 100% moving. I don't want to leave you, Aiden. I love you so much.*

*And if you love me back, please just hold my hand, kiss me, and let me go. Because this will be the hardest day of my life.*

*I love you so so so much*
*Mateo*

When I look at Mateo, I can't see anything. Tears blur my vision. I open my mouth to speak, but I can't find the words.

Tears spill from eyes, harder than I've cried in some time. Mateo holds me. He holds me, and he whispers, "I love you. I'm so sorry. I love you so much."

When I catch my breath several minutes later, I look up at him.

I hold his hand.

I pull him toward me, and I gently kiss his lips.

When I pull away, he stands.

I look down. I can't watch him walk away, but I hear his footsteps.

I've fallen a lot in my life, especially these last two years—from literal fights to breakups and heartache.

When I look up, Mateo's back faces me, and he walks home.

I want to run after him. Grab him, kiss him one more time, and tell him that he can just live with me, that we'll find a way. That when we put our minds together, we can figure out anything.

Looking at his letter, I reread the last part.

*And if you love me back, please just hold my hand, kiss me, and let me go. Because this will be the hardest day of my life.*

So, I do as Mateo asks. For now.

Another voice speaks in my mind. "When you learn how to fall, you learn how to rise." But it's more than that. We can't expect to find joy if we don't get back up and try.

And so, I watch Mateo leave. Then I rise. Each step feels heavy, impossible. But, somehow, I put one foot in front of the other and move forward.

## *Author's Note*

THANK YOU FOR following Aiden and friends on this journey. If you loved this story, tell others about it. Post a review online. Take a pic or video with the book and share it. Tag me (@joechianakas) so I get to see it, please.

Follow me on your favorite socials so I can tell you when the next book drops. It's the most joyful book in the series yet, and I can't wait for you to keep reading!

And thank you for celebrating diverse stories.

JOE CHIANAKAS is an author and a college professor. He's won multiple teacher-of-the-year awards and inspiring students in his greatest passion. He loves long walks with his furbaby Bailey, a mini-Australian Shepherd. He lives in Peoria, IL with the love of his life, Brian.

Joe's known for his horror series *Rabbit in Red*—a three book trilogy that became a huge hit after multiple subscription boxes bought and mailed thousands of copies to horror fans around the world. Joe's next horror novel, *Darkness Calls,* will be releasing soon.

Chianakas is currently represented by Amy Brewer of Metamorphosis Literary Agency and has multiple publishing contracts with Roan & Weatherford Publishing Associates. Learn more about Joe and send him a message at **www.joechianakas.weebly.com** or follow him online at www.facebook.com/chianakas or search for him on your favorite socials.